PRAISE FOR NANCY HERNDON'S ELENA JARVIS SERIES

"Nancy Herndon's characters, descriptions, and situations are both intellectual and laugh-out-loud funny."
—*Mostly Murder*

"Nancy Herndon's mysteries are notable for some of the most varied, inventive, and bizarre murders in the realm of crime fiction."
—*El Paso Inc.*

"Refreshingly different . . . Herndon's characterizations are wonderful."
—*The Mystery Review*

"[Herndon's] characters are believable and human—often touchingly and irksomely so . . . Her books are always fun to read."
—*Las Cruces Sun-News*

"Herndon has a gift for humorous dialogue rivaled by very few in the mystery genre."
—*El Paso Times*

"Herndon's comic touch is delightful and seems to become more deft with each book."
—*El Paso Herald-Post*

. . . and don't miss the other Elena Jarvis Mysteries:

ACID BATH
WIDOWS' WATCH

MORE MYSTERIES FROM THE
BERKLEY PUBLISHING GROUP...

CAT CALIBAN MYSTERIES: She was married for thirty-eight years. Raised three kids. Compared to that, tracking down killers is easy...

by D. B. Borton
ONE FOR THE MONEY   TWO POINTS FOR MURDER
THREE IS A CROWD   FOUR ELEMENTS OF MURDER
FIVE ALARM FIRE   SIX FEET UNDER

ELENA JARVIS MYSTERIES: There are some pretty bizarre crimes deep in the heart of Texas—and a pretty gutsy police detective who rounds up the unusual suspects...

by Nancy Herndon
ACID BATH   WIDOWS' WATCH
LETHAL STATUES   HUNTING GAME
TIME BOMBS   C.O.P. OUT
CASANOVA CRIMES

FREDDIE O'NEAL, P.I., MYSTERIES: You can bet that this appealing Reno private investigator will get her man... "A winner."—Linda Grant

by Catherine Dain
LAY IT ON THE LINE   SING A SONG OF DEATH
WALK A CROOKED MILE   LAMENT FOR A DEAD COWBOY
BET AGAINST THE HOUSE   THE LUCK OF THE DRAW
DEAD MAN'S HAND

BENNI HARPER MYSTERIES: Meet Benni Harper—a quilter and folk-art expert with an eye for murderous designs...

by Earlene Fowler
FOOL'S PUZZLE   GOOSE IN THE POND
KANSAS TROUBLES   DOVE IN THE WINDOW
IRISH CHAIN   MARINER'S COMPASS
     (Available in hardcover
     from Berkley Prime Crime)

HANNAH BARLOW MYSTERIES: For ex-cop and law student Hannah Barlow, justice isn't just a word in a textbook. Sometimes, it's a matter of life and death...

by Carroll Lachnit
MURDER IN BRIEF   A BLESSED DEATH
AKIN TO DEATH

PEACHES DANN MYSTERIES: Peaches has never had a very good memory. But she's learned to cope with it over the years... Fortunately, though, when it comes to murder, this absentminded amateur sleuth doesn't forgive and forget!

by Elizabeth Daniels Squire
WHO KILLED WHAT'S-HER-NAME?   WHOSE DEATH IS IT ANYWAY?
MEMORY CAN BE MURDER   IS THERE A DEAD MAN IN THE HOUSE?
REMEMBER THE ALIBI

CASANOVA CRIMES

NANCY HERNDON

BERKLEY PRIME CRIME, NEW YORK

CASANOVA CRIMES

A Berkley Prime Crime Book / published by arrangement with
the author

PRINTING HISTORY
Berkley Prime Crime edition / April 1999

The Penguin Putnam Inc. World Wide Web site address is
http://www.penguinputnam.com

ISBN: 0-425-16812-3

Berkley Prime Crime Books are published
by The Berkley Publishing Group,
a member of Penguin Putnam Inc.,
375 Hudson Street, New York, New York 10014.
The name BERKLEY PRIME CRIME and the BERKLEY PRIME CRIME
design are trademarks belonging to Berkley Publishing Corporation.

PRINTED IN THE UNITED STATES OF AMERICA

10 9 8 7 6 5 4 3 2 1

Acknowledgments

Many thanks to fellow writers Jean Miculka and Joan Coleman, who, as always, provided help and encouragement in the writing of this book. I am particularly indebted to Raul Tellez of the Tillman Clinic in El Paso for information about the symptoms and treatment of HIV and AIDS. Last but never least, thanks to the El Paso Police Department, whose officers have been my best source of information throughout the writing of the Elena Jarvis series.

N.R.H.

1

Saturday, April 5, 8:00 P.M.

Angus McGlenlevie, Professor of English at Herbert Hobart University and author of the best-selling poetry collections *Erotica in Reeboks* and *Rapture on the Rapids*, was hard at work in his office responding to a sudden attack from the poetic muse. He had just chosen *Scattering Seeds of Love* as the working title for his newest book of verse and begun the first poem when the telephone rang.

The caller was evidently a scatteree, for she screamed into his ear, "*I'm pregnant!*"

Gus was delighted. Having witnessed the birth of quintuplets to the wife of a police officer—having, in fact, been the birth poet to the charming babies—Gus had been overwhelmed with the desire to be a father, to savor the delights of domesticity and the excitement of seeing himself replicated in a new life.

An unromantic judge, who issued a restraining order, had forced Gus to give up his pursuit of Sarah Tolland, his ex-wife and first choice to mother Gus junior. Gus had then widened his sights, looking for a younger, more nubile candidate, one who would appreciate being the focus of attention from a famous poet. His students, both the dreamy-eyed young poetesses in his classes and the healthy, firm-bodied volleyball Amazons he coached on the women's intramural team, were always suitably receptive.

And now the long-anticipated event had occurred. A lady

1

of his choice had conceived. He could look forward to the first stirring of his child in the womb, to sonograms, to birthing classes, to the delivery, to dandling the little one on his knee, to reading it his poetry.

"My dear, I am delighted." He tried to guess which of his choices had been the lucky winner, as it were, of the McGlenlevie Reproductive Sweepstakes.

"Delighted? You're *delighted*?" she gasped.

To McGlenlevie the young woman sounded rather hysterical. Perhaps her hormonal balances were changing in response to the coming blessed event.

"You were supposed to be taking care of things," she said accusingly.

"I did," said Gus, who *had* taken care. He'd punched holes in all his condoms, but he didn't mention that to the mother of his child. "We'll have to think of this as our little miracle," he advised her cheerfully.

"Don't be an ass," she snapped. "I'm not having a baby."

"Nonsense, my dear. We'll marry, have a delightful family life—"

"You, me, the baby, the girls' volleyball team, and every female on campus who writes poetry," she interrupted angrily. "No one but you would consider that family life."

He was glad to note that her hysteria seemed to have abated. "Fatherhood will make a new man of me," Gus promised.

There was a moment of silence. Then she said, "You wanted this baby, didn't you?"

"Of course I want our child," he replied. "What man would not want such a lovely girl as his wife and the mother of his offspring?"

"You *planned* this!"

"Well, ah—" She wasn't taking her good fortune as well as he'd expected. And which one was she? She hadn't identified herself. It might seem a bit tactless to admit that he didn't know which girl he'd impregnated. "Ah—we must think of names. If it's a girl, we'll want to name her after you. Try it out with McGlenlevie, my dear. I long to hear the name of my future daughter from your lips.''

"You don't even know who I am, do you? I could be any volleyball player.''

Gus chuckled. She had given herself away. He had chosen four girls initially: two volleyballers, two poetesses. Therefore, he now knew to whom he was speaking. Kimberly Sweet. The other athletic darling, a center, had a deeper voice. "Of course I know, Kimberly. If we weren't on the telephone, I'd go down on bended knee to propose, but since—''

"Don't bother. I'm getting an abortion.''

Gus felt a moment of panic. "I'll get a restraining order.''

"And I'll have you arrested for—for statutory rape or—or impregnating a minor.''

"Now, Kimberly, you were charmingly willing, and you're not a minor.''

"I hate you!'' she cried and hung up.

Gus sighed. He'd expected a better response. If Kimberly was going to be difficult, perhaps one of the other girls would turn up pregnant. Although he doubted it. He'd been trying since December, and Kimberly was the first. He had a date with Carla in—he glanced at his watch—an hour. Should he try with her? Or attempt to change Kimberly's mind about the abortion? Surely the father had some say. Gus didn't really know. He'd never been in this position. Heretofore, he'd preferred that his ladies not become pregnant. He'd taken pains to see that they didn't.

Trying to look at the matter from Kimberly's point of view, to be sensitive to her concerns, Gus was reassured to realize that girls tended to panic when they found themselves pregnant. The result of some ancient female instinct no doubt. But after all, these were the days of legal abortion. Here at H.H.U. the Nazi doctor at the Health and Reproductive Services Center would provide an abortion for any coed who could bear to sit through an unpleasant lecture on sexual responsibility.

Gus himself had been the target of such a lecture. It had occurred—where?—ah, at the Wednesday afternoon prayer and cocktail party held every other week by President Sunnydale. No wonder Kimberly was upset! It was the prospect of facing Dr. Greta Marx. And who could blame the girl for being wary of such a belligerent woman? Satisfied that he'd found the source of Kimberly's doubts, Gus decided that a face-to-face interview would calm his future wife and restore her happiness, for she was usually a perky, good-humored girl.

He'd have to stop dating, he mused. During his first marriage, Sarah had always been unduly irritated by his female admirers. Still, a few sacrifices were little enough to make in return for the anticipated pleasure of fatherhood.

Gus reached for the telephone to break his date with Carla. That done, he reread the poem he had started for *Scattering Seeds of Love*. The blessed news from Kimberly should be a source of special inspiration.

2

Gretchen Farber turned to her date, Wayne Quarles, Jr.
"I'd love to come up for a drink," she said. "Which floor
are you on?" As if she didn't know that the creep had rooms
on seven, three floors above her own in the student dormitory. She knew all about Wayne, who had lured her roommate up there, then wouldn't take no for an answer. Nita
had hit him with the base of a Nefertiti bust and come home
crying, her blouse torn, tooth marks on her neck and breast.
The poor girl had been so upset that she had to take tran-
quilizers and missed the trip to Chichén Itzá with her class
in Mayan Culture.

Gretchen patted her purse and, smiling, preceded Wayne
into the elevator. They'd just been to see a very sexy movie,
which was, no doubt, meant to get her in the mood. And she
was in the mood! She could feel the outline of the Mace
canister in her handbag. As soon as Wayne made his move,
she was going to give him a shock he'd never forget. Then
if he ever got another date with an H.H.U. coed, he'd remember how a noseful of Mace felt. He'd think twice about
forcing himself on unwilling women.

"Nice suite," she said as they entered the sitting room,
which was decorated with an Egyptian motif. She couldn't
decide which was worse, the hokey Egyptian stuff here on
the seventh floor or the flowery style of the floor her own
room was on, all the furniture fussy with inlaid blossoms.

5

Each level of the dorm building featured some aspect of Art Deco, another passion of the late, weird founder, Herbert Hobart, Video Game King of the U.S. "Aren't your roommates home?" she asked ingenuously.

" 'Fraid not," Quarles replied, "but they'll be along shortly. With their dates."

Sure they will, she thought. *They're probably both out of the country.*

"Can I fix you a drink?"

"Nonalcoholic," she replied, not about to take any chances. "I'm thinking of becoming a Muslim. They don't drink, you know."

Quarles grinned. "Bet you've always fantasized about life in a harem."

"It does sound romantic." Gretchen managed to twitter a bit. Since he didn't know her very well—they'd met in the Jazz Classics course—he wouldn't know that she wasn't the twittery type. She thought of herself as the in-your-face type—of necessity. She was the youngest of four children, with three older brothers.

"I can hardly wait for the class trip to the New Orleans jazz clubs," she said.

Quarles agreed as he handed her a Coke which he'd taken from the small refrigerator and poured into a glass with ice. "There's some pretty good jazz in Houston, too," he said. "My sister lives there. Maybe we could fly over for the weekend, stay at her place in River Oaks, and hit some of the clubs."

"Sounds wonderful," she replied, thinking, *In your dreams.*

She sipped from her glass. Blah. He must have given her Diet Coke or something. She didn't like the taste at all. Well, he'd make his move any minute now; she'd douse him with Mace; then she'd take the elevator to her own room and tell Nita all about it. The Revenge of the Roommates. Maybe she'd write it up for the university paper. The story would make a dandy feature article and embarrass the little cretin, a fate that he richly deserved. She glanced at her good-looking, blond date, who was sprawled casually beside her on the sofa with a Scotch and water in hand, seemingly in no hurry to put the make on her. Nita hadn't wanted Gretchen to do this. She considered Quarles dangerous. Gretchen considered him a prick in need of a lesson in how to take no for an answer.

God, she felt tired! She drained the Coke, wishing it had some caffeine to give her a boost, wishing he'd get on with it so she could leave him whimpering, go back to her room and get a good night's sleep. She'd had a real date last night and stayed out late, then got up early for tennis.

"Want another?" he asked, taking the glass from her hand.

Gretchen thought about answering but yawned instead. Suddenly dizzy, she laid her head back against the upholstery and blinked. Inexplicably, she felt as if she were flying backward, moving farther and farther away from her body. On which he now had his hand. She opened her mouth to protest, but no words came out.

Reach for that Mace, she told herself fuzzily. *Now's the time.* But she couldn't move her hand.

Couldn't move any—

What . . . ?

3

When Graham Fullerton awoke in his suite on the fifth floor of the Herbert Hobart dorm tower, he was sprawled, half-dressed, across his own bed, suffering from a terrible headache. And he was alone.

The digital clock on the nightstand said 3:25. What the hell? He groaned and, in trying to sit up, experienced a wave of nausea. If he hadn't known better, he'd have sworn he had a hangover, but Graham had given up alcohol months earlier. Therefore, familiar as that morning-after feeling was, it couldn't be the result of alcohol.

The fact that his belt was undone, his trousers unzipped, his shirt open and, if his investigating fingers didn't lie, buttonless, was certainly a clue to what he'd been doing earlier when it was still Saturday and he'd had guests. Through the pulsing headache he grinned at the thought of what a hurry they must have been in to avail themselves of his fabled sex drive. Unfortunately, he couldn't remember a damn thing after the preliminaries.

Had they slipped some of that date rape drug into his Evian? That didn't make sense. When had he ever needed any encouragement—unless the girl was a complete dog? And nobody gave Rohypnol to a man. Most men couldn't perform if they were bordering on comatose, although Graham thought he himself might be able to. He'd done a lot of very satisfactory screwing around in his drinking days.

8

So why did he feel like the tail end of a three-day binge? An edge of panic crept into his consciousness. Could he be getting sick? Quickly he squelched that thought. No way. He was living healthier than he ever had in his life, and he'd seen the doctor just last—well, whenever. He wasn't taking any chances in that regard.

He took a series of slow, deep breaths, which helped the nausea if not the headache, then idly scratched his chest. What the—his fingers had encountered a small square of paper stuck to his chest hair. Wincing, he pulled it off and dragged himself to the head of the bed, where he pressed the switch of the bedside lamp. The light cut like glass slivers in his eyeballs.

Squinting, he read the note—and laughed. The little minxes! He reached up to turn off the light, wishing that he could remember the "hot time" they had thanked him for. Maybe it would come back to him tomorrow.

Angel Guadaramma was on the night cleaning crew at Herbert Hobart. Among her responsibilities was the university chapel, a place of strange gods. It made her nervous. Still, every Saturday night—actually Sunday morning—she cleaned the chapel in preparation for services the next day, at which time she herself would be attending early Mass at San Isidro del Valle before going home.

The pews here were made of wood such as she had never seen, and had outlandish, twisted arm rests. The stained-glass windows pictured varied gods, a fat one sitting cross-legged; a woman with many arms, a red god all afire. Among them, however, was a crucifix over the altar. It gave Angel reassurance that perhaps her employers were not wholly heathen. Best of all was the glowing woman in blue robes and halo, holding flowers in her hands. Angel took her to be the Blessed Virgin Mother, for there were babies around her feet and a land of flowing water and plentiful crops behind her— heaven perhaps.

Angel always said a quick prayer to the Virgin before beginning her tasks, a prayer asking protection from the evil influence of the strange idols and another prayer when she had finished her work, asking that she arrive safely at Mass, where she would make her confession and take communion. At Herbert Hobart the money was good, but her Anglo employers were very peculiar, and she needed the cleansing of the soul that she experienced by finishing the week in God's hands.

When she had dusted the last pew, sprayed and polished the last crystal candlestick, and vacuumed the last plush carpet, she knelt once more at the Virgin's window and looked up, her hands folded reverently. It was then that she saw a marvelous thing, a miracle. Glistening in the lights from the crystal chandeliers, Angel Guadaramma saw tears on the cheeks of the Holy Mother. She crossed herself in wonder and stared.

4

Tuesday, April 8, 11:50 A.M.

After stopping for an early lunch, Detectives Elena Jarvis and Leo Weizell returned to Crimes Against Persons from the investigation of a brawl between neighbors in South Central—one bloody scalp wound inflicted with a garden hoe, one shotgun blast sideswiping the hoe-wielder's left buttock. They backtracked from the stroll down the aisle to Homicide Row when their sergeant leaned out of his cluttered office and called to them. Manny then wheeled his gray-blue tweed chair to his desk and replaced his telephone receiver in its cradle.

"H.H.U.," said the sergeant.

Elena groaned.

"Come on, Dr. Jarvis," said Manny, who was still amused that his only female detective had been awarded an honorary doctorate by the grateful university for her prompt solving of their peculiar crimes. "You owe them. You too, Leo."

Leo Weizell, father of quintuplets, had been furnished by H.H.U. with support for his children and an upscale house (repossessed from a drug dealer and sold to the university). In return for H.H.U.'s largess, the Psychology Department got to study the seven Weizells in their natural habitat.

"What now?" Elena demanded. Having taken the sergeant's exam and done all the interviews, she was waiting nervously for the results and feeling decidedly grumpy.

11

"With graduation next month, I suppose the fraternities are up to something." The previous May the frat boys had disrupted graduation by kidnapping the academic regalia and then, during the ceremony, turning the sprinklers on, with unexpected results. The sprinkler heads had blown up during the closing prayer.

"They've got a dead body," said Manny, returning Elena's attention to the crime of the day. "Don't know whether it belonged to a fraternity. Why don't you two go over and find out?"

"Where and who?" Elena asked.

"Male student," Manny Escobedo replied. "Found in his dorm bathroom, pills on the tiles, fifth floor."

"Overdose," Leo guessed.

Elena nodded. There were druggies at H.H.U. She'd assisted in the arrest of a dealer and knew about at least one user. She assumed there were others. In fact, her ex, Frank the Narc, had said as much.

The crime scene team, headed by Charlie Solis, and the medical examiner, Onofre Calderon, arrived in the lobby of the student dormitory at the same time that Leo and Elena entered. They all stepped into an elevator just vacated by a group of students coming downstairs for a gourmet lunch in the dining room.

Elena could smell it—something French and laced with wine and cream, she guessed. It was a wonder the entire student population hadn't turned into butterballs after eating that kind of stuff every day. But then they no doubt worked it off playing golf on the university course or tennis on the university courts, polo on the polo field or racquet ball in the gym, or flying off to exotic foreign countries to assess resort facilities and study languages and cultures of interest only to the idle rich. They certainly didn't get their exercise cleaning their rooms. H.H.U. had maids for that, more maids per student than any university in the country.

The law enforcement contingent exited on the fifth floor and trailed down the hall after the housemother, Mrs. Monserrat, who was showing signs of shock. Until today no one had died in the dorm, she informed them. In the faculty apartments, yes. In the library, certainly. But not in her dormitory. She ran a refined operation. If the young man had been sick, he should have gone to the clinic instead of dying on his bathroom floor.

Mrs. Monserrat opened the door to 507 without knocking—a terrible breach of etiquette, Elena imagined—and introduced Chief Clabb of the university security force, an officer of his, and two nervous young men, at whom she pointed while reading their names from a file folder. "Mr. Mayhew, Mr. Fullerton."

"Carswell," corrected a short, slender student with a plain face but teeth of absolute perfection. "Fullerton's the one who's dead."

"Ah," said Mrs. Monserrat disapprovingly and left.

Elena greeted Chief Clabb, shook hands with his officer, introduced her colleagues, then watched the hasty escape of the lavender-uniformed university policemen. H.H.U.'s security personnel hated crime and avoided having anything to do with it if they could.

Then she studied the two roommates and wondered whether Mr. Carswell's teeth were false, crowns from front to back, or the product of heredity, a perfect diet, and expensive dental care. Her own teeth weren't bad, but she was just lucky. She had relatives on the back roads in New Mexico who were on their way to being toothless before they hit thirty.

"Where's the stiff?" asked Charlie Solis, drawing on latex gloves.

The roommates looked shocked. "G-g-graham's b-b-back h-h-ere," stammered Mr. Mayhew.

"Lawrence stammers," said Mr. Carswell unnecessarily. "I'm Pete. Can I go down to lunch?"

"No," said Leo.

Charlie Solis and Onofre Calderon followed the stammerer through a door on the left. Elena knew that it led to one of three bedrooms, each of which had its own bath. However, she'd never been on this floor with its peculiar brand of nutty decorating. How could the students stand to live in a place that reeked of blood sacrifice in steamy jungles? Elena recognized the Mayan decor: the temple-backed sofa and love seat, the mosaic lizard offering snacks in a basket on its tail and, from its snout, wine in a bota. You poured the wine anywhere from your forehead to your mouth from a long spout reminiscent of the watering can she used on plants inside her adobe house on Sierra Negra. And botas were Basque, not Mayan, if the waiter at a restaurant in Juarez was to be believed. She personally didn't have anything to do with botas. She didn't like pouring wine on her face and certainly not on her clothes, as often happened. Red wine was the devil to wash out.

"We'd better have a look," said Leo.

Elena had seen enough dead bodies to satisfy any curiosity she might have had, but duty demanded that she follow her partner into the bedroom, where they could see into the connecting bath. A young man, naked, lay sprawled on the floor, face twisted, skin surprisingly pink. Sunburn? Had he been a nudist, given to exposing himself in the altogether to Los Santos's intense desert-mountain sunlight?

Elena judged that he had been handsome when alive, but he looked as if his death had been a hard one. The smell of vomit lingered in the small room. Capsules and pills were scattered on the tile floor around the body. Suicide? If so, he hadn't picked a gentle death. If Elena wanted to off herself, she'd have gone for sleeping pills. Just drift away, no agony. Lawrence, the roommate, stood just in front of them, trembling, staring at the body with horrified fascination.

Leo and Elena led him back and pushed him onto the love seat beside his roommate. Charlie Solis followed almost immediately. "Calderon wants to know if the victim was always that pink?" he asked the two students.

"N-n-n-"

"No," said Carswell helpfully when Mayhew couldn't get the word out. "He was tanned, but otherwise as white as any of us."

All the Hispanics in the police contingent stared at him.

"Here in the dorm," Carswell added nervously.

"A-a-a-an-a-a—"

"We had a black girl named Analee Ribbon," said Carswell, anticipating Mayhew. "But she got killed."

Elena knew. She'd investigated that case. The young woman was killed by a pushed statue. "Does the pink mean anything?" she asked Solis.

"Onofre's guessing cyanide poisoning," Solis replied. "The victim threw up—"

"God, yes," Carswell agreed. When they turned to him, he added hastily, "I smelled it. Saw it. I wasn't there when it happened. I was in class. I—"

"Probably had convulsions," Solis continued. He turned back to the roommates, consulting a notebook. "Did you smell bitter almonds when you found him?"

Mayhew looked blank. Carswell asked, "What do they smell like?"

Solis yelled in to Calderon that they hadn't smelled anything but vomit.

Calderon came out of the bedroom, waving a photographer toward the deceased. "Maybe Wilkerson will smell almonds at the autopsy when they cut him open."

Mayhew turned greenish.

"What were those capsules on the floor and in the bottles?" the medical examiner asked.

"Vitamins, I guess," said Carswell. Mayhew just shook his head, hand over his mouth. He'd evidently given up hoping anyone would wait for him to stammer out a reply. Or else he was so close to throwing up at the thought of his roommate on an autopsy table, he dared not try to answer.

"You sure?" Solis asked.

"Graham was a real health nut," said Carswell, "popping vitamins all day, jogging, hassling the chef about whether the menus covered the four basic food groups, whatever they are. He even quit drinking."

"Was he ever sick?" Solis persisted.

"He never said so," said Carswell.

Mayhew poked him. "L-last y-y—"

"Well, yeah, last spring," Carswell agreed.

"What was wrong with him last spring?" Solis prodded.

Mayhew scratched his head. "M-m-mono." The two roommates laughed.

"The kissing disease," Carswell amplified. "Graham did a lot of kissing." More laughter. "A whole lot."

Calderon had re-entered the sitting room, nodding as he listened. "Symptoms?" he snapped impatiently.

Mayhew looked surprised.

Carswell replied. "Well—ah—he was tired. Ran a low-grade fever. You know the drill. It's something college students get." He shrugged.

Solis said to Calderon, "They claim the pills in there are vitamins."

"Uh-huh." Calderon went back into the bathroom.

Leo and Elena elicited from the roommates the information that they had last seen Fullerton the evening before when he came into the suite at 12:30 from a date. He said he was going to skip class and sleep in, so neither had gone into his room to wake him for breakfast. Mayhew had, however, according to Carswell, knocked, then entered Graham's room before lunch and found him on the bathroom floor. That was about eleven-fifteen.

Elena glanced at her watch. Almost eleven hours during which Graham Fullerton could have died. They'd have to depend on Onofre's estimate and autopsy results for a time of death. Of course, it was possible that Fullerton had killed himself, she mused. "Did he seem depressed lately?" she asked. "Been having problems? With classes? With girls? Money?" The last seemed unlikely. Almost every kid at H.H.U. came from a wealthy family.

Mayhew laughed, then looked embarrassed. Carswell explained, "Graham didn't care about his grades, he had plenty of money, and, like I was saying, girls invariably fell all over him."

Ah, thought Elena. Maybe a jealous girlfriend had done him in. *If* he'd been murdered. At any rate, she thought of poison as a woman's weapon, although that was sexist thinking, not her style at all. She grumbled to herself, sick to death of cases at Herbert Hobart University, where poets got dissolved in bathtubs, coeds had their heads bashed in by naked statues, and sprinklers exploded, injuring panicky parents in designer clothes.

Calderon came back into the sitting room. He was holding a bottle of red capsules, staring at it thoughtfully. "See that," he said to the four people in the room. "The bottle says Vitamin C—"

"Yeah, he took Vitamin C," Carswell agreed.

"But I've never seen a red Vitamin C capsule," Onofre Calderon continued.

"Maybe it's sulfa," Leo suggested. "Maybe he had a bladder infection. I remember my grandmother—"

"Sulfa's not used much anymore," said Calderon. "Not since your grandmother's day. Maybe if he was allergic to antibiotics—" Onofre stared at the red capsules, turned the bottle this way and that. "You know, this one looks like it's been tampered with," he said, fishing a capsule out with tweezers.

The roommates stared at the capsule, uncomprehending. Elena, however, understood the implications immediately. Los Santos might have some nut going around putting poison in over-the-counter medications. Or whatever that red stuff was.

5

Tuesday, April 8, 12:30 P.M.

Mrs. Monserrat, the hovering housemother, actually came up from the dining room to rescue Mayhew and Carswell when she discovered that they were missing from their chairs at her table, an honor that rotated among reluctant students. When Mrs. M., as she was called by the residents, promised that she would personally escort them back upstairs, Elena agreed to their departure, mostly because Onofre Calderon insisted.

"They're suspects," said Leo. "We wanted to question them."

"Right," Elena agreed. "And Leo doesn't think they should get to eat before—"

"Sit down," Calderon ordered and plopped down himself on the temple-back sofa. He carefully placed three plastic bags on the coffee table. In one were white capsules with a dark blue band. The second contained diamond-shaped tablets, the third, some of the red capsules he had puzzled over earlier. "Like I said, I found the red ones on the floor and in a Vitamin C bottle. I got no idea what they are, but they're not Vitamin C; I'm pretty sure of that. These—" He pointed a pen at the diamond-shaped tablets. "—were on the floor and in a plastic bottle labeled for a generic acetaminophen, but I've never seen acetaminophen in that shape."

"So maybe he did overdose," said Elena. "He was taking

18

uppers or downers or some garbage and hiding it in innoc-
uous bottles."

Calderon frowned at her. "These," he resumed, tapping
his pen beside the white capsules with the blue band, "are,
I think, zidovudine."

Leo stared at the capsules, puzzled. "Some new street
drug? Crack in a capsule."

Calderon gave him a disgusted look. Charlie Solis said,
"Retrovir. AZT. You heard of that?"

Elena felt a shock go through her. Had she touched the
body? Got any of the vomit on her? Did vomit carry the
virus? "AIDS?" she asked in a hushed voice. The cops on
patrol, rousting the hypes downtown, worried about getting
stuck with infected needles, but it wasn't as big a problem
for detectives. They put on gloves at the crime scene, but
mostly so they wouldn't contaminate the evidence, not to
protect against the evidence contaminating them.

"Not necessarily AIDS, but maybe HIV," Onofre said
quietly. "I can't be sure, but the colors of the capsule and
the unicorn, that's the Glaxo-Wellcome emblem, make me
think it's AZT even though he was keeping it in a vitamin
bottle."

"The roommates said he had mono last spring," said Leo.

Calderon nodded. "Some of the same symptoms."

"But he was O.K. in the fall and turned into a health nut,"
said Elena. "Vitamins, jogging, healthy food."

"That's the way you stave off the onset of AIDS," said
Calderon. "Medication to keep your viral loads down and
your T-cell counts up. And you want to live as healthy a life
as you can, including safe sex."

"What difference does that make if you've already got
it?" Leo muttered.

"Well, you don't want to reinfect yourself, and if you're
not a complete bastard, you don't want to spread it around,"
Calderon replied.

Elena and Leo exchanged glances. "Oh jeez," she said.
"All that kissing."

"Kissing doesn't do it," said Calderon.

"I know that," she retorted, "but the roommates were

doing enough snickering to indicate that this Fullerton was screwing everything that moved.'' She thought a minute. ''Maybe guys too. Unless he was an IV drug user.''

''No tracks,'' said Calderon.

''And hiding the medication. That would mean he wasn't telling his partners he was infected,'' she continued.

''Probably not,'' Calderon agreed.

''Which means if he passed it to someone, they'd have a real good reason to kill him,'' said Leo.

''No question,'' Solis concurred. ''HIV's a death sentence, sooner or later.''

Elena bowed her head, palms against her temples, fingers pressed into the thick, black hair that fed into her French braid. ''So we've got to question all his girlfriends, boyfriends, whatever, tell them they may have been exposed to AIDS.''

''Hey, isn't that City-County Health's job?'' Leo protested, ''warning the girls.''

''It's nobody's job,'' said Calderon, rising from the sofa. ''Without written consent from the infected person, it's a Class A misdemeanor to reveal his condition.''

Leo shrugged. ''He's dead.''

''So he can't sign,'' said Calderon. ''It's not only a criminal offense to reveal HIV infection; you expose yourselves and your department to civil lawsuits.''

''He's dead, Calderon,'' Leo reiterated.

''He's got family, doesn't he?''

''I don't know,'' Elena muttered.

''In Texas the newspapers can't even say someone died of AIDS without written consent from the family,'' Calderon told them.

''So we've got to conduct an investigation without ever mentioning the motive?'' Leo looked chagrined.

''And everyone we talk to could need testing and treatment, but we can't warn them?'' Elena added. ''And they may be spreading the virus to other students and starting a damned epidemic, and we can't—''

''It's a bitch,'' Calderon agreed.

6

Calderon had supervised the loading of Fullerton's corpse into a body bag and the removal by gurney. The ID & R team headed by Charlie Solis had taken the last photographs and the last fingerprints and headed back to Five Points, leaving Elena and Leo to eat a light lunch sent up to them by the housemother: liver pâté on crackers, French onion soup, a chicken-and-vegetable dish reeking of white wine, and a fresh raspberry tart.

Elena wasn't crazy about rich-kid food, especially pâté, but if she ate heartily now, she'd save the price of lunch and wouldn't have to cook dinner. So she cleaned her plate, as did Leo, although he complained about being fed mashed chicken livers. Then they both pulled on latex gloves to search Graham Fullerton's room. "Maybe Fullerton just said he was getting it on with everyone," Leo suggested hopefully as they began going through the belongings of the deceased. "Maybe he quit screwing around as soon as he found out he was positive, which must have been—When?"

"Last summer," Elena guessed. "He thinks he's got mono. He gets a blood test. Turns up positive for HIV. Starts on medication. Comes back seemingly healthy." She finished with his underwear drawer, having learned only that he wore bikini briefs. Why wear those if he wasn't exhibiting them to lovers? she asked herself. Then she had a thought and turned to Leo. "I'll bet he went to the clinic. I'll bet Dr. Marx knows he was HIV positive."

"*If* he was," Leo added. "We don't know that for sure. Onofre just *thought* he recognized the AZT capsules."

"Right. Maybe he wasn't." She had started on the desk while Leo continued to rifle through the closet. "Oh, boy." Elena had been examining a small black notebook she found in the middle drawer. It contained a hundred pages, thirty-one of which had been filled, each one with the name of a female, her phone and dorm room number, and comments on her looks and sexual expertise, or lack of it.

"I hope he was using condoms," said Elena. "Otherwise, we may have an AIDS epidemic right here on campus. That is, if he actually had the virus." She handed the book to Leo.

"Wow," he said. "That's more women than I've had in my entire life."

"How many more?" she asked, curious.

"None of your business. And he did use condoms. Or at least, he kept them around. I found some in his pockets."

"I found one in his billfold," said Elena. "So maybe— Hello, here's phone numbers for two doctors. One in Chicago, one on the other side of town."

"Call them," Leo suggested. "Maybe they'll confirm that he was HIV positive."

"Sure. Some doctor is going to commit a Class A misdemeanor while talking to a cop on the phone." She dialed the doctor in Los Santos. What kind of doctor treated AIDS? she wondered. "Could you tell me what Dr. Conway's specialty is?" she asked the receptionist.

"Infectious disease," said the woman.

Bingo! Elena thought. AIDS was certainly infectious. Add that information to the fact that Fullerton didn't just take his medical problems to the university clinic and Dr. Greta Marx. Elena found that significant. When she was Fullerton's age and had an infectious disease, like the flu, she staggered into the clinic at the University of New Mexico because it was free and convenient. Even if the money didn't matter to him, why would Fullerton bother to go all the way around the mountain to a doctor on Lomaland unless he wanted to keep his ailment quiet?

She asked to speak to the doctor. The receptionist told her that the doctor was busy and asked if Elena was a patient. Elena replied that she was a police detective and needed to talk to the doctor about someone he had treated. The receptionist said they didn't give out information about their clients. Elena told her that this particular one was dead. The receptionist said, "Even so," then changed her mind and put Elena on hold.

After what seemed like an interminable exposure to elevator music, a male voice said brusquely, "Dr. Morton Conway. What's this about a patient of mine being dead?"

"Graham Fullerton," Elena replied. "Could you tell me the nature of his illness?"

"He died of natural causes?" The doctor sounded puzzled.

"Probably not," said Elena. "I'm a Crimes Against Persons detective. So could you tell me about his health?"

"He was under my care. Any information other than that is confidential."

"He's dead," Elena pointed out. Maybe Dr. Conway wouldn't be as sticky about Texas rules and regulations as Onofre Calderon.

"Suffice it to say, I doubt he died of anything I was treating him for."

Elena sighed, remembering the questions about cyanide and the smell of bitter almonds that Solis had asked the roommates, who didn't know what bitter almonds smelled like. For that matter, Elena didn't either. "Maybe not, but he may well have died of his medication."

"If he was having problems with his medication, I'd have known about it," said the doctor.

"The medical examiner thinks one of his pills is AZT."

"I can't comment."

"But you don't deny it?"

"Detective, I've already told you that—"

"You can't break confidentiality. O.K. But he had three

kinds of pills, all in over-the-counter medicine bottles, vitamins—''

"Vitamin bottles?" Conway sounded surprised.

"Including the stuff that looked like AZT. It was in a multivitamin bottle. There were red capsules in a Vitamin C bottle, and diamond-shaped stuff in an acetaminophen bottle."

"I see." The doctor fell silent.

"And the medical examiner thinks the red capsules had been tampered with. And he's sure they weren't Vitamin C. Do you know of any Vitamin C in red capsules?"

"No."

Lord, the man was close-mouthed. He wasn't about to get arrested or sued for spilling the beans. "So if the red capsules had cyanide in them—''

"Cyanide!"

That got his attention. "That's the medical examiner's best guess. Before the lab work tells us for sure. Would you know of anyone who'd want to kill Mr. Fullerton?"

"No."

"Or any reason someone might have to murder him? Would the nature of his illness cause someone to—''

"If this is another way of asking me to reveal protected information, Detective—''

"O.K.," she snapped. Then took a deep breath. "Is there any reason he'd want to kill himself? Was he depressed?"

"Not that I'm aware of."

She tried a different tack. "Let's say those red capsules turn out to have cyanide in them. In that case, we need to know what they were and where they came from. At least you can tell me what pharmacy Mr. Fullerton used."

"A minute," said the doctor. Elena could hear the rustle of papers. "I don't know," Conway admitted. "Graham had the prescriptions filled himself."

"Then he did have prescriptions? At least you can confirm that the stuff in the bottles here wasn't Vitamin C or acetaminophen or—''

"I can't confirm that," said the doctor.

"But can you tell me if there was any reason for Mr.

Fullerton to hide the nature of his medication?''

"Detective, this whole conversation is a waste of time. I can't help you."

"What if someone tampered with his capsules at the drugstore? Or at the drug company? Other people taking his sort of medication could die.''

"Dear God,'' muttered the doctor.

"Isn't there any way you could—''

"No!''

"I guess I'd better come to see you, Dr. Conway,'' she said, sounding as grim and threatening as she could.

"With the idea of forcing me to break the law?'' he asked dryly. "You could find yourself under the same legal constraints that apply to me, Detective.'' With that warning the doctor hung up.

Leo had moved to the communal sitting room and called through the door, "Doesn't sound like you got anywhere with him.''

"Well, he's an infectious disease specialist,'' Elena replied. "But he wouldn't tell me a thing.'' She dialed the number of the doctor in Chicago, who, according to his receptionist, was another infectious disease specialist, one who was out of town. Did the lady need a referral to the doctor covering his practice? the receptionist asked. Elena declined and asked about Graham Fullerton.

"We don't give out information on our patients,'' the woman replied. "If you have questions, maybe you should ask Mr. Fullerton himself.''

"He's dead.''

"Oh, my. Poor lad,'' said the receptionist.

More hints, no confirmation, Elena thought as she put the receiver into its cradle. Would Dr. Marx at the university clinic be as hard to wheedle information out of? Did she have any?

7
..

"O.K.," Elena said to Leo as she dropped onto the sofa. "Both the doctors are infectious disease specialists, so he's had something or other since last year. Onofre thinks he was taking AZT, so his infectious disease is probably AIDS."

"Or HIV," said Leo. "There's a difference."

"Right."

"But they wouldn't confirm or deny?"

"Right. You know what? This is crazy. Either we've got some nut tampering with the capsules before they came to Fullerton—someone at the drugstore or at the drug company, in which case we need help from the feds—"

Leo groaned.

"—or someone got into Fullerton's medicine cabinet, maybe someone he gave the virus to, and killed him for revenge. In that case, we may be able to solve this one ourselves."

"But either way we've got to dance around the fact, if it is a fact, that he was HIV positive." Leo sighed. "This is going to be a bitch," he muttered glumly.

"Amen," Elena agreed. "Maybe we should be glad we don't have to get in touch with all the girls in that book and tell them that he had AIDS."

"Yeah, weeping females are hard on a guy. I oughta know. I got four at home if you count my wife."

"Babies don't count," said Elena. "Wives do. Anyway,

26

it sure seems unfair that no one's going to warn those young women. I read that you can take the drugs while you're asymptomatic and keep yourself from getting sick."

"At least he's dead and can't infect anyone else."

"His partners can," Elena pointed out. "And not even know they're doing it. We'll have to talk to Dr. Marx. She'll know if she's been getting HIV positives from student blood tests, and she's rabid on the subject of safe sex."

"Looks like she has good reason," said Leo.

"So even if she can't give us names of people who tested positive, she can say if it's starting to be a problem."

"If it is, there's still nothing we can do," said Leo, "about the girls. And without names, we don't have any leads."

"But we've got the notebook he kept. His little black book." Elena scowled. "What a scumbag! There are at least thirty-one girls with a reason to kill him."

"*If* they knew they were at risk," Leo reminded her. "We better talk to those two roommates again, too. They may know who's had access to his medication."

"Well, *they* sure did," Elena pointed out. "I wonder if he was AC/DC. They might know that, too. They might even have been—"

"If they were, they're not going to be anxious to tell us about it," Leo interrupted.

"When has anyone ever been anxious to talk to us?" Elena grinned at her partner. Then the two went back to searching Fullerton's room. "He sure had a lot of money in his account," Elena remarked.

"Don't all the kids here?" Leo replied. "Wonder if he really got it on with all those girls. I guess he was good-looking, but—"

"Maybe he was a fantastic lover," said Elena absently. She had found a laundry bag under the bed and begun to go through the pockets of shirts and trousers. "More condom packets," she remarked. "Maybe there won't be an epidemic."

"Let's hope." Leo lifted the last chair cushion, then opened a drawer in the nightstand beside the bed. "And more condoms," he announced.

"Wonder what this is?" Elena murmured. She had unfolded a piece of paper that she'd found in a shirt pocket and read the message aloud to Leo. "Thanks for a hot time. The Ménage à Trois Twins." Carefully she refolded the note and slipped it into a plastic bag. "Kinky," she remarked. "Think he really had twins?"

"Nothing would surprise me about this guy," Leo replied. He closed the nightstand drawer. "Sounds like the roommates are back." Elena stood and brushed off the knees of her slacks. They could both hear voices in the sitting room.

Then Mrs. M. called out, "Detectives, I've returned your suspects." Carswell and Mayhew protested loudly at being called suspects. Leo and Elena went out to meet them.

"Sit down," Elena invited, taking out a notebook.

"I presume you're not addressing me," said the housemother. She stuck her head into the hall and ordered a maid to collect the lunch trays. "Was your repast acceptable?" she asked the detectives, making it clear that their failure to acknowledge her thoughtfulness was a severe breach of good manners.

"It was very—" Elena paused, searching for a word.

"High cholesterol?" Leo suggested.

Carswell snickered, Mayhew looked astounded that anyone would dare offend Mrs. M., and the lady herself departed in a huff.

Elena followed her into the hall to make amends with a courteous thank you. After all, they might need Mrs. M.'s cooperation in the future. Having assured the housemother's good will with a compliment on the raspberry tart, Elena returned to find the roommates wandering nervously around the room. "Sit," she ordered. "We'd like to know about Mr. Fullerton's associates—friends, lovers, enemies."

Between Mayhew writing down names, after a few stammering attempts to voice them, and Carswell dictating names, Leo and Elena accumulated an impressive list of girls with whom Graham Fullerton had had dates or longer associations and male students from whom he had stolen girls.

"He even had two girls at once—when was it, Lawrence?" Pete Carswell remarked enviously.

"S-s-s-at-t-t—"

"Saturday. Right."

"And their names?" Elena asked, wondering if she was being told about the Ménage à Trois Twins.

"I don't think he said," Carswell admitted. "In fact, he was so hung over Sunday, he didn't say anything about it."

"M-m-maybe, h-he m-m-made it up-p-p," said Mayhew. Carswell shrugged.

"I thought you said he didn't drink," Elena objected.

"Well, not this year—except for Saturday I guess. Last year he really liked to party, and partying meant alcohol and sex. I can remember him bragging that he could perform if he was half conscious."

"Great guy," Elena muttered. "Do you know of any twins he dated?"

The roommates looked at one another blankly. "We don't know any twins," said Carswell.

"Who had access to his bathroom besides you two?" Leo asked.

"Hey, we never went into his bathroom," Carswell objected. "Except today when Lawrence went in to wake him up and found him on the floor." Elena stared, waiting for more helpful information.

"Well, any girl he brought home could have used his john," said Carswell.

"So any of the girls you mentioned could have been in his bathroom?" She guessed at the number of capsules the empty bottles would have held. If he took twenty a day— hadn't she read somewhere that an HIV-positive person might take that many? And spend a fortune doing it. Well, the money wouldn't have been a problem for Fullerton. But say he took twenty pills a day. Given the size of the bottles, wouldn't that mean his meds had been poisoned within the last two weeks if the tampering was done here? Of course, she didn't know the dosages. This was guesswork because the damned doctor wouldn't—well, hell! Why speculate?

She brought out Fullerton's date book, which, unfortunately, was studded with initials, and tried to get the roommates to identify the girls who belonged to the initials jotted down between March 15th and April 7th. Mayhew and Carswell protested that they couldn't be expected to remember who passed through the suite and when. They hadn't kept notes on Fullerton's activities.

"Just match up the names we gave you to the initials in his book. Oh, and the maids had access to his bathroom. They cleaned it," said Carswell.

"Was he intimate with one of the maids?" Elena asked.

The two roommates looked at one another. "Maybe Socorro," said Carswell. "He had his eye on her. Who wouldn't?"

"Sh-sh-she's g-g-gorgeous," said Mayhew.

"What's her last name?" asked Leo, pen poised above his notebook, which rested on one bony knee.

"Who knows," said Carswell. "You don't get introduced to the maids. They wear nametags. Rosa . . . Socorro . . . Maria . . . whatever."

All Hispanic, Elena noted, wondering if they were legal. "What about men?" she asked.

The roommates looked blank. "Did he screw around with men?" Leo clarified impatiently.

Carswell flushed. Mayhew looked astonished. "You've got to be kidding," said Carswell. "He never said *anything*—"

"What about you two? Either of you ever—"

Mayhew shook his had indignantly. "I'm strictly hetero," said Carswell.

"Both of you willing to take a lie detector test on that?" asked Leo.

The expressions of the two young men turned stubborn and angry.

"Just to eliminate you as suspects," Elena added as winningly as she could.

"Not without advice of counsel," said Pete Carswell. "In fact, if we're suspects, shouldn't you have—"

"—read you your rights?" Leo finished for him. "You're no more suspect than anyone else Fullerton knew."

"We'll get lawyers," said Carswell. "Right, Lawrence?"

Lawrence nodded. He looked scared. Did that mean he had done Fullerton in? Elena wondered. "Thanks for your cooperation, gentlemen." She rose from her position beside Leo on the temple-back love seat. "We'll be in touch."

8
..

Tuesday, April 8, 2:45 P.M.

Elena didn't want to visit Dr. Greta Marx at the H.H.U. Health and Reproductive Services Center. Specifically she didn't want to be lectured on her sex life and her provisions for birth control, which is what happened to anyone unfortunate enough to encounter Dr. Marx anywhere at all. The woman had once delivered a diatribe on population control at a funeral. Consequently, Elena said to Leo, "Let's save some time. I'll go over to the English Department and ask Lance Potemkin if he's heard any rumors that Fullerton was gay. You go over to the clinic and ask the doctor if she's had any AIDS cases. If she claims confidentiality, tell her she doesn't have to give us names. But you never know. She might not care, so don't—"

"I think I know how to work a witness," said Leo, scowling at her.

"Right. Well, I'm off to the English Department." Elena departed as hastily as she could. Before Leo decided it was safer to talk to Lance than the doctor. Of course, Leo might think the doctor wouldn't consider him a target. Much he knew!

In the Humanities building Elena found a new secretary in the outer office of the English Department. "Doesn't Lance Potemkin work here anymore?" she asked the woman. Lance had once been a suspect in the murder of his father. That investigation had caused waves of resentment in the homosexual community and brought Elena's mother, Harmony, hurrying forth to defend Lance, as well as to schedule poetry readings for him in New Mexico.

"He's the editor of our journal," said the new secretary, a redheaded woman with large overlapping teeth. She put through a call, and Lance, wearing glasses, carrying a red pencil, and reading from a manuscript, came out to meet Elena. He looked much too hard-working and normal to be a successful poet. Elena thought of successful poets in terms of Angus McGlenlevie, who was weird, both in appearance and behavior.

"Elena?" Lance brushed back blond hair, worn longer than in the past, and invited her back to his office, which was littered with manuscripts and galley proofs. He had to remove a stack of magazines to clear a place for her to sit. "How's your mother?"

"She's fine. Making a fortune selling hand-woven clothes to rich tourists in Santa Fe. This the magazine you edit?" Elena asked, craning to look at the top copy where the stack had been pushed into the clutter on his desk.

"*Icarus*," he agreed. "We've been nominated for a prize this year."

"Congratulations." She studied the figure with flaming wings on the cover. "Nice picture. Is it an angel?"

Lance shook his head. "A character from Greek myth. He and his father tried to fly with wings made of feathers and wax. Icarus flew too close to the sun, the wax melted, and he plunged to his death." He gestured toward the picture on the cover. "I'm not sure why the magazine was named after him. Some peculiar whim of McGlenlevie's, I guess."

At a loss for a tactful opening to the subject she wanted to discuss, Elena barged ahead. "I hope you won't take this question amiss, Lance, but since you're gay, I thought of you. Do you know if a student named Graham Fullerton had any homosexual relationships?"

"Not with me," said Lance coldly. "I'm in a stable partnership."

Lance's friend was Colin Stuart in Electrical Engineering, as Elena knew, having been on a date with Colin when he

and Lance found one another. "I didn't think you were seeing Fullerton. I just thought—"

"We keep track of one another? There's a gigantic gay
gossip machine? Maybe a scandal sheet that—"

"Come on, Lance. I told you—"

"Why do you want to know?"

She sighed. "He's dead."

Lance looked furious. "Do I need a lawyer? Am I a suspect?"

"Heavens no!" said Elena. "You weren't even in his address book. It's just—" She stopped talking because voices
coming from the hall had suddenly escalated into shouting,
followed by the sound of a *thwack* and a howl of pain. Having turned to look before the blow was administered, Elena
saw a young woman, dressed for tennis, hit Angus Mc-
Glenlevie over the head with her racket. Then the coed
smashed the erotic poetry professor on the cheekbone with
a powerful backhand.

"Estie, love," cried Gus, "be careful. You might injure
the father of your child."

"I ought to kill you, you treacherous lech," the girl thun-
dered. She hurled the weapon at him and stormed down the
hall and out of the English Department.

Gus spotted Elena and grinned. "Just a little misunder-
standing," he said. "Pay it no mind. Estie is a high-strung
girl but a wonderful volleyball player and altogether charming."

"She's pregnant?" Elena asked. "With your child?" Just
last year Gus had been after Elena's friend Sarah Tolland to
remarry him and bear children.

"So it would seem," said Gus cheerfully. "Wonderful
news, isn't it?"

"She doesn't seem to think so," said Elena dryly. She
doubted that the administration would think so either.

"Have the proofs come back on the poem I submitted to
the journal, young Lance?" Gus asked Potemkin, then explained to Elena that he himself had been editor of *Icarus*
until his failure to put out "just a few" scheduled issues
prompted the chairman to remove him from the position.

"Your poem won't run until next month," Lance replied.

"Why not?" Gus demanded. "It seems to me you might have got it in, even if I was a bit late submitting. After all, I am the foremost person on the creative-writing staff."

"We're doing three short stories by Langston Lee Ribbon," said Lance.

Elena knew Langston, brother of the victim in one of her cases, newest assistant professor of creative writing at H.H.U., a gloomy, young black man with a doctorate from the University of Houston.

"—as well as some student contributions," Lance added.

"Any of my students?" Gus asked, evidently having forgotten about his own poem. "I told the lovely Linda Morell to submit."

"I can't imagine why," said Lance. "The girl has no talent. She doesn't even have an adequate vocabulary. And there wasn't one image in the poem—"

"Could you two discuss this later?" Elena interrupted. "I just want to know if you've heard anything about Graham—"

"His name has never been mentioned among my friends," said Lance. "Nor do I know anything about the sexual orientation of the students. Unlike McGlenlevie here, I don't fraternize with them."

Gus laughed. "You should try it." He went bouncing off toward his office, an aviator's scarf trailing behind, leaving Elena to wonder if he had really impregnated a coed. Dr. Marx wouldn't like it at all if Gus wasn't taking due precautions in his student liaisons. Happily, Gus's pecadilloes, and they were many, were not her concern; finding out who had killed Graham Fullerton was. She drew Lance into his office and closed the door.

Although she knew she shouldn't even mention AIDS, Elena couldn't resist asking, "Have you heard any rumors about AIDS on campus?"

"No," said Lance sharply, "and I don't have it."

Elena sighed; the question had been a bad idea. "I didn't think you did, Lance. And please forget I asked." She picked up her handbag, heavy with the weight of her gun and badge, and prepared to leave. "Say hi to Colin for me."

Lance relented and said, "I guess I'm a little defensive, but you can't blame me. After all, you've had me on your arrest list."

"Not lately," she pointed out, trying a smile on him.

He smiled back reluctantly. "Actually, I did hear something odd."

She turned questioningly. "What?"

"There's a rumor floating around campus that those wack-os—the Antifornication Brigade—are poisoning AIDS meds because they think everyone with AIDS is a sinner."

Elena tried to quell a tidal wave of foreboding.

"Now, let *me* ask a question," said Lance. "Did your corpse have AIDS? Was he poisoned?"

"That's two questions, and we don't know. Where'd you hear that rumor?" Somehow Elena couldn't see Ora Mae Spotwood, the head of the Antifornication Brigade, tampering with medicine. On the other hand, there had been a man, a fanatic named Chester Briggs—but he was dead.

"Colin."

"Who told Colin?" she asked, surprised.

"He heard some students talking."

"You think he knows who they were?"

"No idea. If they were in one of his classes, I suppose he would."

Elena made a note. *See Colin.* "You believe it?" she asked.

Lance shrugged. "It doesn't affect me, so I didn't give it much thought. But since you ask, I'd have to say that I wouldn't put anything past that bunch of self-righteous fanatics."

Elena left feeling depressed. Poisoning AIDS medications to punish sinners? It was an idea that sent shivers up her spine. She needed to talk to Colin.

9

The Herbert Hobart Health and Reproductive Services Center was a one-story, salmon-colored, Art Deco building still bearing the silhouettes of H.H.U. policemen who had been spray-painted by abortion protestors. Inside, the receptionist huddled behind her desk with her hands over her ears. Several students sat giggling in the waiting room while, from Dr. Marx's office, came the boom of the doctor's voice delivering a lecture on the duty of married couples to limit their offspring.

"Five children is ludicrous," she shouted.

Ah, thought Elena, poor Leo was the subject of the attack.

"And it doesn't matter that your wife is Catholic. *You* could have used birth control. Why didn't you?"

Mumble, mumble from Leo. Elena couldn't make out his reply.

"*Fertility drugs?* That's insane. If you couldn't have children in the usual way, you should have been responsible citizens of an overpopulated planet and left well enough alone."

Mumble, mumble.

"Detective, any idiot knows fertility drugs produce multiple births, not to mention huge medical expenses because the babies are born prematurely. I suppose all your children are suffering from birth defects and—"

Mumble, mumble, mumble.

37

"The university's supporting your children? No wonder I can't get a larger appropriation for sex education here on campus. I'd *like* to lecture throughout the city, no matter what Bishop Chavira thinks. But, no. Harley Stanley doesn't want anyone to say anything controversial, especially me."

Elena murmured to the receptionist, "I'll just go back and rescue him."

"What measures are you taking *now*, Detective? Surely, you're not trusting to luck that you and your wife won't have another five—"

"Hi, Dr. Marx," said Elena cheerfully. She glanced at her partner, usually a happy, easygoing man. His face was red, his hands clenched, and he looked ready to leap from his chair and throttle the doctor, who had risen from her chair to berate Leo.

"Don't interrupt me, young woman!" snapped Dr. Marx, who then turned back to Leo. "Los Santos has a huge percentage of young people. While the rest of the nation is aging, people like you, Detective, are overcrowding our schools, raising our poverty rate—"

"AIDS," said Elena loudly.

That shut the doctor up. "Are you saying you have it?" she asked Elena. "Since you're not a student, I can't treat you, but I can refer you to—"

"We think a male student, who was just murdered, was HIV positive, at the least. Of course, that information's confidential."

The doctor's forehead furrowed.

"He was sexually active," Elena continued. "Extremely active, if gossip and his date book are any indication."

Dr. Marx dropped into her chair, face pale. Elena couldn't remember seeing Greta Marx in anything but attack mode, except for the time she was hit over the head with a statue, but even in the hospital, she had been pretty aggressive.

Leo frowned at Elena. "For God's sake, we're not supposed to—"

"I didn't mention his name." She stared meaningfully at the doctor. "I thought you ought to know, so I'm sort of breaking the rules. Don't dump me in hot water. Have any other students tested positive for HIV?''

The doctor's face seemed to age. ''Unless a patient asks, I'm not allowed to administer the tests—an idiot regulation from the state of Texas, as backward and benighted a—''

''Has anyone asked?'' Elena interrupted quickly.

''No,'' said the doctor grimly, ''and I couldn't give you a name if I had one, any more than you gave me a name just now. More regulations about patient confidentiality. Not that the student body here pays any attention to the dangers of sexually transmitted diseases. I presume they think rich people can't get AIDS. Or if they avoid public toilet seats, they're safe. Can you imagine? One young ninny informed me that she was at no risk because she was too intelligent to use a public toilet without spraying the seat with an antibacterial aerosol her mother provided. When I told her that both she and her mother were idiots if they thought HIV was caught from toilet seats, she reported me to the administration for insulting her mother, who had recently made a sizable contribution to the Hobart Fund. I received a letter of reprimand from Harley Stanley.

''All the warnings on television and in the newspapers, and she thought she could get AIDS from a toilet seat.'' Dr. Marx fumbled in the bottom drawer of her desk and came up with a clutch of pamphlets.

''I am constantly appalled at such ignorance.'' She handed a pamphlet to Elena and one to Leo. ''I *wanted* to hold an assembly, give a lecture on the dangers, but the administration wouldn't let me. All I was allowed to do was send out this pamphlet.''

In large red letters it said, DEATH IS STALKING YOU.

''You can imagine how many students read it,'' said Dr. Marx bitterly. ''None, would be my guess. Then I suggested that HIV testing be a requirement for admission. Dr. Stanley said absolutely not. I should have done it anyway, paid for the labs myself, sent anonymous letters to anyone who tested positive.''

''Isn't that illegal?'' asked Leo.

''Of course it is. This is Texas. Land of rugged individualists. Bastion of Bible Belt types who think AIDS is God's answer to homosexuality. Was this fellow homosexual?''

"No evidence that he was," Elena replied. :''If he went for males, it would have been a sideline to a very active hetero lifestyle.''

"He could have infected dozens of girls. If he was bisexual, he could have infected both sexes. We could have a silent epidemic. My God!'' The doctor's volume suddenly rose again, no doubt jarring the students in the waiting room.

"Lower your voice," Leo hissed.

"And all that idiot Harley Stanley cares about is appearances. He doesn't want any scandal. Don't they know people *die* of AIDS? Fools!'' Greta Marx's voice had trailed off. "Fools!''

For the first time, Elena felt sorry for the woman. As obnoxious and embarrassing a person as Greta Marx was, she did have the welfare of her patients at heart. "We've been told that City-County Health can't contact his girlfriends without his written permission, and since he's dead . . .'' Elena spread her hands.

"Cowards!'' snapped the doctor. "It's their duty to make the calls. Even if his family sues them, they have a responsibility to protect the health of the public.''

"I don't think they're going to,'' Leo remarked.

"Then we'll have to,'' said Dr. Marx. "Somehow I'll have to convince the university that it's more dangerous to court a silent epidemic than offend one family.''

"You think they'll—''

"No,'' sighed the doctor. "In which case I ought to quit in protest, but then there wouldn't be anyone to look out for these young people.'' She leaned back in her chair, hands clasped at chest level, thinking, then shot up straight and eyed Elena with her usual mixture of aggression and stubborn fanaticism.

"There is one thing I can do something about. I want to report a rape.''

Both Leo and Elena were caught by surprise. "That's not exactly our—''

"It's a crime against a person, isn't it?" snapped Dr. Marx, glaring at Elena.

"Yes, ma'am, but another division of our—"

"You're here. You can do something about it." The doctor slapped her hands down on the desk. "There is a young woman named Gretchen Farber, a sensible, strong-minded person, very responsible. But she made the mistake of going out with a student who has a very bad reputation with women. Gretchen confessed that she planned to spray him with Mace if he tried anything with her; in fact, she looked forward to it. However, after drinking a Coke with him in his room, she began to feel very sleepy and remembers nothing after that with any clarity until she woke up in his bed the next morning, horrified and, as you can imagine, very confused.

"He told her that she was, and I quote her on this, 'great in the sack.' She stumbled out of his bed, got her purse, and sprayed him with the Mace. Then she came over here and burst into tears.

"I suspect she was given Rohypnol. She certainly had had intercourse, although there were no signs of force. Still, if Rohypnol was administered, force would be unnecessary."

Elena sucked in her breath in dismay. The date-rape drug. It came across the border from Mexico and was easily available to anyone who had the money. "Did you take semen samples? Is she willing to press charges?"

"I did, and she isn't." The doctor shook her head glumly. "Farber has gone completely to pieces. Thinks what happened is her fault. I've begged her to press charges. I've begged her to at least get counseling. She won't do either. But *you* can arrest him."

"Not without her cooperation," said Leo somberly.

"Who was the man?" Elena asked. "Did she name him?"

"Wayne Quarles, Jr. That should ring a bell with you, Detective. You put his father in jail."

Elena nodded. The father would have his day in court sometime during the summer, and the son—she remembered very well the rumors she'd heard about him: drugs and forced sex. "I'll look into it," she said grimly.

Leo protested, "Elena, we can't—"

"We can ask a few questions," she insisted.

"Good," said the doctor with angry satisfaction. "I'm breaking patient confidentiality even telling you this, but poor Gretchen isn't going to sue me, and his arrest will give the girl some closure."

"And a hell of a time if she has to testify in court," Leo muttered.

"Look, if I go after Quarles, you ought to do me a favor in return," said Elena. "I'd like to know if you've had any students with symptoms of AIDS or HIV, even if they wouldn't let you test. Maybe someone who's left school for health reasons under circumstances that would—"

"Sorry, Detective," Greta Marx replied crisply. "I don't make deals of that sort."

"Why not? You broke confidentiality for Gretchen Farber. Why won't you give me names—"

"Gretchen is a victim. Any girl who shows HIV or AIDS symptoms, even if I had one as a patient, would also be a victim, but you'd be looking for her with the idea of victimizing her twice. Isn't that the thrust of your inquiry? To find out who killed your unnamed corpse? Therefore, if I had such a patient, I certainly wouldn't expose her to questions or suspicion. Gretchen, on the other hand, will never recover from what happened to her unless the disgusting Quarles boy is punished. She has to understand that he, not she, was to blame for what happened."

Then the doctor smiled. "However, I will do this much for *you*, Detective Weizell." Leo looked hopeful while the doctor disappeared into an adjoining room.

"You did say your wife is Catholic?" she asked, returning with a box under her arm.

"Yeah," said Leo cautiously.

"Then holding the line at five children is *your* responsibility." She thrust the box into his hands.

"What—"

"Condoms," she said smugly. "Would you like instructions on how to—"

Leo turned red and grumbled, "I know how."

"Good. Then use them." She turned to Elena. "I believe we're finished here."

"I guess so," Elena agreed. "Well, Leo, now that you're all taken care of, we'd better see if we can run down that maid Carswell mentioned."

"I can't walk past those giggling students with a box of condoms under my arm," he muttered.

"Men!" said Dr. Marx in disgust. She made another quick trip into the next room, returned, and wrapped the condom box in a white towel. "Satisfied?" she asked.

Elena choked on laughter, while Leo glared at her.

"So, do you think she has a patient who's sick after going to bed with Fullerton?" Leo asked once they were out of earshot.

"No. It takes a long time for anything to happen, doesn't it? And if she did have an HIV patient, like she said, she wouldn't tell us. We need to see Colin Stuart, too."

"Why?"

"Because he heard a rumor that L.S.A.R.I. is poisoning AIDS medication."

Leo looked more cheerful. "Maybe we can wrap this up quick and get away from this campus. It gives me the creeps."

"We should be so lucky," Elena replied pessimistically.

10

Tuesday, April 8, 3:45 P.M.

They found Colin Stuart in his office in the Engineering building and asked where he'd heard the rumor about AIDS medication.

Colin laughed. "Good lord, I should never have passed that on. It's manifestly ridiculous." Then he glanced curiously from Elena to Leo. "Isn't it? Why are you asking?"

"Obvious danger to public health," Elena replied casually. "We have to follow up what would be a crime against persons. That's our mission." She tried to look jaunty.

"In other words, mind my own business and answer the question?" Colin leaned back in his swivel chair. "All right, but I can't think of anyone I told except Lance. Did he tell you?"

"He did."

"I wonder why."

Elena looked at him expectantly without answering.

"You're not looking at him as a suspect in some murder, are you? He told me about the time his father—"

"He's not a suspect," Elena assured Colin.

"Has there been a murder? I mean other than the usual things you read in the paper—drive-by shootings, Juarez drug-war executions, jilted lovers killing the—"

"Professor." Leo frowned at Stuart.

"Well." Colin Stuart crumpled an interdepartmental memo and lofted it into a wastebasket. "Where did I hear

44

the rumor in question? Or more to the point, from whom?'' He dropped his chair back into upright position. ''I believe it was after my Monday ten o'clock class. And the student was . . . Carswell. Can't remember his first name.''

''Pete?'' asked Elena. Colin shrugged; he didn't remember. ''What does he look like?'' In case there were two Carswells on campus, she wanted a more positive ID.

Stuart thought a moment. ''Short height, small frame, light brown hair.''

That sounded like the victim's roommate. ''What about his teeth?'' she asked. ''Does he have great teeth?''

Stuart stared at her. ''All the students here have good teeth,'' he replied. ''Obviously there wasn't anything wrong with Carswell's teeth. *That* I would have noticed.''

Leo nudged Elena. ''Sounds like the same guy to me,'' he observed. Elena had to agree. In the meantime Stuart had pulled out a grade book, run his finger down the list, and pointed to the name Peter Carswell, who had a low C average. Satisfied, they thanked Colin Stuart and left quickly.

As they walked back to the dorm, Elena said to her partner. ''Carswell? Does that mean he knew Fullerton was HIV positive and had a good idea, which he didn't share with us, about how and why Fullerton got killed?''

''Or that, protests to the contrary, he's gay and has reason to keep track of rumors about stuff like AZT?'' Leo suggested.

''Or maybe he made the rumor up to throw suspicion on outsiders even before we found out for sure that Fullerton took poisoned AIDS meds,'' Elena speculated.

''Right,'' Leo agreed. ''Because Carswell poisoned the capsules or knows who did,''

When they arrived on the fifth floor again, Mayhew was out and Carswell was watching a soap opera on TV with several friends in the end-of-the-hall lounge. The detectives dragged him away from some convoluted drug-deal plot involving a voluptuous blonde and walked him back to his room.

''Don't see why you couldn't wait for the commercial,'' Carswell complained.

"We just heard you've been telling people about poisoned AIDS medication. We'd like to hear about that." Leo stared at the young student.

Carswell stared back. "How come?"

"Just tell us about it. What did you hear? Who did you hear it from?"

"You think Graham—" Carswell seemed to be considering the implications of their questions and coming up blank. "I mean he's the only person who—" He scratched his head. "But Graham was taking vitamins, not AIDS stuff. Why would he—"

"You remember the question?" Elena prodded. "What did you hear, and who did you hear it from?"

"Graham didn't have AIDS . . . Did he?" Carswell suddenly laughed. "I guess you think because he did a lot of screwing around he might have, huh? But listen." He turned earnest and sober. "People like us don't get AIDS. Don't you read the papers? It's the gays and the minorities. Graham used condoms. Everybody with half a brain does. Well, when they remember."

"Thanks for sharing that," said Elena dryly. Dr. Marx had been dead on when she said H.H.U. students thought they were immune. "Now, back to our question."

He shrugged. "Some girl told me. She said there was a rumor floating around campus that those wackos—what are they called?—the Antifornication Brigade. That they poisoned AIDS medications because they thought everyone with AIDS was a sinner or something."

"What girl?" Elena asked.

"I don't remember," said Carswell. "Since it didn't have anything to do with me, I didn't pay much attention."

His roommate Lawrence Mayhew came in with a gym bag in one hand and a Danish pastry in the other. "You hear that rumor, Lawrence?" Carswell asked.

"W-w-what—?"

"About someone doctoring AIDS medication. That anti-abortion, antisex group."

Mayhew nodded.

"Remember where you heard it?"

Mayhew shook his head. "G-g-girl."

"Just what I said. I think it was going in to dinner. Were we together?"

Mayhew nodded and unzipped his bag to take out a bottle of Perrier, which he sipped between bites of pastry.

"Why would someone tell you something like that?" asked Leo. "Either of you on AZT or any of that stuff?"

"No, man," cried Carswell, obviously insulted. "It was just gossip. Probably not even true. I mean how would anyone do that? Like would you soak the pills in something? Or substitute something in the person's pill bottle? Or—"

"How come you don't remember who told you?"

"Well, actually she told someone else, and I overheard," said Carswell. "She was behind us in line, wasn't she, Larry?" Mayhew nodded, mouth full of Danish.

"If you remember who told you the story, give me a call," said Elena, handing him her card.

That was very convenient, a rumor with no source, from a guy who might want to deflect suspicion from himself or his roommate or other students who might have had reason to kill Graham Fullerton. So he encourages the police to blame it on the crackpots. Still, she wrote herself a note as they boarded the elevator. *Check L.S.A.R.I.* The initials stood for Los Santoans Against Rampant Immorality. The group was divided into the Antifornication Brigade and the Antiabortion Brigade.

Then she paged back in the notebook. *Look for maid named Socorro,* she read. "Shall we check out the gorgeous maid that Fullerton had his eye on?" she asked Leo.

"Beats talking to those two guys," Leo replied. "You believe them? That they actually heard that? And that they don't remember who told them?"

"Seems convenient, doesn't it? We'll have to find out how they got along with Fullerton. Maybe he was screwing their girlfriends."

"If they have any girlfriends," Leo responded.

11

Tuesday, April 8, 4:20 P.M.

The roster of maids, which Elena and Leo got from the office of Vice-President for Financial Affairs Joel Smith, contained two Socorros, Rascon and Treviso. No one in the business office could predict which one might have caught the eye of the late Graham Fullerton, but Mrs. Poleby, the director of Housekeeping, revealed that both Socorros were just going off shift and might be intercepted at their lockers in the "maids' retiring room," as she so quaintly called it.

The detectives rushed off to the locker room, where Elena—Leo wasn't allowed into a female enclave—located Socorro Treviso, a stocky, no-nonsense woman of fifty or so with a brown face scarred by acne or one of the poxes. She did not seem a likely candidate to have attracted the victim. Consequently, Elena went in search of Socorro Rascon and was told she'd just left.

"Maybe you can catch her at the bus stop," said the woman who had the adjoining locker. Her nametag said Luz.

"She's gone to the chapel," volunteered a soft-voiced woman who looked no older than sixteen.

"Which chapel?" Elena asked.

"*Aqui. De la universidad,*" replied the teenager.

"Who are you?" Luz asked Elena. "You new here?"

Elena produced her identification, after which both women backed away, looking conscience-stricken, as if they had betrayed Socorro Rascon.

48

"I knew what she was," said the older Socorro, who had been listening. "*Policia!*" She made a sound of disapproval and went back to folding her lavender uniform and placing its pieces, skirt, blouse, apron, and cap, into a large shopping bag.

"Which bus stop?" asked Elena. "In case she's left the chapel."

All the women turned away. Sighing, Elena walked out of the cement-walled room—no Art Deco touches here—and rejoined Leo.

"Not very liberated," he said as they headed for the chapel. "How come I can't go into the ladies' locker room? Female reporters insist on barging into male locker rooms."

"Although how they can stand the smell is beyond me," retorted Elena.

"It's not the smell; it's the principle," said Leo loftily. "As the departmental femiNazi, you ought to know that. I just might file a complaint of sexual discrimination here."

"Good idea, Leo," Elena agreed.

"Which you'll support me in?"

"Absolutely. I'll even try to protect you when their brothers and husbands come after you, all being proper Hispanic males who don't want their women's underwear ogled by cops like you."

"What's that supposed to mean?"

"Male. What else?"

They had walked from the housekeeping offices over paths edged by lush grass, palm trees, and flowering bushes—none native to the desert southwest, all devourers of scarce water supplies. Last year the sprinkler system and wells had been bombed because of the university's flagrant water wastage. But even so violent a warning seemed to have gone unheeded, for Elena could see no evidence of conservation. The shrubbery, which had withered before the wells were redrilled and the sprinkler systems replaced, now flourished again. She could see sprinklers in action over by the Engineering building, where they had just interviewed Colin Stuart.

Elena wondered what Socorro Rascon was doing at the

chapel since her shift was over. When they arrived, a number
of Hispanic women were clustered in the Sacred Vestibule,
where cocktail parties were held after services. Chief Clabb
of the university police and two of his men were remonstrat-
ing with the women.

"It's not the Virgin Mary, ladies," said the chief, wiping
sweat from a brow furrowed with alarm.

"They are keeping the miracle for their Anglo students,"
a woman beside Elena whispered in Spanish to her friend.
"We are not good enough to see the Weeping Virgin." She
sounded highly resentful.

Her friend shouted at the beleaguered chief, "Miracles are
meant for all. God does not care what is the color of the
worshipper's skin."

"True," cried Chief Clabb, "but—"

"We'll go to the bishop," cried a young woman with
flowing black hair.

"All right," said Clabb, looking confused, "but he'll tell
you—"

"—that it's our right as Christians to visit a weepin' Virgin."

"It's *not* the Virgin!"

"What are you going to do? Shoot us if we go in?" called
the woman beside Elena.

Elena was amazed at how religious fervor could make
normally reticent women so outspoken.

Clabb swiveled and stared at his challenger desperately,
then noticed for the first time that Elena and Leo were in
the crowd. "Reinforcements," he cried with relief and wiped
his forehead again. "Detectives, could you please tell these
ladies that they can't just occupy our chapel?"

"Why do they want to?" Elena asked. Considering how
strange the chapel was, she couldn't imagine why any sensible Hispanic Roman Catholic would want to enter, much
less "occupy" the place.

Clabb shook his head wearily. "One of the stained-glass
windows appears to be weeping. I mean the image on the
window appears—well, it's *not* the Virgin Mary. I don't

know who it is. Some fertility goddess. No one seems to know.''

''Angel Guadaramma says it's the Holy Mother an' that she weeps,'' said the young woman with long hair, her mouth set in a stubborn line.

''We have come to lay flowers at her feet,'' said another woman, speaking Spanish, which the chief and his minions did not appear to understand. She waved a spray of blossoms that Elena was sure had been plucked from a campus bush.

''Where did you get those flowers?'' demanded one of Clabb's officers.

Elena could feel the resentment growing among the women. They took their devotion to the Virgin seriously. Quickly, Elena cut through the crowd, which had grown by five or six women and three men she took to be gardeners. Standing beside Chief Clabb, she said loudly enough to be heard by all, ''You should consult with the bishop or your priest. If it's some pagan idol instead of the Virgin, it wouldn't be proper to honor her with your flowers. If it's the Virgin, then you'll want to arrange visits to the chapel, perhaps through Mrs. Poleby. Isn't she your boss?''

''My boss is Hector Montes,'' said a gardener.

Elena nodded. ''I know him. You guys can take the problem up with him.''

''What are you saying?'' whispered Clabb nervously.

Elena had been speaking in Spanish, gauging her audience to be mostly Hispanic. ''Is any of you Socorro Rascon?'' she asked as the crowd began to break up, still muttering.

''I am,'' said the long-haired spokeswoman. She was slender and moved with the grace and strength of youth that had outgrown awkward teenage self-consciousness, but her eyes snapped with an anger and cynicism beyond her years. ''Whadda ya want with me?'' she demanded.

Elena and Leo identified themselves.

''I gotta bus to catch,'' said Socorro in English and turned to leave.

''We'll give you a ride home,'' Elena offered quickly.

Leo frowned. ''I got five kids and a wife expecting me just about now.''

"I'll drop you off at headquarters, Leo, then take Ms. Rascon home. Where do you live?" She smiled at the young woman, who looked ambivalent. Elena knew just what she was thinking: a ride home was better than a long wait at a bus stop and a longer ride on the bus, perhaps standing; on the other hand, a ride with the cops—no one wanted that.

Then Socorro shrugged, still speaking English, which meant that she wasn't accepting Elena as one of *la raza*, one of her people. "I ain't done nothin', so I'll take the ride. But I live in Canutillo."

Upper Valley, Elena thought, and Leo wanted to get home, but he hadn't driven in to headquarters today; Concepcion had dropped him off on her way to the pediatrician with the five babies. What a ride that must have been!

"Chief Clabb," Elena called. "Can one of your men give Detective Weizell a ride? He lives up the mountain in Sussex Hills."

"I'll do it myself," said the grateful Clabb, who, as usual, had panicked at the first sign of trouble.

"O.K.?" she asked her partner. Leo nodded. Elena turned to Socorro. "Let's go." The young woman looked relieved, probably because she wouldn't be riding with two officers, one of them male. And she proved to be quite talkative as they drove northwest to Canutillo, a small town in the Upper Valley. However, she never switched back to Spanish, which would have been more comfortable for her and a sign that she accepted Elena.

"Fullerton? Room 507, right?" she said when questioned. "A creep. You oughta arrest him. He sees me; he tries to grab a titty. *Pinche* bastard. I hit him with a mop last time."

"Where was this?" Elena asked.

"Inna shoulder. Big tall guy. Thinks he's a great lover or somethin'."

"No, where were *you*?"

"Moppin' his bathroom."

"When was that?"

"I don' know. Three, four weeks ago. I got Señora Poleby to move me to another floor. Now Socorro Una does his rooms."

"Come again?"

"We got two of us maids named Socorro. Socorro Una, she was hired before me. When the university opened. Me, I only been here like six months. The other Socorro, he gives her any trouble, she'll kill him."

By poisoning his medication? Elena wondered. "You know of any of the maids who've—ah—"

"Fucked 'im? No way. Hey, one of us gets tight with a some stuck-up Anglo student, we're out on our asses. But I'll tell you, if it wasn't for the good money, I'd quit. No wonder the Virgin's weepin'. She's weepin' for what we gotta put up with. Weird food, long bus rides, guys with wanderin' hands, girls who want us to wash their dirty hose an' underwear, like we don't have to finish half a floor every day. Some of us do the washin' 'cause they pay, but not much. You'd think a *gringa* with so much money would share a little of it, huh? No way.

"Well, I don' wash no one's underwear. But I'm savin' my money. Gonna learn computers an' get a real job. I could kick myself, I didn' pay no attention to that kinda stuff in high school. Like I graduated, but I didn' learn nothin'. I thought the gangs was more important than the classes. Now look at me. My boyfriend's in jail, an' I'm cleanin' rich kids' toilets. An' how come we ain't good enough to go look at the Virgin?"

"They say it isn't the Virgin," Elena replied.

"They lie. I seen it once. Helped clean the chapel when Angel was pukin' with mornin' sickness. They was gonna fire her. You believe that? 'Cause she's pregnant. We oughta organize a union. That's what we oughta do."

"Good idea," Elena agreed. That would give the administration something to think about.

"Call it la Virgin de H.H.U. Union."

"What if it's not the Virgin? You gonna call it the Pagan Fertility Goddess of H.H.U. Union?"

Socorro glared at her, a tough kid who still had that in-your-face gang attitude. She'd probably make a great labor organizer if she actually followed through on the union idea.

Just then Elena got a call on her radio informing her that

she had to attend a meeting in the office of Dr. Harley Stanley, vice-president for Academic Affairs at the university. What now? Had they heard about Socorro's subversive plans to rally the maids?

Elena dropped the young woman off at a rambling adobe on a dirt road in Canutillo and headed back. She'd check to see just when Socorro had stopped working Fullerton's floor and if there was any gossip about her and the victim. For sure, Socorro Una wouldn't have been on the receiving end of any passes from the deceased. But what if she had a beautiful daughter—and Fullerton had gotten to the beautiful daughter? Elena shook her head. That was a long shot. She had other paths to follow first. One of which led, unfortunately, to Harley Stanley's office. And someone had to notify the victim's parents.

12

Tuesday, April 8, 5:30 P.M.

When Elena arrived at Harley Stanley's vice presidential suite of offices, she found that she had not been invited to a private tête à tête. She was directed to the conference room by Dr. Stanley's angry secretary, who thought secretaries should be allowed to go home at five o'clock, not asked to remain for the foreseeable future, making themselves available should they be deemed sufficiently trustworthy to take notes on the rude, noisy conference being conducted behind closed doors. "I can't even take you in," she said to Elena. "It's too top-secret, according to Dr. Stanley—as if I can't hear every word they're shouting at each other."

Elena made sympathetic, if noncommittal, noises.

"Oh, and I've been instructed to ask you to let the university get in touch with the dead student's parents."

Elena readily agreed. She hated family notification. "Ask Dr. Stanley to let me know after he's talked to them. We may need to interview the relatives."

The secretary made a note. "He probably wants to hit them up for a memorial donation," she said, voice dripping with cynicism.

Elena could easily believe that. Harley Stanley just loved contributions to the Hobart Fund, no matter what the occasion. She opened the door for herself and was struck immediately by the magnificence of the room: heavy turquoise drapes held back by giant replicas of the university seal,

55

salmon and gray carpeting with an elaborate, repeated pattern; chairs upholstered in a matching fabric, with backs, arms, and legs of a highly polished wood that matched that of the long gleaming conference table.

And the table! Inlaid at its center, and along the border, was a pattern of stylized leaves and flowers. The remaining, smooth surfaces had been waxed and buffed to a mirrorlike finish that actually reflected the faces of the angry combatants. Elena wondered if anyone ever dared to lay conference materials on that imposing, if gaudy, piece of furniture. Had it known the weight of pens, pads of paper, tape recorders, academic schedules?

All this splendor was noted in a second, for the heated argument in progress was even more striking. Seated around the table were Dr. Greta Marx of the H.H.U. Health and Reproductive Services Center; Dr. Juan Geronimo Morelos, Commissioner of City-County Health; Medical Examiner Onofre Calderon, Police Chief Armando Gaitan; Dr. Stanley himself, and Leo. As she dropped into an empty chair next to her partner, Elena was thinking that the only person missing was her superior, Lieutenant Beltran. However, he arrived before she had settled her tired body on the cushioned seat and nodded to Leo, who looked less than pleased to be here. Sighing, Elena tuned in on the confrontation. No one had paid any attention to her arrival.

"I consider your bringing public officials into what is a private university matter a breach of your contract, Dr. Marx," Harley Stanley shouted.

"There's nothing private about an AIDS epidemic in Los Santos," said Dr. Morelos. "It's a public disaster."

"You don't know that that poor fellow had AIDS," Dr. Stanley pointed out, moderating his tone for someone over whom he held no power. "Your medical examiner is guessing. Capsules look alike, I would imagine. There are probably hundreds of medications that particular color."

"Maybe he was only HIV positive," Elena suggested. "He didn't necessarily have full-blown AIDS."

"Which would make him just as able to pass the virus on to any poor girl foolish enough to have sex with him," snapped Dr. Marx while Harley Stanley cried, "Dr. Jarvis!" acting as if Elena, the recipient of an honorary degree from H.H.U., had betrayed her alma mater by suggesting that a student of the university might be in any stage of such an embarrassing infection.

"Detective," she corrected.

"The pills found in his bathroom are AZT and 3TC," said Onofre Calderon. "We haven't identified the third capsule."

"There," declared Harley Stanley. "You're unable to say our student was ill. Perhaps he just overdosed on some illegal substance."

"He may have," Dr. Morelos admitted, "but since he was taking Retrovir and Epivir, it's reasonable to assume that he had the virus and that his CD4 counts were under five hundred."

"Proof positive," said Greta Marx triumphantly. "We owe it to our students to initiate immediate campus-wide testing."

"We don't know that they were his pills," protested Dr. Stanley.

"Best guess is that those pills killed him," said Onofre Calderon. "Three or four of the capsules on the floor had been tampered with, and I'd bet my next month's salary someone put cyanide in them."

"Chief Gaitan." Stanley appealed to the chief as a city functionary who might support him. The city customarily went out of its way to please an institution that provided jobs, salaries, and great buying power in a poor community, as were most such cities on the Texas-Mexico border. "A scandal of this sort—good lord, it could close the school," Dr. Stanley warned. "Certainly donations to the Hobart Foundation would fall off disastrously. Students would drop out. Potential new students would not enroll. Think of the economic consequences to the city if we close."

Chief Gaitan cleared his throat, no doubt considering how the mayor would view such an outcome. "State law forbids us to identify the deceased as HIV positive without his written consent, which, for obvious reasons, he can't give. That being the case, the investigation will have to be handled with discretion. The press hasn't got wind of this, have they?" He turned toward Elena and Leo. They didn't get a chance to answer.

"Because our hands are tied, as Chief Gaitan pointed out," interrupted Morelos, "the university will have to find some way to warn anyone with whom this young man may have been intimate and to advise testing."

"I told you so," said Dr. Marx smugly to Harley Stanley.

That attitude wasn't going to help matters, thought Elena. The woman really was tactless.

The vice-president scowled at his medical officer, as if the whole public relations problem could be laid at her door. Greta Marx turned to Elena and Leo. "As soon as you find out who he's been sleeping with, let me know. I'll call them in one at a time and have a talk with them."

"You'll do no such thing," barked the vice-president. "Not only would that expose us to scandal and cause a wave of gossip and panic among the students, but you'd leave us open to law suits."

"Don't be such a weenie," retorted the clinic doctor. "You want to be responsible for an epidemic?"

"Gentlemen—and ladies," Chief Gaitan intervened in his best peace-making voice, "now that it's been established that notification is neither the intention or responsibility of the LSPD, we'll just conduct a quiet investigation, get this cleared up, and—"

"Chief, we don't know whether someone tampered with Fullerton's medication after he got it or before," Elena pointed out, finally getting a word in by dint of interrupting her own superior, which was never a smart move. "Maybe the tampering was done before the capsules were dispensed. His weren't in properly marked bottles. Where did they come from? His doctor doesn't know what drugstore."

"Well, find out," snapped the chief. "Canvass the pharmacies. They'll have a list of their customers."

"And the doctor won't divulge what kind of medication Fullerton was taking. And there's the red ones," Elena went on doggedly. "We don't even know what they are. Maybe he was buying something weird in Mexico, ground peach pits or something."

Morelos stared at her over the top of his glasses. "I believe you're thinking of apricot pits, a quack cancer treatment, Detective."

She flushed. "Whatever. It's going to be hard to investigate this without mentioning AIDS."

"The thought of a year in jail and/or a five-thousand-dollar fine should be an incentive," said Onofre, grinning at her.

"If these capsules came to him already poisoned, there may be other AIDS victims at risk," Elena said quickly. "We'd need to call in the feds."

"Much too early in the game for that," snapped Gaitan.

"Well, at least other people with AIDS need to be warned of the possibility that their medication might be—"

"Do you have any reason to think this crime wasn't aimed specifically at the victim?" asked Morelos.

"We've heard rumors about AIDS medication being poisoned," said Leo.

Morelos drummed his fingers on the gleaming table, leaving fingerprints that caused Dr. Stanley to wince. "We'll need to warn doctors and pharmacies if that's the case," said the Public Health honcho.

Elena felt a measure of relief. She'd been afraid no protection would be offered to either Fullerton's sexual contacts or AIDS patients city-wide because everyone was afraid of that year in jail and the five grand fine—not that she could afford it herself.

"But the warning doesn't have to be connected to the university," said Gaitan soothingly.

"I should hope not," Harley Stanley chimed in, looking horrified at the possibility.

"Have you had any other students who tested positive, Dr. Marx?" asked Dr. Morelos.

"You *did* call him, didn't you?" accused Harley Stanley.

"No," snapped Greta Marx, "but I should have."

"Yes. Why didn't you?" demanded Morelos.

"I'm going to have to report you to the board of trustees, Dr. Marx," said Dr. Stanley.

"I'm the one who called Public Health," said Onofre Calderon.

"It doesn't matter who called me," said the City-County Health commissioner impatiently.

"Well, even if Mr. Fullerton was ill, I doubt that his— er—problem would affect other students. At least not many," said Harley Stanley confidently. "We're making a mountain out of a molehill."

"Around thirty," said Elena.

"*What*?"

"He had the names of at least thirty girls in his book. Maybe we'll find more when we crosscheck what his roommates said against his little black book and his calendar."

"But many would have been friends, not lovers," insisted the vice president.

"Then why was he writing in sexual comments beside their names?" Elena retorted.

"Thirty?" Dr. Stanley dropped his head into his hands.

Dr. Greta Marx said, "I must ask you, Dr. Stanley, to authorize HIV testing for the entire student body. If he infected thirty girls, and they infected, say, two boys each, and those boys—well, you can see the implications. Campuswide testing is the only safe course."

Harley Stanley raised his head. "No," he said. "Absolutely not."

"At least not without their permission. You do understand that, Doctor?" said Juan Geronimo Morelos. "You can counsel testing, but you can't insist. How many cases have you had so far?"

"How should I know?" snapped Greta Marx. "Our students aren't sensible enough to ask for a test."

"There," said Dr. Stanley. "Not a single student has tested positive."

"Fullerton evidently did," she retorted.

"But you didn't test him, and I don't want you even mentioning AIDS from now on, Dr. Marx. I forbid you to subject our students, or faculty, for that matter, to any lectures or pamphleteering or nagging about diseases that they, doubtless, don't have.''

"You wish," said Dr. Marx.

13
..

Tuesday, April 8, 7:00 P.M.

By the time the meeting ended at seven, hunger and irritation were the only feelings Elena had left. "We ought to check out Wayne Quarles, Jr.," she murmured wearily to Leo.

"Not me," he replied. "I'm going home, and to hell with H.H.U." He stalked off through the pink marble lobby of the Administration building, climbed into his own car, which he had parked in the university president's space, and drove away.

Unable to banish the thought of Gretchen Farber, someone she didn't even know, but who had probably been victimized with Rohypnol by the slimy Quarles son and heir, Elena decided to find him on her own while she was feeling especially mean. Did he live at home or in the dormitory? Probably in the dorm since there was no longer anyone at home, his mother being dead, his father in jail. Elena would be testifying in that trial this summer.

She walked across the quadrangle to the high-rise dorm and checked with the lobby clerk for Junior. "Seventh floor," said the clerk, "but they're still at dinner. Nonetheless, Elena took the elevator up and knocked at Quarles's door. No response. Shrugging, she wandered down the hall to a social area. Decorated in Egyptian style, it had several of those creepy bronze snake lamps casting mellow light over rounded sofas upholstered in Pharaonic prints. After

inserting coins into what passed for vending machines at
H.H.U., Elena retrieved a chocolate eclair with real whipped
cream inside and a cup of cappuccino, which she carried
over to a sofa, sinking into welcoming cushions with a sigh.
She'd just sit here, resting, pigging out, until she heard people coming off the elevator.

How bad did she look? she wondered, running a hand over
the front of her hair, then down her French braid. There were
definitely escaping strands. No doubt her mascara was
smudged. Her lipstick had probably worn off, and her slacks
and blouse were wrinkled, but what the hell. Her blazer, at
least, was a jewel. It could be wadded up and stuffed in a
corner and still come up looking respectable. Unfortunately,
it did have to be dry cleaned because some idiot designer
had put a dry-clean-only lining in it. And dry cleaning was
expensive.

Then thinking of her budget, she hoped the mild weather
would hold. During the last week there'd been no need to
heat her adobe house nor cool it. In fact, she'd turned the
furnace off and the swamp coolers on in March during a
warm spell. As a result, she couldn't use the furnace without
getting back up on the roof to turn off the coolers, which
were cheap to run but a pain to service up there on the roof
what with their pumps and fans and wetpads. She'd resisted
the impulse to build fires in her round corner fireplaces on
nippy nights because the logs cost a fortune. Not surprising.
There were no forests within a hundred miles of Los Santos.
She sipped the last of her cappuccino, wiped her mouth with
the napkin that accompanied the chocolate eclair, and leaned
her head back against the soft cushions, eyes closed.

"I'll bet you ten bucks Fullerton was killed by some girl
he dumped," said a voice coming on the heels of the musical
bong that signaled the arrival of the elevator.

"Suicide," said a second voice. "I heard he was found
with pills all over the floor."

"Not the type." That was a female speaking. "Certainly
not for suicide. Why would he? He was really popular."

"Unlike Wayne here, who has to date high-school girls
most of the time," said one of the males.

"Fuck you," said Wayne Quarles, Jr.

Recognizing his voice from her last case, Elena rose.

"Not interested, buddy," said a male voice. "And neither are any girls I know."

Elena reached the group as they broke up to head for separate doors. "Quarles," she said and showed her ID.

"Hey, hey, hey," whooped a young man in a tartan vest and baggy pants. He had turned back to watch. "Is *Quarles* a suspect in Fullerton's death?"

Elena glanced at him but didn't answer. "You want to talk in your room or down the hall?" she asked Quarles, pointing toward the area where she had been sitting.

"I don't have to talk to you at all," snapped Quarles.

"O.K. We'll go down to headquarters."

He turned pale and waved her into his room. The other three students were snickering. Evidently Junior was not popular. "I hardly even knew Graham Fullerton," he protested. "I haven't been living on campus that long, which you should know since you're the detective who arrested my father and broke up my family."

Elena ignored the accusation and, unasked, took a seat in his sitting room.

"Dad didn't do any of that stuff he's accused of," snarled Wayne. "Now every cent the family's got is tied up by the government as drug profits—which is a crock—or going to pay for lawyers, and he didn't do anything! You can bet we're going to sue for false arrest and get those attorney's fees back from the state and get Dad's money back and—"

"Not my concern," said Elena, shrugging, "and I'm not here about your father or Graham Fullerton."

Quarles's face fell into lines of sulky puzzlement. "Then what? I'm not on drugs." He glanced into a mirror inset in a sphinx head and admired his blond hair. "I've been through rehab, and I'm clean." He whirled back to Elena impatiently. "So you've got no cause to hassle me. I—"

"It's about Gretchen Farber."

His expression didn't change an iota.

"Remember her? You gave her Rohypnol and raped her."

"Did she say that?" he asked, almost casually. "She's

lying. I slept with her, but it was consensual sex, and she's old enough to say yes.''

"It's not consensual if one partner can't protest because she's been doped up.''

"Why would I do that?'' Innocence personified. As if he didn't have an ugly record with reluctant young women.

"Because every girl who's heard the stories is leery of you,'' Elena snapped. "That's why Farber was carrying Mace. That's why she sprayed you the next morning.''

"I don't know what you're talking about.'' Quarles dropped languidly onto the sofa, his body obscuring a tapestry pyramid.

"She came out of it the next morning,'' said Elena, consulting her notebook as if reading the scenario back to him. As it happened, the notes were on the Fullerton case, but the ploy seemed to unnerve the oh-so-cool Wayne. "You told her she was a great lay, and she got the Mace out of her purse and zapped you.''

"Bull,'' he said angrily. "Do I look like someone who's been Maced?''

"Shall I ask your roommates whether you were in discomfort that morning?''

He shifted on the sofa, where he had been stretched out in an arrogant sprawl. "I was having—allergy problems that morning. I think it was hair spray—her hair spray!''

"She went to the clinic,'' Elena continued doggedly. "Dr. Marx did a vaginal smear for sperm and a blood test for Rohypnol, not to mention combing for pubic hair. The lab work will come back, you know.''

"Listen,'' he said earnestly, "you may find my sperm, even hair. I told you we spent the night together, but if there's any drugs in her, I didn't give them to Gretchen.'' He was beginning to look seriously agitated. "I remember now! *She* offered *me* something.'' His words tumbled out faster and faster. "I told her, no way. I was clean. I couldn't afford to get mixed up with any drugs, not with the cops watching me because of my father.'' At that point, he stopped abruptly and took a deep breath. "So she had something with her all right. Maybe she took it when she went into the bathroom.''

Elena was pleased to note beads of sweat along his blond hairline. "How come you didn't use a condom?"

"She said she was on the pill."

"She say that before or after she passed out?"

"She never passed out. She was fine. Real—ah—responsive. I gave her a good time."

"Too bad she can't remember it," said Elena dryly. "From what I've heard, she may be the only girl you ever gave a good time."

"What's that supposed to mean?"

"That you've got a reputation: Never-Take-No-For-An-Answer Quarles."

"Listen, I don't have to put up with this. If you keep bothering me, I'll get a lawyer."

"Sure." Elena rose. "Maybe your father's lawyer will give you a family rate. Half-price for kids or something."

"My dad didn't do anything. Neither did I." Junior was looking decidedly pale.

"So we'll wait for the labs, ask some questions, see what we come up with."

"No matter what the lab work says, it doesn't mean I did anything. So leave me alone."

What a lame story, Elena thought as she left the building. Gretchen Farber gave *herself* Rohypnol? "Get real, Junior," Elena muttered.

Sunlight was almost gone when she hurried down the dorm steps, only to be stopped by a voice saying, with obvious delight, "Serendipity!"

It was Rafer Martin, the trombone player in the H.H.U. jazz band with which Elena sang, and she knew what serendipity meant. It was a sixties word that her hippie mother used, causing confusion among her Hispanic neighbors in Chimayo, New Mexico. But why was Rafer talking about serendipity?

Before she could reply, he stopped just short of running over her and gave her a hug, somewhat awkwardly since he was tall and she—well, she just missed being short by a few inches. "On this very special day in my life," he said exuberantly, "you're just the person I want to see."

"I am?"

"You said to call you when I was a free man. Well, my divorce was final today!"

She couldn't remember her ponytailed, physics-professor friend looking happier. "Congratulations, I guess."

"Thank you very much. Will you have dinner with me tomorrow night before the jazz band meets?"

"I didn't know we were meeting."

"No? Well, there should be a message on your answering machine when you get home. Bernie's calling everyone. So how about dinner?"

Elena hesitated. Helen, his ex-wife, was a very unpleasant woman. "What about Helen?" she asked.

"I told you. We're divorced."

"But how's she taking it?"

"I imagine she's already left town with all my worldly goods. Thank God we never bought a house, or she'd have got that, too. Actually, I don't even have a car," he added. "So I'll pick you up in a cab. Want to go to the Airport Hilton? I hear they have a fantastic Italian restaurant there."

"If she really cleaned you out," said Elena dryly, "maybe we'd better go to McDonald's." Rafer looked crestfallen. "O.K. How about Pizza Academmia?" She regretted that suggestion immediately, having had her first date with another professor, Michael Futrell, there, the start of a relationship that had not ended well.

"Great," said Rafer enthusiastically.

"And you don't have to call a cab. I'll meet you there at six tomorrow night."

"You're an angel." He hugged her again, earning good-natured whistles from passing students.

The administration ought to slap a curfew on them, Elena thought. Like no leaving the dorm after dinner. Still, student rudeness wasn't enough to put a damper on her high spirits. Even though he had a mean ex-wife, she did like Rafer and had always found him attractive, both with and without his trombone. Physics, his area of academic expertise, was another matter, but maybe he wouldn't insist on telling her about it.

She cheered up at the prospect of a real date. They'd been few and far between, except for several friendly evenings with Sam Parsley, who had been her therapist during a very trying bout of posttraumatic stress, but evenings with Sam weren't real dates. Sam was just a friend. Albeit, a very nice one.

14

Tuesday, April 8, 8:05 P.M.

Elena stretched out on her living room sofa with a beer
and a bag of tamales that she'd picked up on her way home.
It had been a long time since she'd devoured that fancy tray
lunch at the university. After eating the last tamale, she sat
up, put her feet on the coffee table, and reached for the
morning paper. She'd only had time to read the front page
before she left for work, and there was no longer an evening
paper. It had gone under, more's the pity.

Preacher Lashes Out Against
Gays and Their Supporters

The Reverend Wesley Hardin of the Evangelical Fountain of Faith Ministry called a news conference today
to demand that more Christians initiate and observe
boycotts of companies that "endorse homosexuality by
providing health insurance and other benefits to the
partners of gay employees."
  "Countenancing perversions is as sinful as practic-
ing them," said Hardin.

Well, that was certainly shooting from the hip, Elena
thought. Was the preacher a descendant of John Wesley Hardin, the famous gunfighter? She shook her head and read on.

Hardin demanded that the local police enforce laws against sodomy and advocated the quarantine of persons with AIDS. "If someone's got AIDS," said Hardin, "you know he or she's been going against the laws of God."

Elena sighed and thought, *Dumbhead.* Did he know that ninety percent of hemophiliacs had contracted AIDS from transfusions? She'd read that in some magazine. Did he know that in Africa the spread of AIDS was heterosexual? And getting more so every day among minorities and IV drug users in the U.S.? More to the point, did he care?

"For the protection of God-fearing Christians, people who are HIV positive or homosexual should be treated like lepers used to be, forced to make their disease known or kept in AIDS colonies."

She toyed with the possibilities of what Hardin would advocate when he heard about the problem at H.H.U. Bricking up the gates to keep the sinners inside? Rounding up the students, testing them, then tattooing *AIDS* on their foreheads? Maybe he already knew. And if this campaign of Hardin's set off a round of gay-bashing, something Los Santos had not heretofore been troubled with very often, the police were in for a rough time.

On the other hand, if the state wasn't so sticky about confidentiality, someone could notify Fullerton's girlfriends that they should be tested. If City-County Health had asked Fullerton, she wondered, would he have given his permission for notification? Probably not. He'd been pretty careful about hiding his condition.

"Los Santoans Against Rampant Immorality, a group I belong to, is behind me on this," said Hardin, "as are all those who read and follow the dictates of the Bible and our Lord Jesus Christ."

Elena put the paper down, thinking of the rumors at H.H.U. that AIDS medication had been poisoned. Was it

true? Were Hardin and L.S.A.R.I. actually behind it? And if
so, how had they known Fullerton was HIV positive? And
how had they got to his medication? This was going to be
a hard case. She felt depressed even thinking about the com-
plications presented by the death of Graham Fullerton.

Well, there was nothing she could do about that tonight,
but . . . her mind jumped back to Dr. Marx's request and her
own subsequent interview with the obnoxious Wayne
Quarles, Jr. Tomorrow she'd call a detective in Sex Crimes
to start the ball rolling on the rape of Gretchen Farber.

Elena shuddered, imagining how she'd feel if some bastard managed to have sex with her because he'd slipped Rohypnol into her drink. With any luck Gretchen Farber had
managed to squirt her whole container of Mace into young
Wayne's rotten face.

Stretching, Elena rose and headed toward the front door.
Today was one of the three watering days allotted by the
city water-rationing program to householders with even-
numbered addresses. She'd turned on the drip irrigation before entering the house. Now she had to turn it off before
she went to bed or risk sending her desert landscaping into
water shock, afflicting it with mold or some other unlikely
plant killer. She was returning when her telephone rang.

"I have Gretchen's blood tests," said the caller without
even greeting Elena.

"Dr. Marx?" Who else could it be?

"Positive for Rohypnol. Now do something about it!"
The doctor hung up.

Elena thought a moment—back to another case in which
a young policewoman had been shot last November. Monica
Ibarra, doing well with her transplanted lung, was back on
patrol downtown. She'd be getting married to her deputy
sheriff pretty soon, or so Elena had heard. And Monica
wanted to be a detective, so why not give her a leg up and
start the investigation of Wayne Quarles, Jr., at the same
time? The most satisfying aspect of this idea, but maybe not
the smartest on Elena's part, was that Monica had a score to
settle with the Quarles family because she'd been framed for
the death of the mother. After calling the Downtown Re-

gional Command to get Monica's home phone number, Elena called the young patrolwoman.

"Want to do a little detective work for me?" she asked after they'd exchanged news.

"Really?" Monica exclaimed. "I'd love to."

Elena told her about the alleged rape. "Tomorrow morning I'll have a photo of Junior faxed to you. I imagine you know who's bringing Rohypnol across the border."

"Sure," Monica agreed. "We know most of the *roche* mules and dealers." *Roche* was the street name for Rohypnol, *roche* or roofies.

"Show his picture around. See if you can find anyone who sold to him."

"I'd love to," Monica agreed. "This rapist is the son of—"

"Right. But don't let that influence you. We need to get the information in such a way that it's admissible in court. If we get the kid into court."

"I'll be very careful," said Monica. "Extra careful. I can always catch the dealers on something illegal and do a little horse-trading for information. That's O.K., isn't it?"

"Sure. As long as they're not just feeding you what you want to hear in order to make themselves a deal."

"I'm getting pretty good at telling who's lying to me. Which is what most of the people I talk to do, actually."

"Yeah," Elena agreed, remembering her own days on patrol. "So. If you find the dealer he bought from, we'll turn it over to Sex Crimes."

"All *right*! And thanks, Elena. I'm going to take the detective's exam next time it comes up. If I find this guy, it should help me get an assignment. Providing I score well."

"You will," said Elena, wondering how she herself had done on the sergeant's exam. "Good luck with it. Both the case and the exam."

15

Wednesday, April 9, 8:00 A.M.

The Wednesday workday began with a flurry of activity. First, Elena faxed a picture of Wayne Quarles to Monica Ibarra at Central Command. Then she took a call from Wilkerson, the coroner, who told her that Graham Fullerton had indeed died of cyanide poisoning, which had been obvious as soon as they opened him up. "The guts reeked of bitter almonds," said Wilkerson and went on to give more information from the autopsy report, which would be faxed to headquarters within the hour.

"What about AIDS?" Elena asked.

"Have to wait for the blood tests on that, but I can tell you, I hate to do autopsies on people with AIDS," muttered Wilkerson. "I'd rather cut up a body that's been left in the heat for three days and stinks to ..." Elena tuned out the graphic descriptions of three different types of corpses Wilkerson would rather autopsy than an AIDS victim, who, even dead, was a danger to all who came in contact with the remains. Elena herself didn't even like to *attend* autopsies, although she had to from time to time.

While she was listening to Wilkerson, Leo was fielding a call from the DPS lab about the medications found scattered on Fullerton's bathroom floor and in bottles in his cabinet. The 3TC tablets had been clean, but not the AZT. Three of those from the multivitamin bottle, plus one of the red capsules on the floor and four more in the Vitamin C bottle had potassium cyanide replacing the original powder. Each doctored capsule contained enough poison to kill him. "Your murderer wasn't taking chances," the lab tech told Leo, who repeated the information to Elena.

Then they repaired to the office of Lieutenant Beltran, head of Crimes Against Persons, for a meeting with the lieutenant and their sergeant, Manny Escobedo. Both were receiving pressure from the chief, who was being pressured in turn by H.H.U. to solve the case expeditiously and with the greatest discretion. "No statements to the press," said Beltran sternly. "The paper this morning had nothing beyond a suspicious death at H.H.U., police investigating. That's more than enough."

Beltran looked like Elena's father, Ruben Portillo, Sheriff of Rio Arriba County, New Mexico—a stocky, graying Hispanic of middle age and old-fashioned views. And he expected to be obeyed when he issued an order. Leo and Elena agreed that they would avoid the media.

"To get this solved fast, I'm giving you Mosconi and the new guy, Jaime Sandoval. They'll help with the interviews."

That did surprise Elena. Every detective in the department had a forty-plus case load. That four detectives would be assigned to one case was another indication of how important the department considered the murder. And why not? The threat of a local AIDS epidemic was enough to get a reaction, and with H.H.U. involved, Los Santos's own academic pot of gold, a solution became even more imperative.

Mosconi and Sandoval were called in and briefed. Never having worked with Sandoval before, Elena watched him closely. Too young, too handsome, and too cheerful, she decided gloomily. They'd have H.H.U. coeds fluttering their eyelashes, simpering, flirting, and in general paying more attention to the young detective than to information they might have that would forward the investigation.

When Manny had finished the briefing, the group discussed the division of labor and what directions the investigation should take.

"We need to know what the red capsules are and where he got both those and the AZT. We need to know whether

they were poisoned before or after Fullerton bought them,"
said Elena. "Did you read about that sermon given by the
preacher who thinks people with AIDS should be treated like
lepers?" Leo and Mosconi nodded. Sandoval looked blank.
Great! He didn't even read the papers.

"Hardin could be behind this," she pointed out. "A sort
of kill-off-the-sinners campaign. In which case, there'll be
more people dying."

"Sounds like a stretch to me," said Beltran. "So, let's set
up a plan of attack. Suggestions?" He eyed each of the four
detectives in turn.

Elena thought a minute. "Call the drugstores. Talk to the
doctor who prescribed the medication. So we can find out
where it came from and who had the opportunity to tamper
with it before it reached Fullerton."

"But we also have to talk to all those girls he dated, in
case someone from the university got into his medicine cabinet," Leo added.

Elena agreed. "Why don't I go to Dr. Conway's office,
Sandoval can call the pharmacies, and you two guys can start
with the women in Fullerton's little black book." She nodded toward Mosconi and Leo.

Harry Mosconi grinned. Although still hung up on his ex-
wife, Harry yearned after women of all ages. Maybe he
thought a day spent with a bunch of pretty young coeds
would inspire him to start dating again—someone other than
his ex.

"No dating the suspects," said Elena, grinning back at
Mosconi. Then she glanced at Sandoval out of the corner of
her eye. He'd be the one to worry about in that respect, once
he'd finished calling pharmacies. Word was in C.A.P. that
no less than four patrolwomen were smitten with him and
that when he'd given a talk at the academy, two female re-
cruits had swooned, and not from the 100-degree heat. Sandoval was a member of the SWAT team; he'd been accepted
while he was still on patrol. Which meant that he was more
than a pretty face; he was also in great shape and just a little
crazy.

Her attention snapped back when the lieutenant muttered,

"You should talk, Jarvis." He was staring belligerently at Elena. For a minute she was confused, then irritated.

Before she could point out that it had been several years since she'd dated a murderer, Sandoval said, "When do *I* get to talk to coeds?"

"When you finish talking to druggists," said Leo.

Sandoval grinned. "Sounds like we're gonna think we've died and gone to heaven, getting to interrogate a bunch of sexy chicks."

Beltran frowned. Elena mumbled, "Even if they all have AIDS?" Sandoval looked chagrined.

"Let's not forget that no one mentions AIDS on this case," Beltran warned.

"Most of the coeds I've met over there are feminist ball-busters," Leo assured the young detective.

"Melody Spike graduated last spring," said Elena, referring to a former star in the Feminist Coalition. "Since then, feminism hasn't been the same at H.H.U., so all you chauvinists can rest easy. They're more likely to flirt with you than lecture you."

"Can we get serious about this?" snapped Beltran.

16
··

Wednesday, April 9, 9:45 A.M.

Dr. Morton Conway was so thin that Elena wondered whether he himself might not be infected with the disease he treated. "Detective, I've already told you that I can't discuss my patient," said Conway. "Even though he's dead."

Elena sat down across the walnut desk from him and rested her heavy shoulder bag on the floor. "We've identified two of the three things he was taking: AZT and Epivir." She had to consult her notes for the second name. "So you don't need to tell me that Fullerton was either HIV positive or had AIDS. Since his roommates think he was super healthy, I don't suppose it was the latter." Still no reaction from Conway. "You want to nod?" she asked sarcastically. "Or do we have to keep playing this game?"

The doctor said nothing, just stared at her expressionlessly from deep-set, heavy-lidded eyes.

"So." Elena stared back. "You'll want to know what he died of. You were right. It wasn't his viral infection, however far it had progressed. His AZT had potassium cyanide in it. He was poisoned."

The doctor frowned.

"We're canvassing the drugstores to find out where it came from. Assuming that he couldn't get it under a false name. I mean you didn't write him any prescriptions under an alias, did you?"

77

"I don't write prescriptions for people who use aliases, not knowingly anyway," the doctor replied.

"A bigger problem is that the red capsules were poisoned too. I guess the Department of Public Safety Lab will find out what the medication was sooner or later."

"Which department?" The doctor looked surprised and a little pale.

"DPS. They do most of our lab work. But not real fast. They've got their own work and every other police force's that doesn't have a departmental lab. While we're waiting to find out what the stuff is, other people taking it could die. So if you know—"

"Other people? Why would anyone else—"

"There are rumors floating around that crackpots are poisoning AIDS medications to kill off sinners. Fullerton might be the first of God knows how many poor suckers to turn pink, throw up, convulse, and die. That's how cyanide poisoning affects—"

"I know that, Detective," he snapped, "but if you think anyone here—"

"Are you saying the red capsules came from your office?" Elena pounced on that slip. Her job might be easier if Conway was dispensing the red capsules.

"Even if that were true, Detective, you just said another capsule, AZT, which I don't dispense, was contaminated."

"O.K. So someone tampered with the AZT somewhere else. I want to know about the reds."

Conway sat silent, engaging in what was obviously anxious thought. "Without revealing anything about Graham Fullerton's condition—"

"Which everyone's too scared to mention," Elena interrupted sardonically.

"Do you want to hear this, or do you want to make smart remarks?" he snapped.

"Sorry."

"The red capsules are part of an experimental treatment regimen, now in clinical trials."

"And he got them—here?"

"Yes."

"And you got them . . ."

"Arbin-Meldorp-Proxem." When Elena looked up from her note-taking, he added, "It's a pharmaceutical company. Graham was part of a carefully monitored clinical study being run by A.M.P." He paused. "They send the medication to my office. I dispense it to selected patients. Actually, I only have two enrolled in this particular test, although I'd like to have more." He sighed. "It's been very successful for patients who present—certain progression patterns."

"So he did have AIDS?"

"Please, Detective. I'm trying to cooperate. Don't make it impossible. Suffice it to say, the new combination was successful. How long it will keep the patients healthy—well, it's too early to tell. Last summer Graham was—experiencing problems. Then his doctor in Chicago got him into this test group. Must have connections. I couldn't have managed it. Because of Graham, I have one other patient involved."

"So Fullerton was contagious?" Elena persisted. Research data was all very well, but she had a murder to solve.

"Of course. Even asymptomatic, he'd be contagious, but he wasn't sexually active, so—" The doctor stopped, face grim with the realization that he had said too much.

"Why do you think that?"

"What?"

"That he wasn't sexually active."

The doctor hesitated. "Because he told me so." Conway then hastened to add, "Questions about a patient's sexual practices are commonplace during any physical examination."

"He lied."

"What?" Cut off in mid-evasion, Dr. Conway gave her an anxious glance.

"He may have had intercourse with thirty or more young women," she told Morton Conway.

"Good lord!" Dr. Conway looked sick. "We'll need to notify City-County—"

"What good will that do? He's dead. He can't give written permission for contact notification. But he did use condoms," Elena added, relenting a bit in their game of cat, mouse, and guilt because the doctor seemed so stricken. "Or at least I found lots of those foil packets, some empty, among his things."

Dr. Conway swung his chair and stared at the desert landscaping outside the long, one-way window that ran up the wall beside his desk. Elena followed his glance toward the boulders, the gnarled vegetation, the tiny birds pecking for seeds among the landscaping rocks. When the doctor turned back to her, he said, "Unfortunately, even with condom use, one in ten can be infected by sex with an partner who is HIV positive. Those are the latest figures. If he was actually intimate with thirty young women—"

"—three caught it," Elena finished for him. She was shocked, after all the publicity about the efficacy of condoms, that they were only ninety percent safe. "Any chance that the medication could have been tampered with at—what was it?—A.P.—"

"Arbin-Meldorp-Proxem. I wouldn't think so, but after this, I suppose anything is possible."

"How is it stored here after you receive it?"

"You think someone here—" He looked nonplussed. "This office is dedicated to keeping—ah—patients alive, not killing them. Many medical professionals wouldn't take a job here. You can be sure that those who have are dedicated—"

"Any religious fanatics on your staff? Are you yourself—"

"I'm agnostic," said Dr. Conway brusquely, "and if I hadn't been, my practice would have converted me. As for my staff, I'm not familiar with their religious preferences, but the information might be on their employment records, I suppose. No, that's not legal anymore. However, it's a question on their medical insurance forms, I believe. Why in the world would you care?"

"Just one line the investigation is taking," said Elena evasively. Connecting the Reverend Wesley Hardin, or even L.S.A.R.I., to her case was probably a long shot. "So is the medication locked up?"

"No," he said slowly. "It wouldn't have occurred to me to do so. It's not like narcotics, you know."

"There's an underground market for all kinds of drugs, Doctor," said Elena. "You said yourself that you wish more of your patients could have this combination."

"Yes, but it wouldn't benefit anyone to steal it. These cocktails are only effective with the right dosage and careful monitoring."

Elena nodded. "Well, stealing isn't what I'm worried about, anyway. Tampering is. So could we say that anyone in your office, given a motive, could find the opportunity to poison Fullerton's capsules?" A fanatic in the doctor's office would answer the question of how someone, other than a sexual partner infected by Fullerton, could have known that he was HIV positive and how a poisoner could have gained access to the medication . . . well, the red ones.

"Ye-e-s," the doctor admitted reluctantly, "but someone else would surely see if—"

"The storage facility is in plain view, and no one is ever alone in the room?" she asked.

Conway sighed. "The capsules are stored in bottles placed in a cabinet in a small room at the end of the hall."

"How are the bottles marked?"

"With the name of the medication, the drug company, and the patient who will take it."

"So someone here could poison the bottles for both patients or just Fullerton's?"

"I suppose, but no one—"

"I'll need the names and the records of everyone on your staff."

"Really, Detective, this is surely illegal, an invasion of privacy at the very least."

"You're not interested in finding out who killed your patient?"

"Of course, but—"

"I can get a warrant."

He sighed again and called his receptionist in to gather the information.

"That will take several hours, Doctor," she said, casting

a curious glance at Elena. "I'm helping with the billing right now. In the meantime, you have three patients waiting, including Kurt, who is having a particularly bad day."

"As soon as I've finished talking to Detective Jarvis, send Kurt in," said Morton Conway, "and give the detective what she asks for, except, of course, access to patient files." The woman, a slender, pinch-faced brunette, graying and plainly dressed, clacked out on sturdy, stacked wooden heels.

"I don't need patient files," Elena assured Dr. Conway, "but it would help to know when Graham Fullerton last came in to get new medication."

The doctor pulled a chart from a drawer and told her that Fullerton had received a month's supply fifteen days earlier.

Elena nodded and made a note. "How many pills would that be?"

"Ninety. He took three of them a day. The dosage was on the bottle."

Except, thought Elena, Fullerton had switched bottles in order to conceal his illness from anyone who visited his bathroom—like his sex partners.

"You do realize that you can't afford to give your other patient any more of that stuff?" she murmured, tapping a pen on her notebook. "In fact, you should call him and tell him not to take what he's got."

"But that would be very dangerous. If you stop medicating—" Conway cut himself off. "Anyway, I'm sure no one here—"

"Sure enough to risk the other guy's life?" Elena demanded.

The doctor fell into a glum silence from which he roused himself to say, "This is appalling. It will set the clinical trial back, and endanger the patient. And A.M.P. will be very upset."

"Yes," Elena agreed. "You'll need to call and warn them of the possibility that the poisoned capsules are coming from their facilities."

"I meant I'll need to ask that more medication be airmailed for my other patient. The virus is opportunistic. Stop taking the medication, the virus attacks."

"Right, the virus we can't name. Even so, the red capsules have to be checked before he takes any more," Elena warned.

"*She*," muttered the doctor. "We're seeing more and more infected women." Conway scowled at Elena as she rose to leave. With the information he had given her, she calculated that she now had a rough idea of when the red capsules had been poisoned, that is if it hadn't happened before Fullerton got them.

17

Wednesday, April 9, 11:30 A.M.

When Elena left Dr. Conway's office, she met Jaime Sandoval coming up the sidewalk toward the patio around which several doctors' offices were built. "What are you doing here?" she asked. Sandoval was supposed to be back at headquarters calling pharmacists or, having completed that task, interviewing people at H.H.U.

"I was around the corner, so I figured I might as well see if you were still here." He turned companionably and walked toward the parking lot with her. "Found the pharmacy," he said, obviously pleased with himself.

"You were bound to sooner or later."

He grinned. "Sooner, in this case. I called the one closest to Dr. Conway's office first, and guess what? Graham Fullerton got his prescriptions filled there."

Elena turned and stared at the young detective. He'd gone about his assignment in an eminently reasonable way, and it had worked. "Good," she said. "So how come you're not on your way to H.H.U. to enjoy some coed interviews?"

"Thought we could catch lunch before we go over there. Unless you're not hungry. I sure am. There's a McDonald's a couple of blocks from here."

"You like McDonald's?" Elena watched his face light with enthusiasm.

"I'll say. Not that I don't love enchiladas and gorditas and frijoles, but my mom and sisters cook all that stuff. Mom

84

used to send me to school with tamales and rice. I never have got over thinking a Big Mac's an exotic treat.''

Elena laughed. ''O.K. Meet you there.''

She paid for her cheeseburger, Coke, and fries, carried the tray to a window table, and sat down to look at her notes. Sandoval was still at the counter. While she was setting out her food, she did some quick mental math. Fullerton had got his new meds on Monday two weeks ago. If he'd started taking them Tuesday, he should have had forty-five of the red capsules left when he took the pill that killed him. She checked her notes. He'd had forty-four. So one of the A.M.P. capsules from Conway's office had been ingested in the fatal dose. Of course, an AZT could have killed him and the red capsule been clean, or both of them could have—Grimacing at the uselessness of her calculations, she took a bite of her burger.

''That bad?'' asked Sandoval, sitting down across from her.

''The case, not the food,'' she replied and dipped a French fry in ketchup. ''What did the pharmacist tell you?''

Before answering, Sandoval had spread his lunch—two Big Macs, a large order of fries, and a Sprite—out in front of him and admired it with a happy smile. ''The AZT capsules are 100 milligrams each. The usual dosage, including his, was five a day, one every four hours while he's awake. He got a prescription for them, hundred fifty caps, fifteen days before he died. There were seventy-five left when we found him.''

Elena smiled. ''Then he was probably killed by one of the red ones because there were fifteen days less one capsule of those gone.''

Sandoval nodded. ''Problem is that some of the AZT was poisoned too. Isn't that what the lab said?''

''Yeah.'' Elena took another bite of her cheeseburger, and they ate in silence for several minutes.

Then Sandoval said, ''You wouldn't believe what I had to go through to talk to the pharmacist about this. Course, I'd called him, but when I came in, he dragged me back behind some shelves full of pills and stuff and whispered in my ear.''

"What about?"

"About how careful—'discreet,' is what he said—they have to be about AIDS meds. How the patients can have their lives ruined, lose their jobs, insurance, friends, families, and so forth if people find out what they've got. I felt like telling him why wasn't anyone worrying about the patients ruining the lives of their sex partners, who didn't know what they were getting into.''

Elena sipped her Coke. "It can take ten years before it causes problems.''

"I guess. This guy was really upset at the idea that his AZT supplies might be poisoned. 'How am I supposed to tell?' he asks me. 'If my customers start dying, I'll be open to law suits.' I guess he gets a lot of AIDS patients. And that AZT doesn't come cheap. Wonder what his profit margin is?"

"More than if the patient loses his job and has to get his medication through the state, I imagine," Elena replied.

"Yeah." Sandoval started on his second Big Mac. "This is really a depressing case. I hate to start interviewing co-eds.''

"I thought you were looking forward to it.''

"Well, I had time to think about it. Poor girls. They could be sick and not even know it, and we can't tell them. I got four sisters, real sweethearts, all of them, and I guess I'd want to kill anyone gave them AIDS. Not that they're out screwing around or anything, but still—"

"So you think you'd pull apart some capsules and stuff them with cyanide?" Elena asked curiously.

"Nah. I'd probably just shoot the son of a bitch." Then he looked embarrassed. "Sorry about the language.''

She grinned. "Hey, you're SWAT. You're supposed to be macho and foul-mouthed.''

Sandoval looked shocked. "I am not. That's a real great bunch of guys. In fact, we've got a girl now too.''

"Really? Girl? She's what—twelve, ten?''

"O.K. Woman. Whatever. She's a hell of a shot.''

"So were you and the *girl* out there twiddling your thumbs while I was held hostage for days by the bomber nut?"

"How do you know I wasn't the sharpshooter who got him?"

"I met the guy."

"Well, they didn't leave you in there for days," he pointed out, "and I wasn't on the team then. Her either, but she could have made the shot that took down the bomber. She's that good. I'm only fair."

Elena looked at him approvingly. He was a nice guy. Liked his sisters, admired his female colleague, not unduly stuck on himself.

"So anyway, we should be looking at brothers for this killing, don't you think?" he asked.

"Sure," Elena agreed. "Brothers, fanatics, nut cases, girl-friends, boyfriends of girlfriends, roommates. No shortage of suspects."

"You want an apple pie?" he asked. "I'm gonna go back and get one."

"You can't still be hungry!" she exclaimed.

Sandoval looked embarrassed. "That's what my mom is always saying."

18
..

Wednesday, April 9, 12:30 P.M.

Elena and Sandoval pulled their unmarked departmental cars in side by side and stepped out into the parking lot behind the H.H.U. dorm tower. She nodded for him to follow, and they entered the lobby, where they met their disgruntled fellow detectives. "Find the killer?" Elena asked.

Harry Mosconi glared at her. "I'll bet you knew just what we were getting into when you offered to go to the doctor's office," he said accusingly. Elena gave him her most ingenuous smile.

"Tears," said Mosconi. "Jesus, how I hate crying women. We've talked to ten girls from the list, and every damn one of them has cried all over us."

"Yeah," Leo agreed, "and they don't even know they've got something serious to cry about."

"Actually, one of the girls said Fullerton used a rubber when they were an item, so I guess she's O.K.," Mosconi remarked.

"Not necessarily," said Elena. "Dr. Conway told me that ten percent would get AIDS, even with a condom. And we can't warn them. You didn't say anything about—"

"Damn straight, we didn't," Mosconi assured her. "We asked questions about his health, but—"

"For Pete's sake!" Sandoval exclaimed. "They're not dumb. They're going to catch on if we—"

"Most of them *are* dumb," Elena interrupted. "That's

88

why they're here and not someplace where they'd get a real education instead of a pampered lifestyle and lots of *research* trips to exotic locations."

"And hey, we were subtle," said Mosconi. "We made out like we thought he might have killed himself over health problems. We asked about both physical and mental stuff. No one caught on."

"And no one looked like they knew he had—ah"—Leo glanced around in time to see a bevy of young women flitting across the lobby—"the problem he had. Ten percent? The doctor said ten percent would—"

"Right," Elena confirmed glumly. "Anyone act like they had any reason to kill him? Or knew of anyone who did?"

"Not so far," Mosconi replied. "Every girl we talked to is in mourning for the all-time great stud. Take a look at his obituary in the campus newspaper." He handed over a tabloid-sized publication called the *Campus Enquirer*.

The headline read THREE-TIME STUD OF THE MONTH DIES. Elena skimmed the article, which ended with the touching statement, "Graham Fullerton led the life that every red-blooded H.H.U. male fantasizes about. He'll be missed. Especially by the ladies."

"I had one who didn't cry," said Leo. He glanced through his notes. "Minette LaFaure—short, cute, curly black hair. She said she dated him off and on before the Christmas break, but she didn't like sharing him with other girls, so they split. Friendly split."

"Has she visited him lately?" Elena asked.

"Says other than seeing him in the dining room from time to time, no."

"Anyone admit being in his rooms lately?" she asked.

Both Leo and Harry shook their heads. Then the four detectives divided the remaining names and headed to different floors to conduct more interviews. Elena thought for a minute about Minette LaFaure, the one interviewee who hadn't wept, and decided to revisit her. "Hi," she said cheerfully when LaFaure, recognizable by the curly black hair, answered her knock. "My partner, Leo Weizell, was by to see you this morning, and something you told him stuck in my mind.''

Minette gestured Elena into the sitting room. ''What did I say that would interest the police, aside from having dated Graham for a while?''

''You said you didn't like to share. Not that I don't agree with you. What bothered me was that no one else said that. In these days when having lots of sexual partners is pretty dangerous, I'm surprised so many girls were willing to go out with him.'' Elena knew she was treading on dangerous ground, but she wanted to see this girl's reaction to the subject. Maybe, just maybe, Miss Minette had known something about Fullerton the mourners didn't. Maybe she'd done something about it, or told someone else who had done something. Like sneak in and stuff his capsules with potassium cyanide. ''Weren't they worried? For that matter, weren't you? Was that what you meant by not liking to share?''

Minette laughed. ''I meant just what I said. I found out he was dating a couple of other girls at the same time he was dating me, and I thought, 'I don't need this.' As for being worried, I suppose you're talking about HIV, but he used condoms. Religiously, from what I've heard, and he was astoundingly good in bed. Any girl who was just out for a good time, short-term, couldn't do much better than Graham.''

''Condoms don't always work,'' said Elena.

Minette shrugged. ''That's why you get tested.''

''You've been tested?''

''Hasn't everyone?''

Elena thought about herself. There'd been Michael, but that was a while ago, over a year. She'd trusted him at the time, but he hadn't turned out to be the sweetheart she'd taken him for. Should she get tested?

''Maybe you ought to be worried about that professor. He could be giving students AIDS as well as babies,'' said Minette, her pretty mouth quirked in a smart-aleck smile.

''What professor?'' asked Elena, thinking for just a minute that LaFaure meant Michael.

"McGlenlevie," said Minette. "It's in the *Campus Enquirer*. And I've got to get to class. So unless there's something else . . ."

Elena shook her head as she left the suite. Minette La-Faure wasn't much of a suspect, she decided as she glanced down at the first name on her list. Jennifer Newton. Jennifer wasn't in her room, so Elena went on to Marilyn Fone, who said she used to call Graham the multiple man because he could give a girl multiple orgasms, "unlike my fiancé, who is a really boring lover."

"You're engaged?" Elena stopped taking notes and looked up.

"Oh, sure," said Marilyn. "It's a family thing. Daddy likes him. So I fly up to New Haven on the weekends, or he flies down here. Graham was my weeknight recreation." She looked woebegone. "I'm really going to miss him."

"What's your fiancé's name?"

Marilyn giggled. "F. Martin Mowbry IV, and if you think Mowb killed Graham, forget it. He didn't have a clue."

Elena wrote down the name so that she could follow up on the fiancé, who might have known more than Marilyn Fone thought. "Can you think of anyone who might have wanted to kill Graham?"

"Gosh, no. The man was a national treasure."

"Maybe he killed himself," Elena suggested. "How was his health, for instance?"

"Oh, he had a wonderful body. He even quit drinking this year. He said a man, if he didn't watch it, could be over the hill by the time he was twenty, but girls were like the Energizer bunny. We just keep going and going." Fone giggled. "Graham claimed he didn't want to get left behind. Isn't that cute?"

Absolutely, Elena thought. "Were you ever in his bathroom? Ever notice what kind of stuff he kept in his medicine cabinet?"

"Vitamins and condoms," said Marilyn solemnly. "I always look. You can tell a lot about a person by what's in their bathroom and whether a boy is sloppy about peeing on the toilet seat or on the floor. Graham wasn't. And you never had to provide your own condoms with Graham. He had something for every taste.'' She giggled again. ''You ever used a Hungarian zinger?''

Elena took a deep breath. The conversation was beginning to embarrass her, something she wouldn't have thought possible. ''Ah—when was the last time you checked his medicine cabinet?''

Marilyn pressed a blue-polished fingernail to her lip. ''I don't know. Two or three weeks ago.''

''Maybe you could check your date book.''

''Oh, dropping in on Graham isn't something I'd put in my date book. Our relationship was—spontaneous.'' She grinned. ''And hot!''

''I'll bet,'' Elena muttered. Well, two or three weeks. If it was two, Fone was a suspect. She could have got at the medicine after the new bottle came in. And her initials hadn't appeared in Fullerton's date book, just her name on his sexual-comment list, so her claim to a ''spontaneous'' relationship checked out. Putting a star beside Marilyn Fone's name, Elena closed her notebook and rose to leave.

19

Wednesday, April 9, 1:40 P.M.

Candace Lott—who was not called Candy because "Candy sounds like a topless dancer or a manicurist, don't you think?"—told Elena that no *girl* would have killed Graham Fullerton; everyone she knew who had dated Graham just loved him. He was so sweet, so personable. The murderer was probably some jealous ex-boyfriend of a girl that Graham had charmed away. Candace herself had been dating Buster Pelham before Graham swept her off her feet, and Buster had not been happy about it.

Not that Buster would have killed Graham. Buster was a gentle soul who wrote poetry and brought her flowers he gathered himself. Of course, he could *afford* to buy them, but picked flowers were so sweet and personal, didn't Elena think so? On the other hand, poetry, even written especially for you, wasn't as good as great-in-bed, which was Graham all over. You hadn't *lived* until you'd had sex with Graham Fullerton.

And you might not live long afterward, Elena thought wryly. She had to bite her tongue to keep from telling Candace-not-Candy to go out and get herself tested for HIV.

Candace thought Graham was "super healthy," and she didn't "go poking around in people's bathroom cabinets," because that wasn't at all "cool." Elena managed to wrangle a list of boys who might have been jealous of Graham, all of whom, on second thought, Candace doubted would have

93

killed him. They were just too nice, even if they were upset at having their girlfriends whisked away.

Elena was left with the impression that Candace Lott had a high opinion of most males. She also doubted that Candace had killed the very sexy Graham Fullerton herself, because she hadn't dated him since January or seen him, except in the dining room, for at least a month. "Not to talk to, you know," she explained. "He had the sexiest voice. I'd remember." She and Buster were back together again. She might even marry him if he'd stop letting people call him Buster, which was as silly a name as Candy, didn't Elena think so?

Elena then called on Buster, whose considered opinion it was that Graham Fullerton had probably "fucked himself to death" which wasn't a "bad way to go, right?" He didn't seem unduly chagrined by Candace's interim relationship with Graham because she'd definitely "learned a thing or two from good old Graham."

Jennifer Newton had returned by the time Elena escaped from Buster. "Call me Jen," said the young lady, who had a memorable turned-up nose. However, when she discovered that Elena wanted to interview her about Graham Fullerton, she demanded, "How did you get my name?"

"You were in his date book."

Jen groaned. "My mother thinks I'm a virgin. She'll put me in a convent school if she hears any different. You won't tell her, will you?"

Elena assured Jennifer Newton that she did not expect to be talking to Mrs. Newton.

"I heard from Pete and Larry, his roommates, that Graham was poisoned. Can you believe it? My mother will kill me if she even hears I dated someone who was murdered. Mom just hates scandal. I hope the out of town papers don't pick this up."

Elena swallowed the impulse to say that Jen's mother might not have to "kill" her for scandalous associations; the relationship with Fullerton could turn out to be a surer path to death than an angry mother.

"Well, all I can say is, he was really cute and scrumptiously good in bed, and I certainly didn't have anything to do with his murder. Imagine, poisoning someone's vitamins. Next, people will be poisoning moisturizers and mascara and—boy, I don't know what! Have you ever had a case like that?''

"Not yet," said Elena, thinking that if such an M.O. materialized, it would be at H.H.U. Poisoned moisturizer. What an idea!

Graham's roommates had evidently been spreading the poisoning story around. At least Ms. Newton wasn't in tears. In fact, Elena had yet to question a weeping suspect, while her male colleagues had encountered nothing but. Maybe coeds were less likely to weep all over a female cop.

"And what reason would anyone have to murder him? That's what I want to know," said Jen. "I've never heard anyone say they wanted to kill Graham."

Given the efficacy of the university gossip mill, Elena reasoned that the deceased's infection hadn't been widespread knowledge, so the medication must have been laced with cyanide by someone who was infected with HIV by Fullerton or before the medicine was brought onto campus. That would pretty much rule out the jealous-boyfriend theory advanced by Candace. Elena sighed. She couldn't completely discount the possibility, but it was a secondary angle at best.

Call-me-Jen didn't remember anything about Graham's bathroom except the Aztec mirror over the sink, and she hadn't noticed his medications because she was trying to put on mascara in front of that silly mirror. But the mascara attempt had been just a week ago. Elena starred Jennifer Newton on her list as a definite suspect.

Elena then went on to interview a coed named Barbara Chalmers, whose roommate said she was in the shower, but Elena was welcome to wait. "We've been playing golf. Fifty dollars a stroke, sudden death. Missed lunch."

The young woman was devouring a thick sandwich, sprawled out in a comfy chair, and looking as if she could use a shower too, or at least a comb taken to her hair. Hadn't she worn a golf hat? And fifty dollars a stroke? Elena would have suffered a heart attack and sudden death before they

ever got to the last hole and the play-off. And if Barbara had
missed lunch and the gossip had been spread then, that meant
the poisoning story might be new to her. How would a golfer
react to having a former boyfriend murdered? According to
Graham's records, Chalmers had dated him once in October.

"Is Barbara the emotional type?" she asked the roommate
cautiously.

"Why, are you going to arrest her?" The young woman
grinned, pushing frowsy hair away from her face and reach-
ing into a white box for a second sandwich.

Elena wondered if Mrs. Monserrat provided a box lunch
for those who missed the midday meal. Champagne? Pâté?
Lobster-salad sandwiches? Before her imagination ran away
with her, she spotted the *Campus Enquirer* on an end table
and picked it up, remembering that Minette LaFaure had said
something about a professor spreading AIDS. She'd even
mentioned McGlenlevie. Either Elena had remembered
wrong, or Minette had.

In the gossip column "Willie's Whispers" Elena read:

> What erotic poetry professor has impregnated at least
> two members of the girls' volleyball team? How many
> more expectant mothers are out there? Maybe the mod-
> ern Shakespeare should sue his condom maker, or the
> volleyballers should sue the university.

That was Angus McGlenlevie all right. Elena remembered
the furious young woman who hit Gus with a tennis racket
while Elena was talking to Lance Potemkin. It was a miracle
that the administration didn't do something about Gus. And
maybe they would if he was really getting girls pregnant.
She imagined the headlines: SULTAN OF SEX CAUGHT BY DE-
FECTIVE CONDOMS. COEDS PREGGERS BY POET.

A tall woman with streaked blond hair, wearing a toweling
robe, came in and looked into the white lunch container,
fishing out an apple, then turning to Elena. "Have we met?"
she asked. She had a lean face, handsome rather than pretty,
broad shoulders, long legs, and a mouth that showed no signs
of smiling.

Elena introduced herself, suggested that they might have their discussion in private and, when the roommate went off with a piece of chocolate cake in her hand, asked Barbara Chalmers when she had last seen Graham Fullerton.

Chalmers shrugged. "I used to see him around. He lived upstairs."

"When was your last date with him?" Elena asked.

Chalmers took another bite of her apple and dropped it, half-finished, into a wooden trash receptacle with carved flowers on each side. "October last year."

"Why did you stop dating?"

Barbara shrugged. "He was a superior lover, but you can't spend all your time in bed. With his clothes on, he was a self-impressed bore."

There was something odd, almost defensive, about the young woman's demeanor, and Elena wished that Barbara Chalmers was hooked up to a lie detector. "So you dumped him?"

Chalmers bit her lip and glanced sideways at Elena. "Not exactly," she mumbled.

Caught short, Elena stared. "But you did have sexual relations with him?" According to Fullerton they had.

"That's right. What are you? The chastity police?"

Elena smiled wryly. "No. That's L.S.A.R.I."

Barbara nodded. "I remember them. They tried to burn down the Charleston Dancer. I was a freshman and didn't get in on the fun."

"So how many times were you intimate with Mr. Fullerton?"

"Once," Chalmers mumbled.

Was she lying? Elena wondered. "And after that?"

"He never called again."

To Elena's astonishment, a tear slipped down the girl's face. "I guess I just wasn't—sexy enough." She sounded bitter, but she looked vulnerable.

Elena hated to see that, a handsome young woman whose confidence had been destroyed by someone like Fullerton. "Did you resent that?" she asked, sad to add pain to pain that already existed.

Another tear as Chalmers shook her head. "I hoped that . . .
I hoped he . . . might ask me out again," she admitted. ". . .
sometime. But now—" She blinked hard. "Now that's not
going to happen, is it?"

" 'Fraid not." Elena tapped pen on notebook. "What was
your take on his health?"

"His health?" Chalmers' eyes widened. "Good heavens,
the man ate tofu." She stood, frowning, hands shoved into
the pockets of her terry cloth robe. "Are you saying he killed
himself because he was ill? What did he have?"

Now I've put my foot in it, Elena thought. "Did he ever
seem depressed to you?" she asked, seeking a diversion
from any sharp guesses Barbara Chalmers might make about
this line of questioning.

"Depressed because he was sick? My God, he had a brain
tumor, didn't he?" She bit her lip. "That's *awful*!"

Elena had to quell a sigh of relief. "Have you ever been
in his bathroom? Did you notice—"

"Why would I—" Chalmers flushed. "Oh, I see. You
think we had sex in his room, and I . . . Well, I've never been
in his room. We . . . the one time . . . we did it in the back
seat of his car."

"Oh."

"Not very romantic," said Barbara Chalmers sadly. "And
really uncomfortable. But still, it was . . . good . . . for me."

"When was this?"

"October. I told you."

That checked with his date book. Chalmers probably
wasn't a suspect.

Elena's next interview was with Bitty Cinderhalt, who was
delighted to speculate on all the boys who might have had
it in for Graham Fullerton, including her own ex-boyfriend,
who had been livid with jealousy and threatened to kill Graham. When asked if she'd been in Graham's bathroom, Bitty
said, certainly. She'd chosen the condom herself. She personally loved those French ticklers, which Graham kept on
hand. As for medication, she'd noticed vitamins in the bathroom ten days ago.

A suspect, Elena decided, starring *Cinderhalt* in the notebook, both Bitty and her ex-boyfriend, whom Elena visited next. However, Ned St. Mitas maintained that he planned to send a big wreath to the funeral in appreciation of Graham's having rescued him from a relationship with the clinging Bitty, who wouldn't let him go until he made a huge, public scene about her infidelity with Graham. St. Mitas grinned slyly. "In fact, I asked Graham to have a go at her. Check it out with my fraternity brothers."

In response to a question about Graham's bathroom, Ned said, "Why would I? I've got my own john." Two of his fraternity brothers confirmed that they'd had a big party after Graham seduced Bitty and got St. Mitas off the hook.

To Elena, that scenario sounded like a first-class motive for murder if Bitty had heard it. Yes sir, Miss Bitty deserved a closer look.

The detectives met in the parking lot to compare notes, Elena nominating Marilyn Fone, who had been in the Fullerton bathroom in the last two or three weeks, Jennifer Newton, who had visited it a week ago, and Bitty Cinderhalt, ten days ago.

Jaime Sandoval was looking depressed as he added another name to the list. "These poor girls loved him, and the guy had no morals. And I got another story that would break your heart. This girl had sex with a professor, consensual, but he got her pregnant, and it's not a consensual pregnancy. She's going to get an abortion. What kind of professor would—"

"Was it Angus McGlenlevie?" Elena asked.

Sandoval looked surprised. "She didn't say."

"What was her name?"

"Renee Winter," he replied.

Not the name Elena had heard. Not Estie.

20

Wednesday, April 9, 3:30 P.M.

Of the thirty-one women on Graham Fullerton's list and a few others mentioned by the roommates that couldn't be accounted for in the "sex-commentary book," the four detectives had interviewed all but nine by the end of their shift. Five were scheduled for the next morning; two were out of town on class trips; two had dropped out of school. One or both of those, Elena reasoned, might have tested positive for HIV and left the university, in which case that unfortunate young woman would have a motive to kill Graham if she was in any condition to do it. Or a relative of hers would have a motive to kill him. That made two more possible suspects.

Elena was thinking of going to the registrar's office to get addresses for the two dropouts, when her pager summoned her to a cell-phone chat with Monica Ibarra, who, sounding disappointed, said she had managed to run down every known *roche* dealer except for one who had gone to Sinaloa for his mother's funeral. "None of them recognized Wayne Quarles's picture," she admitted. "And of course, he could have bought the stuff across the river in Juarez. It's sold in the *farmacias*. You're supposed to have a prescription, but everyone knows you can get it without one."

Elena thanked her and asked her to keep an eye out for the last dealer, who would undoubtedly return sooner or later. However, if Quarles had bought the stuff in Juarez and snuck it through customs, no way could they find that out. Discouraged, she told the others the outcome of Ibarra's search.

"Why are you bothering?" Leo asked. "If the girl won't press charges—"

"Exactly," said Elena. "Let's go talk to her."

Leo eyed his partner with disfavor. "I'm about to go off shift. So are you. So's Ibarra downtown."

"Yeah, but we could do one last—"

"Hey, Mosconi, can you give me a lift?" Leo called. "You or Sandoval? Elena, who's bucking for sergeant, wants to keep working."

Obviously, he didn't intend to stay for a talk with Gretchen Farber. Well, Elena reasoned, she could use the overtime even if Leo didn't need it now that his family expenses were being underwritten by H.H.U. On the other hand, she had to stop by the office of Morton Conway to pick up those employee information sheets, and the doctor's office closed at four, so she had to do that first. By the time she'd made that trip and talked to Gretchen, it would be time to meet Rafer at Pizza Academmia, and she'd still be driving a departmental car. Grumbling to herself about having to justify that, she glanced around. She could drop Leo off, after all. Or not. He'd just driven off with Harry, and Sandoval was pulling out of the lot, too.

Elena made the trip to the doctor's office and returned with a seat full of manila envelopes containing the records of the doctor's employees. Her ears were still ringing with the snappish remarks of his unsmiling receptionist, who didn't like the idea of the police pawing through her life without her permission. "We can get a warrant for your files," Elena had snapped back. "Have you got something to hide?"

The woman scowled and dumped the whole pile in Elena's arms. Half the envelopes spilled over onto the floor, and the receptionist didn't offer to help pick them up. She sat down at her desk, looking smug, while Elena scooped the scattered envelopes together, dropping a few more in the process. Evelyn Dietz, said the nameplate on the receptionist's desk. "Thanks for your help, Ms. Dietz," Elena growled.

"Mrs.," said the receptionist and started to type.

Elena was back at the university by five, looking for Gretchen Farber. She got the room number from the lobby clerk, took the elevator, and knocked at the door, which was opened by a pale, slender blonde who peered out apprehensively. Behind her the drapes of the sitting room were drawn, the lights off. Had they been napping? Elena asked for Gretchen. The roommate pointed toward a chair whose occupant was nearly obscured in the gloom. "I'm Detective Jarvis of the Los Santos Police," Elena said to the two young women.

"Neither one of us ever went out with Graham Fullerton," said the blonde.

"I'd like to talk to Gretchen alone, if you don't mind," said Elena politely.

The blonde glanced at her roommate with questioning hesitancy. Gretchen Farber shrugged, and the roommate accommodatingly went to her own room. Elena leaned over to turn on a lamp sitting on an end table, then took a seat across from Gretchen. The room seemed eerie, illuminated by just the one lamp, especially since Elena knew it was still full daylight outside, although overcast and getting surprisingly cold. She thought glumly of her heating and cooling system. Her house was going to be cold when she got home. Still, it would be easier to wait out the cold snap than get back up on the roof.

"Dr. Marx told me about your experience with Wayne Quarles."

The coed didn't even raise her eyes. "She shouldn't have."

"You tested positive for Rohypnol. I assume she told you."

"Yes."

"He drugged you and had sex with you. That's rape."

"It's over," Gretchen mumbled. "I want to forget."

"If you don't charge him, he'll do it to someone else."

"If someone else is dumb enough to go out with him."

"Why did you?" Elena asked curiously.

"See, you think it's my fault. That's what everyone's going to—"

"I think," Elena interrupted, "that he's a lowlife bastard who ought to go to jail, and you don't have to tell me why you accepted a date with him. You just have to file charges."

Gretchen looked up, emotion finally showing in her eyes. "I accepted the date to get even."

"For what?"

"He came on to my roommate, Nita, got rough with her, scared her to death. So I wanted to teach him a lesson."

"How?" asked Elena softly.

"With Mace." Gretchen's eyes filled with tears, and she looked down. "As soon as he made a move on me, I was going to Mace him," she mumbled. "Only he got me first."

"So charge him," Elena urged. "We'll get Nita to charge him too."

"She'd never do it. Nita's afraid of her own shadow, and I—" Gretchen laughed, a hollow, humorless sound. "I'm not much better. I'm afraid to go to sleep at night because I have such awful dreams."

"Believe me, taking him to court will help you get past this," said Elena. "And you need to sign up for counseling. It's something all rape victims should do." She let herself think for just a minute of how awful rape must be. You thought it couldn't happen to you. You thought you could fight an attacker off, but it wasn't always possible. Gretchen had found that out. "The bastard is saying you were the one who wanted to take the drugs." Elena hoped to make her angry, to get her off this self-pity jag. "He said—"

"He's lying."

The denial was weak. Elena studied the sad girl. "We can't arrest him if you won't bring charges and testify."

"It won't do any good. My word against his. People will say I got what I deserved for going out with him in the first place."

Elena sighed. If they'd been able to tie Quarles to a *roche* dealer, she'd have pushed. As it was, this depressed victim wouldn't make a convincing witness. Elena stood, resting a hand on Gretchen's shoulder. "At least think about it," Elena counseled. As she left, it occurred to her that she should fax a picture of Gretchen to Monica. If the *roche* dealers hadn't sold to Gretchen, and Elena doubted they had—she didn't believe Quarles for a minute—then at least there would be some negative evidence to use against Quarles during a second chat.

But again, any defense lawyer could suggest that Gretchen had gone across the border to get the powerful and, in the U.S., illegal sedative. There were a number of cases involving young women in Los Santos who had taken the drug for kicks. Although what they expected, beyond passing out, Elena couldn't imagine.

Glancing at her watch, she saw that she had twenty-five minutes before her date with Rafer, and there was the story told by Sandoval of the nonconsensual pregnancy of—she thumbed through her notebook—Renee Winter. No time to pretty herself up for Rafer; he'd have to settle for end-of-the-day cop disarray. She got Winter's room number and stopped by, just to check that Ms. Winter had been a willing sexual partner to Angus McGlenlevie.

Renee Winter cried, "How could Jamie betray my trust?" Who was Jamie? Elena wondered.

"I told him that in confidence. I ought to sue him for revealing a—a confidential communication."

"McGlenlevie's the one you ought to sue," Elena retorted. It took her a minute to realize that Jamie was Jaime Sandoval. "As for Detective Sandoval, whose name is pronounced *Hymee*, he thought you might need to talk to a woman."

"But I don't even know you. And you're wrong about his name. I have his card right—" She fished around in a backpack that had been flung on the coffee table. "There! Jamie."

Elena gave Renee a brief lesson in Spanish pronunciation, then added, "You ought to be glad he sent me. The man's got four sisters. He might have sent one of them."

"Really?" Renee was softening. "He was so worried about me that he considered sending his own sister?"

Elena didn't comment, as she had no idea whether Sandoval brought his sisters in on his cases. Probably not, since the department wouldn't approve.

"That's so sweet." Renee Winter patted her teary eyes with a hanky. "Do you think he'd ever ask me out?"

Oh-oh, thought Elena. "He couldn't do that, Renee," she said soothingly. "He's in the middle of an investigation. It wouldn't be proper."

Renee flung her arms around Elena's neck. "And I'm pregnant," she cried. "No one wants to go out with a pregnant girl. And I'll bet he's Catholic. He probably doesn't approve of abortion."

Embarrassed, wishing she were elsewhere, Elena patted the weeping student consolingly.

Rafer Martin was a dear, Elena thought as she parked her truck in the driveway beside her adobe house on the east side of the mountain. She'd picked her truck up and turned in the departmental car after her date with Rafer. They'd eaten pizza, drunk beer, and talked for two hours, and never once had he mentioned his ex-wife, Helen, the horrors of divorce (about which Elena knew all she wanted to know from her own split with Frank the Narc), or even physics, which was Rafer's academic area at H.H.U. He'd told a few funny stories about his students, but the anecdotes didn't involve arcane scientific information.

Instead they'd talked music, politics, even religion—Rafer being an atheist and Elena a sometime Catholic, whose closest contacts with the Church in recent years had been the baptism of Leo's five offspring, to one of whom she was godmother, and various investigations that brought her into contact with the crusading priest, Conrad Bratslowski. If he got wind of the latest scandals at H.H.U., Father B. would undoubtedly have a thing or two to say—as publicly as possible.

Anyway, it had been a very pleasant dinner and conversation, followed by an enjoyable few hours with the band, Rafer on trombone, Elena belting out such Dixieland favorites as "St. James Infirmary" and "Sweet Georgia Brown."

Afterward, she and Rafer had made arrangements to see each
other Friday night.

Elena inserted her key in the lock of her carved door and
went in to flop on the sofa in the living room, where the
temperature was about 55°F and falling. If she'd had wood,
she'd have started a fire in the round corner fireplace. In lieu
of that comfort, she pulled up a quilt made by her Grandmother Waite, upper middle-class practitioner of trendy
crafts in Marin County, California. Snuggled under the quilt,
Elena switched on the ten o'clock news.

Nothing yet from Father B. or the Roman Catholic diocese
on events at H.H.U., but Reverend Wesley Hardin was at it
again. A reporter interviewing him got the quotation, ''The
wages of sin are death, and Herbert Hobart University is
beginning to pay the price. Its students flout the laws of God,
committing all manner of sexual sins, and God's plague,
AIDS, is among them. 'Vengeance is mine,' sayeth the
Lord.''

Nice guy, Elena thought, and he had information about
H.H.U. that, as far as she knew, was available only to the
police, a few city and university officials, and probably the
murderer. Was that murderer the knowledgeable Reverend
Hardin?

She listened to a weather report that promised rising winds
and falling temperatures, then began to read through the employment records of the people working for Dr. Morton Conway, whose mission in life was evidently to flout God's
vengeance. He'd been doing a pretty good job on Graham
Fullerton until someone with a bag of potassium cyanide
intervened.

Among all the unexciting information from the doctor's
files, Elena found one hit: a woman who had filled in the
religious preference on her health insurance as evangelical
Christian, possibly linking her to the vengeful Reverend Hardin, who hated homosexuals and people with AIDS. Listed
on her employment application among the organizations that
Evelyn Dietz belonged to was Los Santoans Against Rampant Immorality.

Fullerton's roommates had repeated a rumor that some

group of fanatics was poisoning AIDS medication, and Elena remembered thinking of L.S.A.R.I. Dr. Conway's unpleasant receptionist was a member. She'd been employed at Conway's office for five months, which made Elena wonder whether any more of Conway's patients had died under suspicious circumstances during that time.

Elena would definitely head back to the doctor's office tomorrow. She thought of calling Leo with the lead but decided it could wait until morning. If all the five babies were asleep, Elena didn't want to be the person to awaken one or more. Even with the help of psychology students from the university and a big new house, from which the cocaine had been vacuumed and the false walls for drug stashes removed, Elena didn't know how Concepcion could take it. The kids were all crawling, two standing, one having taken a few staggering steps. Soon the house would be a beehive of terrifying toddlers, all no doubt trying to fall in the swimming pool and drown or bite the new puppy or spit up on the carpeting.

Elena stretched luxuriously under her quilt. Single life had its advantages, many advantages. For instance, she could go to bed right this minute, and no one would wake her up—unless there was a new murder in the city.

21
..

Thursday, April 10, 6:30 A.M.

When Elena was loading her purse for the day, she came across the copy of yesterday's *Campus Enquirer,* which she had stashed there. She settled down to read it with her breakfast. Two jelly doughnuts, a glass of orange juice, and a cup of coffee provided two of the five fruits and vegetables people were supposed to eat each day, she told herself, grinning, that is if a person got to count the jelly in the doughnuts as a fruit.

The front page showed a picture of a young woman kneeling in front of a stained glass window. It was captioned "Miracle of the Maids." The story explained the misconception among H.H.U. domestics that the campus had its own Weeping Virgin. "The lady on the window is more likely Venus weeping for the late Graham Fullerton (see obituary on p. 3)."

If the feisty Socorro Rascon read that, H.H.U. was one step closer to unionization, Elena thought as she skipped to the headline MARX DEMANDS CAMPUS-WIDE HIV TESTING. The doctor wanted testing for all to be implemented in "these dangerous times" and "given rampant promiscuity and unsafe sexual practices among students." Vice-President Harley Stanley was quoted in the next paragraph as saying that the students were adults who were quite able to handle their own lives without Dr. Marx's advice and that her state-

108

ments did not represent any opinion but her own; mandatory testing was not university policy.

"Hypocrite," Elena muttered and drained her orange juice.

Leo and Elena began the morning at the office of Dr. Morton Conway, interviewing his receptionist, whose haughty demeanor evaporated when she realized that she was suspected of tampering with medication. She denied having done so. The detectives then called in an ID & R team to fingerprint everyone in the office and take latents from the medication room. Since no one else protested the fingerprinting, Evelyn Dietz, at first reluctant and angry, grudgingly complied, especially after Dr. Conway said, "Why in the world would you refuse, Evelyn? You're not guilty of anything."

"It's the principle," she mumbled even as her prints were being expeditiously rolled onto a form by Charlie Solis. "It's not against the law to be a Christian. Since when are Christians suspect?" she complained. "Christians are good, moral people."

"Which church do you belong to?" Elena asked. "The Fountain of Faith Ministry?"

"How did you know?"

"We've been reading what your minister has to say about people with AIDS," Leo replied. Actually, he hadn't looked at a newspaper in weeks. While he drove to the doctor's office, Elena had read him the Hardin interview and a story that said the police were being unusually close-mouthed about the investigation of a student found dead under suspicious circumstances at Herbert Hobart University.

"What does the minister say?" asked Dr. Conway, looking surprised.

"That AIDS is a plague visited by God on sinners," Elena answered.

The doctor looked horrified.

"That people with AIDS should be forced to carry clappers or be segregated in AIDS colonies," Elena added. "Like lepers."

The doctor turned to stare at Evelyn.

"I didn't say that," she protested.

"Do you think it?" he demanded.

"I—I feel very sorry for them," she stammered. "That's why I work here. It's the responsibility of good Christians to minister to the sick and dying."

"Ninety percent of hemophiliacs either have AIDS or have died from the disease," said the doctor. "They didn't get it from sinning; they got it from blood products."

"Well—" Evelyn Dietz looked close to tears.

"The cases among gay men are down. It's women, mostly minorities, whose case percentage is rising. Do you think God—"

Evelyn Dietz, her last print having been taken, rushed away, wiping the ink from her fingers and weeping. Conway's nurse, leading a patient back to the waiting room, stared.

"I think we'd better take away whatever you have left of that medication," Elena murmured to the doctor. "Oh, and I'd like a list of any patients of yours who've died in the last five months."

"Why in the world—"

"We're looking to see if there have been any more unrecognized poisonings."

"Since Evelyn came to work for me?" Conway's face went white.

"Whatever. Any unexpected deaths?"

"Not really. I mean AIDS is a killer. Some have died, but—"

"O.K., we'll want their names and death certificates. And the medication."

"I have other patients. What am I supposed to give—"

"Only one now," Leo reminded him.

"But I'm going to ask A.M.P. for a second test spot."

"And if the capsules are contaminated, you'll have two more dead patients," Elena pointed out.

"I'll have my nurse inspect every—"

"Someone—Evelyn, for instance—could have pulled the capsules apart, filled them with cyanide, and done it so neatly that you can't see it."

"I'll have to call A.M.P.," said the doctor, looking glum as Evelyn returned.

Her nose was red and her eyes puffy; weeping did not make her more attractive or sympathetic. "I heard what you said," she hissed at Elena. "About me pulling capsules apart. I didn't. I've never even been in that room. I wouldn't know which capsules were—"

"—meant for sinners?" Leo suggested as they left.

The two detectives next drove to the Evangelical Fountain of Faith Ministry, which Leo recognized as a former Baptist church. There they interrupted the Reverend Wesley Hardin in his paneled study, at work on a sermon. Or perhaps it was another letter to the editor, Elena thought wryly. "We're the detectives working the murder of a male student at H.H.U."

Hardin nodded solemnly. "A fornicator and a carrier of disease."

"You knew him?" asked Leo.

"Certainly not. People of that sort are not among my parishioners. I read about him in the newspaper. I imagine he sinned with men as well as women—which is an abomination unto the Lord."

"Women, yes," Elena agreed. "Men? Not that we've heard. And the paper didn't say anything about disease. So what's your source of information?"

"Look and ye shall find. Seek the trails of sin, that the sins may be rooted out for the saving of the sinner."

"Little too late for Fullerton," Leo remarked. "Where'd you hear this stuff about Fullerton?"

"His sins were widely known."

"No one but you said he was sick."

"A sick soul gleams through the eyes with the glare of hellfire."

"So you'd met Fullerton?"

"No. I knew him by reputation only."

"So you couldn't have seen his sick soul in his eyes," Elena pointed out. "So where'd—"

"I have sources that I will not, as a shepherd who protects his flock, reveal."

"Does he get privilege-of-the-confessional immunity?" Elena murmured to Leo.

"Protestants don't have confession, do they?" Leo replied. "You've had a lot to say about AIDS lately, Reverend."

Hardin nodded again, his long face sallow and sanctimonious. "It is God's judgment on those who practice unnatural—"

"Have you ever visited H.H.U.?" Elena interrupted.

"Why do you ask?"

"Because someone poisoned a man you think should be rooted out—sin and sinner."

"Are you accusing me of murder?" asked the minister coldly.

"We're asking a question, which you haven't answered. Have you ever visited H.H.U.?"

"Perhaps." He shrugged. "I spread God's word in the haunts of evil."

"Ever visited the office of Dr. Morton Conway?"

"I believe not."

"Ever talked to Evelyn Dietz about what should be done with people who have AIDS?"

"Evelyn is a member of my congregation. She has heard me preach on the subject."

"Did she show special interest?"

"Do you suspect Evelyn of something? If so, you err. She is a fine Christian woman."

Elena gritted her teeth. The man answered every question with a question or an irritating generality. However, before she could bore in, the Reverend Hardin followed in the footsteps of his namesake. He shot from the hip.

"If you persist, Detectives, in impugning the character of myself and my parishioner, I shall have to consult a lawyer; there are several in the congregation." He stared at them significantly, waiting for a frightened response. Getting none, he added, "A man's good name is precious. The good name of a man of God is doubly precious, in that his flock—"

"Meaning you refuse to talk to us without counsel present?" Leo asked.

"Slander is a serious offense."

"Questions asked in the course of a murder investigation are not slander," said Elena.

"Mrs. Johnson," the minister called out in an angry, booming voice. Obviously Mrs. Johnson was clerical help of the part-time, volunteer variety, for Elena had seen her pecking erratically on a computer keyboard in a closet-sized room off Hardin's study. Now the woman scurried in, looking confused and alarmed to be summoned in such a loud voice.

"These people were just leaving. Would you mind escorting them out of the church?" said Hardin.

"Me?" Mrs. Johnson looked at Elena and Leo with round eyes. "Where to?" she asked the minister.

"Out," he replied impatiently.

"You want me to—"

"Yes," he interrupted. His grand gesture hadn't worked out very well, and he scowled at poor Mrs. Johnson.

"Slippery character, isn't he?" said Leo as they followed the woman out.

"Reverend Hardin?" gasped Mrs. Johnson, turning around and gaping at Leo. "*Our* Reverend Hardin?"

22

Thursday, April 10, 1:15 P.M.

Elena and Leo met Jaime Sandoval for lunch at a cheap pizza place on North Mesa. Mosconi, who with Sandoval had finished the interviews with Fullerton's girlfriends that morning, had driven downtown to the courthouse, where he was to testify on an assault that had taken place in a Dyer Street bar. Two locals had attacked a soldier from Fort Bliss over the favors of a barmaid who was, in Harry's opinion, "better looking than a dog but not as smart."

As they waited for their pizza, Elena checked her notebook. "Wilkerson never called me back to verify that Fullerton was actually HIV positive," she murmured. "Not that there's much question in my mind. Still—"

"He was," said Leo. "I took the call."

"Thanks for telling me," Elena grumbled. "And Harley Stanley never got back to me about Fullerton's parents. He insisted on being the one to notify them. Did you take that call too, Leo?"

"Not me. You're the one that gets all the attention at H.H.U." Grinning, he helped himself to a piece of sausage pizza, which had just been deposited on their Formica-topped table by a waitress whose chin drooped on the left side.

In an effort not to stare, Elena busily wrote herself a reminder to check with the vice-president to see what the parents had said.

Sandoval reported on the morning interviews. All the interviewees had wept, but none admitted to being in Fullerton's bathroom within the last month. Leo shrugged and said, "We're looking at a lady in the doctor's office. Her and her minister."

"Great," said Sandoval. "I'd hate to think any of those pretty girls iced him. And hey, look at this." He pulled out that day's issue of the *Campus Enquirer*, passing it to Elena and pointing to the column "Willie's Whispers."

Elena read aloud, " 'We're awarding our first Stud-of-the-Month honors to a professor, Angus McGlenlevie. The prof/poet seems to be following in the footsteps of the late three-time winner, Graham Fullerton, although Gus's girls aren't as happy with him as Graham's were, but then Graham, as far as we know, never got anyone pregnant. In fact, he was known for his advocacy of safe and responsible sex. Professor, learn from your students!' "

"Safe and responsible sex?" Leo muttered. "He must have slipped up somewhere."

"Read the rest," Sandoval ordered.

Elena continued. " 'Professor McGlenlevie, when we called to tell him that he was this month's winner, thanked us for the honor but claimed that he is retiring as a stud and opting for happy domesticity. The question is: is he marrying them both (the *Enquirer* was the first to publish the rumor that the good professor had impregnated *two* young ladies), or does one of the future moms have to take care of her own problem? Not cool, Prof. Not too cool.' "

"He must be marrying that poor girl I talked to yesterday, don't you think?" asked Sandoval. "I sure hope so. I'd hate to think of her getting an abortion. That business about him getting two girls pregnant must be wrong, don't you think? I mean the guy's a professor."

Elena didn't tell him about Estie. Leo, however, said grimly, "He probably got the whole volleyball team pregnant." Jaime, a man with four sisters and therefore a man who didn't like to see women taken advantage of, looked horrified. Elena bent her head over her slice of pizza to hide a grin. Leo got up and headed for the men's room.

"Hey, Elena," said Sandoval, making a quick recovery. "How come you're dating Anglos with ponytails? He some kinda hippie type?"

"He's a physicist," Elena replied, wondering how Sandoval knew about Rafer.

"Next thing you'll be hanging out with bikers wearing earrings, when you could be going out with a handsome cop like me."

"Tempting as that idea is, you're too young, Sandoval."

"Nonsense. Women are always better off with younger men. Women get sexier. Men go over the hill."

Now where had she heard *that* before? "You poor guy. You're over the hill?"

"Not me. I'm a late bloomer, so I've got a few good years left."

"Well, I don't date cops. I was married to one, so now I know better. And how come you know who I'm dating?"

"Saw you at that pizza place near the U. I was with my older sister. Say, you think Mosconi might be interested in a blind date with her? She's a widow, and I keep telling her it's time she started going out again."

"He's still hung up on his ex," said Elena.

"Too bad. Rosa is one gorgeous woman, and she's a great cook."

"Who's this?" asked Leo, returning to the table. "Think she'd move in with me? My wife never has time to cook."

"I only set my sisters up with eligible men," said Sandoval. "I got a responsibility here. What if she fell in love with you, Leo?"

"Concepcion would kill her," said Elena.

Returning to campus after lunch with the idea of talking to everyone who had known Graham Fullerton, Leo and Elena were detoured to Dr. Sunnydale's office by the guard at the western gate. Had the University president, usually kept in the dark about knotty problems, heard about Graham Fullerton's death? Elena asked Leo what he thought.

"I expect he'll want us to pray over it," Leo replied gloomily.

President Sunnydale had been a California TV evangelist before the IRS closed him down. Now he spread Christian good will and prayer over the university, his post as president having been willed to him by a convert and the founder, Herbert Hobart. The vice presidents took care of academics, finances, and problems.

To Elena and Leo's surprise, President Sunnydale never mentioned the death of Graham Fullerton. They found him entertaining Bishop Ernesto Chavira, spiritual leader of the Roman Catholic diocese of Los Santos, who had come to inquire about the Weeping Virgin in the H.H.U. chapel.

"Actually, I don't think that figure is the Virgin Mary, Mother of our Lord and Savior, Jesus Christ," Dr. Sunnydale was saying as Elena and Leo were ushered in by Chief Clabb of the university security force.

The bishop's heavy eyebrows folded in toward his nose. "I was led to believe . . ."

"It's a real problem," Clabb whispered to the detectives. "Roman Catholics keep sneaking onto campus to see the window. We caught several people, with their children, climbing over the northern wall this morning." H.H.U.'s lushly landscaped campus was surrounded by five-foot stone walls stuccoed and decorated with mosaic tile borders and occasional designs.

The bishop, who had overheard Clabb, turned to remark, "You must expect the faithful to respond to what they see as a miraculous happening, although why God would choose this particular venue for a miracle—"

"Oh, I assure you, Bishop," said the president, "we're open to miracles here at Herbert Hobart University."

"Some of the students who made the graduation list last year were a miracle," Elena muttered. She didn't know why she and Leo had been summoned but couldn't imagine that the Weeping Virgin was any of their concern.

"However," the president continued, "we don't know that the weeping—ah—lady in question is, as I was saying, actually—"

"I'm told that she is clad in blue," said the bishop, "the Virgin's color, that she has a halo—"

"More like an emanation of light from the whole figure," said Chief Clabb.

The bishop frowned again. "—and that a baby—"

"Babies," corrected Harley Stanley, bustling in to rescue the president. "Many babies around her feet. Hardly the traditional—" He stopped and stared at Leo and Elena, looking alarmed. "Detectives, if you have a report to make, perhaps you'd like to do it in my office."

That meant Fullerton's death and the ensuing scandal were being kept from Sunnydale. Nonetheless, Elena rose and motioned to Leo to do the same. Better Stanley than Sunnydale.

"We'll leave the bishop and the president to chat," said Vice-President Stanley, "while—"

"No, no," cried President Sunnydale. "I particularly asked for Detective Jarvis, who is our university detective." He beamed at her. "Our own first honorary doctor. Since no one seems to know who the lady on the window is, I thought Detective Jarvis could investigate."

"Well," said Leo, heading for the door, "I'll leave you to it, Elena."

He didn't want to get mixed up in some nutty Virgin investigation; that was obvious. And neither did Elena. "That's not the sort of thing I investigate, sir," she said to the president. "No one's dead—in the chapel, anyway—or the victim of an assault."

"One of my officers caught some outsider trying to touch the window," said Chief Clabb. "She was actually trying to climb up on the shoulders of another person, a rather grubby-looking male, to get to the tears." The chief looked to Elena as if he thought she might be interested in investigating a nonviolent assault on a stained-glass window.

"If you got their names, you might have the basis for a trespassing charge," she replied, "but Leo and I don't handle trespass." She had grabbed Leo's arm to keep him from leaving. A minor tug of war ensued.

"Here I am, sir. At your service." A gnomish fellow with a white goatee and suede slouch hat bustled into the office, blocking Leo's avenue of escape.

"Who?" The president looked at him blankly.

"Castor Apulonia, Professor of Multi-Sect Theology. You wanted someone to research the figure on the chapel window? I'm your man. Should make an excellent academic paper—interdisciplinary, too. I plan to bring in someone from Psychology. At the very least, we'll want to investigate the psychology of modern idol worship."

"Idol worship?" The bishop rose, looking highly insulted. "I shall advise my flock to reserve judgment on this Weeping Virgin. I perceive that this may be some hoax practiced on the faithful."

"Maybe you could suggest that they stop climbing over the walls," said Clabb. "It makes my men very nervous."

"Good day," said the bishop severely.

"Won't you stay for a drink, my dear bishop?" asked President Sunnydale. "Perhaps we could go over to view the weeping goddess, whoever she may be, together. A Roman Catholic point of view might shed some light on the issue."

"You haven't mentioned the Fullerton investigation, have you?" Harley Stanley murmured to Elena.

"No," she murmured back, "but we'll need a search of your gate logs." She wanted to find out if Evelyn Dietz or the Reverend Hardin had been on campus during the last few weeks.

"Talk to Clabb," advised the vice-president. "And if you're coming to the memorial service, don't let on to the president that Fullerton was murdered. We don't want to upset him."

"When is it?" she asked.

While they were whispering, Elena heard with half-attention the bishop telling President Sunnydale that he had glanced at their student newspaper in the waiting room and was horrified to see that fornicators were being honored, a very bad precedent to set among young people.

Dr. Sunnydale was stunned and said so.

"And one of the honorees is evidently a professor," the bishop continued.

"I'm sure there must be some mistake," said the president.

"I certainly consider such goings-on a mistake," returned

the bishop. "Good day, sir." He marched out in high dudgeon, leaving the president to exclaim, "I can't believe he wouldn't stay for a drink! I could have offered him an excellent California Chardonnay or, if he preferred, perhaps one of the more piquant Gewurtztraminers."

"You have a sermon to give, sir," said Harley Stanley. "The memorial for Fullerton."

"Oh, yes. Poor fellow. Always so sad when a person dies young, although no doubt he's gone on to a better place."

Elena, for one, doubted it.

"I suppose a few general remarks on fleeting youth and God's welcoming arms will do? What did you say his name was?"

"Fullerton," said Vice-President Stanley.

23

Thursday, April 10, 2:45 P.M.

In the outer office President Sunnydale's secretary was trying to pacify a handsome, enraged gentleman of middle years with offers of tea and scones. "I know it's a bit early," she said, looking plump and cheerful, "but I'd be delighted to provide tea. And I have a lovely marmalade for the scones."

"Stand aside," the visitor said to the secretary, who was fluttering in front of the door as Elena and Leo exited.

"I really can't interrupt the president at just this moment, you see," the secretary twittered anxiously. "He's entertaining the bishop, the Roman Catholic bishop, and President Sunnydale is ever so supportive of interdenominational communication. Why, during his California ministry, I remember—"

"The bishop's already left," said Elena helpfully.

"He has? But I didn't see—"

"Stop blathering, madam," shouted the man with the beautifully waved white hair. "I don't care if the Pope's in there. I demand an explanation of my son's alleged death."

Professor Apulonia and Chief Clabb followed Elena and Leo out.

"Damn it all. How can a healthy young man suddenly die?" the father demanded. "How can the university leave a message announcing it on my answering machine?"

121

Well, that answered Elena's question about whether the parents had been notified.

Dr. Harley Stanley, exiting last, hustled over to the angry man and cried, "My dear Mr. Fullerton. May I assume that you are Mr. Fullerton? We've been trying desperately to contact you since the tragic event, but your servants insist that your wife is indisposed."

"Drunk," snapped Fullerton.

"And you were out of the country."

"Well, couldn't you haven't placed an overseas call? Considering the tuition you charge here, you can afford—"

"Of course, sir, but no one would give us a number," said Dr. Stanley. He was sweating, a clue to Elena that Fullerton was exceedingly rich, probably a past donor to the Hobart Fund.

"What's this nonsense about Graham? And don't tell me he's dead. I don't—"

Dr. Stanley sighed, eyelids at half-mast in a sad droop. "Perhaps Detective Jarvis here can explain the tragic events better than I."

Oh, thanks, Elena thought. "Or Detective Weizell," she suggested.

"I defer to you, Elena," said Leo hastily. "Women are so much more—"

"Right," she snapped. Chief Clabb and the Multi-Sect professor escaped during the buck-passing.

"Well?" Fullerton glared at her.

"Someone poisoned your son's medication with potassium cyanide," she said. "It killed him. Tuesday."

"What medication?" the father demanded.

"AZT, Epivir, and some experimental stuff."

"AZ—" Fullerton sputtered into silence, his face flushing. "If you're implying that Graham had—had—"

"Right," she agreed. "The blood work just came in from DPS, not that we really needed it. They're all HIV medications, so—"

Fullerton's eyes narrowed to hard slits. "He really is dead, then?"

"He is," Elena agreed.

Harley Stanley had been staring at her, horrified, presumably at her lack of feminine subtlety or something. "Most tragically," the vice-president added.

"Who knows about the—the—"

"I assure you, Mr. Fullerton, that is information that will not—I repeat *not*—be released to the public," said Dr. Stanley. "Even if such revelations weren't, thank goodness, against the law, Herbert Hobart University is the soul of discretion when it comes to—"

"You damn well better be," snapped the father. "Or I'll sue you into bankruptcy. Not that I believe he had—it. But I better not hear . . .''

Elena wondered which bothered the father more, the death of his son or the possibility of scandal. But that was probably unfair. The elder Fullerton would be feeling grief soon enough. Sometimes death took a while to sink in.

The memorial service was as strange as such services always were at H.H.U. L.S.A.R.I. had pickets outside carrying signs deploring fornication and proclaiming the dire penalties it brought on the heads of the lustful. The president forgot the deceased's name but called him a "paragon of American youth" and a "young man sure to be remembered forever by his many friends." The females were weeping prettily into lacy handkerchiefs, except for Dr. Greta Marx, who looked like a middle-aged avenging angel. Elena and Leo had requisitioned two campus cops, resplendent in lavender dress uniforms, to take pictures of the mourners for later identification.

The parents sat in the front row of the chapel, the handsome father causing a flutter among coeds, the mother weeping and sipping occasionally from a cloisonné flask.

The chapel was also peopled by male students, who had evidently admired Graham for the wide swath he cut among the ladies or, perhaps, hated him for the same reason. Elena looked them over carefully and listened to the tributes to the deceased. She didn't find anyone looking hateful or violent regarding Fullerton. Many of the attendees seemed to be fraternity brothers who claimed that they would miss "good old Graham," always the life of the party.

At the post-service cocktail party, serenity and restrained mourning evaporated as Fullerton's fraternity brothers told nostalgic stories about him, one example being the time when Graham, always the cut-up, had peed in the beer keg at a party. Horrified, Elena wondered if they could all have been infected from the beer and interrupted Dr. Marx, who was swilling martinis, to ask.

The doctor shrugged. "Since the vice-president"—she aimed a basilisk glance at Harley Stanley, who was chatting earnestly with the Fullertons—"won't let us warn them, what difference does it make? Until they're all tested, we're flirting with disaster." She swept another martini from a tray and drained it, seemingly in one swallow. Then she tossed the olive back onto the tray. "Look at them," she muttered, waving toward the students, "giggling at the doors of death. They haven't a clue."

Before the doctor could shift into loud lecture mode, Elena slipped away and joined Leo. Sandoval was in a corner talking earnestly to Harry Mosconi. One H.H.U. cop was snapping pictures as if he were a photographer at a wedding, grouping students and faculty, begging them to smile. A second had a video camera and homed in when the cocktail party was invaded by a phalanx of young women in sweats labeled:

H.H.U.
VOLLEYBALL

He caught the whole protest as the coeds singled out waiters carrying trays of delicious hors d'oeuvres and snatched them away, depriving Elena and Leo of the tasty snacks they had been enjoying while they observed the show and directed their university minions in the taking of more photos. Many students, thinking their pictures were being taken for the campus newspaper, had been posing accommodatingly. The girls' volleyball team, however, hunted down Angus McGlenlevie, who was talking poetry with a pretty young thing, and pelted him mercilessly with shrimp puffs and pâté de fois gras on melba toast rounds.

During this attack, which drove the astonished poetry professor into the chapel for refuge, Dr. Marx sidled up to Elena and whispered, "You should arrest that man. He's impregnated at least two girls."

"I can't do that," said Elena. "They'd have to bring charges, and if the sex was consensual—"

"What good are the police if they won't address sex crimes?"

"I'm not in the sex-crimes unit," Elena reminded the doctor.

"Have you done anything about Gretchen?"

"She won't press charges."

"I'll work on her. I suppose if Fullerton were alive and you knew he was spreading HIV, you wouldn't—"

"He's dead. If someone hadn't killed him, it's possible he could have been charged with negligent homicide or, at least, endangerment." Elena got out her notebook and a pen. "Has anyone come in for an AIDS test yet?"

"Ha!" cried Dr. Marx. "As if I'd tell you that. You'd probably rush right off and arrest them."

Elena sighed. "We seem to be at an impasse. You won't help me, and I can't help you. Although I'd like to in the matter of Gretchen." Then she remembered guiltily that she'd faxed Gretchen's picture to Monica Ibarra at Central Regional Command, on the off chance that, as Quarles claimed, Gretchen had been the one to purchase the Rohypnol. But Dr. Marx didn't need to know that.

"How many of you young fools have been tested for HIV?" the doctor demanded loudly of everyone at large. An embarrassed silence fell over the group. Graham Fullerton's father stiffened and turned threateningly on the vice-president, who hustled over to Greta Marx, grabbed her arm, and headed her for a side door. ". . . Armageddon . . ." she could be heard roaring as she was dragged away.

Elena overheard the university's public relations person murmuring to the Fullertons that Dr. Marx was an excellent doctor but that she suffered from occasional bouts of "millennium madness."

"What's that?" demanded Fullerton.

"She thinks the world is going to end at the year 2000," said the PR lady. "She's prone to predict disasters after two martinis."

"I always find that two martinis cheer me up," said Mrs. Fullerton, who had one in each hand while tears continued to roll down her face.

Elena wondered if the lady always drank and cried or only during periods of mourning. Had she known that her son was infected with a lethal virus? No way to ask.

Rafer caught Elena on the way out of the Sacred Vestibule and invited her to dinner. "Chinese takeout," he promised.

"But we've got a date for tomorrow night."

"Didn't you have fun last night?" he asked, looking disappointed.

Elena promised to appear at his door by six o'clock. It was nice to be dating again, she thought cheerfully, and considering the Fullerton case, she needed all the distraction she could get. The girls' volleyball team was congregated on the lawn in front of the chapel, giving each other high fives, evidently as a result of the successful canapé attack on their coach.

24
..

After the service and cocktail party, Chief Clabb told Elena that, in order to see the visitor logs from the university entrance gates, she'd have to get permission from Vice-President Joel Smith. She trudged back to the Administration building with Leo and discovered in the vice-president's office a delegation of maids complaining that the student newspaper had attacked their ethnic pride and religious devotion by saying that the stained-glass Virgin was some pagan goddess weeping for that well-known seducer, the late Graham Fullerton.

Joel Smith smoothed his graying mustache and replied condescendingly, "My good women, we all know that boys will be boys. I'm sure in your culture as well as mine—"

"We want an apology," interrupted Socorro Rascon.

"I have no control over the student newspaper," said Smith. "I'm in charge of the financial affairs of the university. However, freedom of the press and constitutional rights no doubt all come into play here."

"I don' give a shit about none of that stuff," snapped Socorro. "I want an apology tomorrow. Onna front page. No apology, you're gonna have a big business problem."

Mrs. Poleby, the head of Housekeeping, said, "Young woman, you are threatening the vice-president for Financial Affairs. It is not your place to—"

"How about a work slowdown? Like we only do half the

127

toilets? Like we don't got time to make all the beds 'cause we're feelin' so bad people are sayin' crap about the Holy Mother? How about that?'' Socorro scowled from one to the other. ''How about you got no maids at all?'' The young woman whirled, long black hair flying, and spotted Elena and Leo behind her.

''What?'' she said, turning back to Smith. ''You called the cops? Well, I know my rights. An' if I wanna go on strike, or I wanna leave the students' underwear all over the carpets or vacuum it up because they're too lazy to pick it up themselves, what are you gonna do? Huh? 'Cause all the maids are with me.''

The other women nodded, but they looked a little scared, much less militant than their tough-talking leader. Socorro turned back to Elena and Leo. ''So you ain't got no reason to arrest me.''

Elena agreed. Leo grinned. The maids departed. Mrs. Poleby said, ''No need to worry, Dr. Smith. They're not going to make trouble over some silly newspaper article. They need their jobs too much.'' Smith concurred, looking complacent.

Elena thought they were underestimating Hispanic pride and the aggressive nature of a young woman who had grown up in a gang, but she let the administrators go on believing they had nothing to worry about. All she wanted was permission to check the visitor logs, which she got, but Leo wouldn't stay to take a look. He wanted to go home now that his eight-to-four shift was over.

Before Elena could check the logs herself, she heard from Monica Ibarra on the cell phone: no *roche* dealer had recognized Gretchen Farber's photo or even sold *roche* to any female in weeks. So much for Quarles's claim that Gretchen had introduced drugs to their evening. Accordingly, Elena decided to have one last try at convincing Gretchen to file charges.

L.S.A.R.I. picketers were still scattered across the campus, some at the clinic, some at the dorm. How did they get in? Elena wondered. And why didn't Clabb make them leave? A nearsighted gentleman in a plaid windbreaker and billed cap took her for a coed as she mounted the dorm steps.

"Fornication is death," he shouted. "Repent!"

Elena stopped, short-tempered after a long day, and turned on him. "Bug off," she snapped, "or I'll have the campus cops run you off."

"Slut! Whore!" shouted the man, waving a sign in her face.

Before she could snatch it from his hand and break the pole over her knee, which was her impulse, Ora Mae Spotwood, head of the Antifornication Brigade, hurried up and murmured into the man's ear.

His face turned red, and he shouted, "The police are as corrupt as the federal government."

Ora Mae smiled nervously at Elena and spoke again to the man.

"If I had my gun, I'd teach her to respect her elders," he replied, then shouted, "Down with gun control! Support the Republic of Texas!"

"Now, Jerry Joe," said Ora Mae, "you know our agreement is no guns, just polite Christian reasoning."

"Balderdash!" shouted Jerry Joe.

"Strange company you're keeping, Mrs. Spotwood," said Elena, who knew the woman from past cases and demonstrations. "What agreement is this? I thought L.S.A.R.I. was banned from campus."

"Not at all," said Mrs. Spotwood. "The president himself issued us a permit for our Christian mission."

Elena rolled her eyes, wondering if Harley Stanley knew what kindly President Sunnydale, who didn't have a clue about much of anything, had done. "Stay out of my face," she told Jerry Joe and stamped up the steps. Her mission, however, was a failure. Even with Elena's assurance that she believed every word of Gretchen's story, the coed wouldn't press charges.

"Why bother?" she said, now seeming more angry than tearful. At least, she was no longer weeping. "I'd be the one who ends up on trial. Everyone knows how rape trials go. And he's a local boy. The jury—"

Thinking of Quarles, Sr., who was in jail, Elena said,

"The family name isn't going to be much help to Wayne. Don't you know that his father—"

"So the jury would feel bad for the poor orphaned Texan, being slandered by some Yankee slut," Gretchen responded bitterly. "Haven't you seen the signs those people outside are carrying? Some old man in a plaid jacket called me names when I came back from class. If he's an example of a sympathetic local juror, I'll just keep my mouth shut."

Evidently Jerry Joe and Gretchen had run into one another. Elena gave up, noted that it was too late to check the visitor logs, and walked over to Rafer's place in the faculty apartment tower, where Elena's friend Sarah Tolland had lived before Gus McGlenlevie's courtship had driven Sarah into home ownership. Now Gus had taken his campaign to become a father to the girls' volleyball team. Elena shook her head, remembering the canapé attack that afternoon. How many girls had he impregnated? And what, if anything, would the administration do about it? In some ways L.S.A.R.I. had a point about H.H.U. Elena just didn't like the way they went about making it.

The Chinese takeout evening with Rafer was a mixed bag. He tried to put the little white cardboard cartons with their metal handles into the microwave. Elena barely got to him before he hit the start button, embarrassing him because a physicist, of all people, should know what happened when you put metal in a microwave. Elena didn't know exactly, but he told her over lukewarm egg rolls and cashew chicken, and the telling didn't make for interesting dinner conversation. As far as Elena was concerned, knowing enough not to put metal in the microwave was more important than knowing what would happen if you did.

She disappointed Rafer by going home early. Her idea was to escape any further science lessons. His idea had evidently been to segue from physics to subjects more intimate, but all he got was a brushed kiss on the cheek as she ducked a warmer goodbye effort. "See you tomorrow night," she called gaily and headed for the elevator.

By the time she had written up her reports and exchanged the unmarked police car for her truck at headquarters, it was nine-thirty. She arrived home to find several of her elderly neighbors milling around in her yard with flashlights pointing toward the adobe walls of her house, where someone had scrawled with red spray-paint, W H O R E.

"I saw him," said Gloria Ledesma. "On the short side, thin. Driving a dark car."

"It was a green car, and he was at least five-ten," said Omar Ashkenazi. Other neighbors, all with poor eyesight, had different versions of the incident and descriptions of the perpetrator. Dimitra Potemkin complained because the police, whom she had called, had yet to arrive. Elena stared at the scrawl and wondered who her admirer was. Jerry Joe? Wayne Quarles, Jr.?

When she went into the house, there was an angry message on her answering machine from Quarles, who said he knew she was trying to talk that lying Farber bitch into pressing charges against him, and he was innocent. He'd sue Elena for false arrest and Farber for slander. He'd——'' The message broke off with voices in the background, evidently dissuading Wayne from continuing the tirade. He sounded drunk.

A patrol car arrived carrying two embarrassed officers, who told her they'd have come immediately, but there had been a hit-and-run on Copia they had to respond to and— she cut off their apologies, suggested that Jerry Joe somebody of L.S.A.R.I and Wayne Quarles, Jr., were possible suspects. She then gave them the tape from her answering machine and went back inside while they interviewed the neighbors, who probably hadn't been up this late or had so much excitement since Boris Potemkin was murdered and his wife blamed God.

Elena's last act of the evening was a call to the Department of Sanitation, which had a new graffiti-removal machine. She left a message asking them to remove the red paint from her house, adding that a Los Santos policewoman, targeted because of her job, shouldn't have to wait the usual three months for graffiti relief. Then she went to bed.

25

Friday, April 11, 6:30 A.M.

Miracle at H.H.U.?

Last Sunday Angel Guadaramma, while pursuing her cleaning duties in the Herbert Hobart University chapel, noticed tears escaping from the eyes of the Virgin Mary, as portrayed on a stained glass window. Guadaramma reported the miracle to her priest, Father Conrad Bratslowski, pastor of San Isidro del Valle.

Yesterday when Guadaramma, who is three months pregnant, feared that she was about to miscarry, she went to the university chapel to pray to the Virgin. All symptoms of miscarriage disappeared. "The Holy Mother has saved my baby," she told a Los Santos *Times* reporter.

When interviewed by telephone, Father Bratslowski proclaimed the "weeping virgin" a hoax perpetrated on good Catholics by an "immoral university administration" and called on his flock to stay away from the H.H.U. chapel and confine their worship to church and personal prayer.

Bishop Chavira and H.H.U. President Sunnydale were unavailable for comment.

Los Santos *Times*, Friday, April 11

Elena put down her paper and poured more coffee. Why hadn't she thought to look at the window when she was at

Graham Fullerton's memorial service? She tried to imagine
what the "tears" were like. Did they drip down and form
damp spots on the carpet? Or did they just sit there on the
glass? And how come a team of scientists-who-investigate-
miracles hadn't turned up to run tear samples through an
NMR or whatever? Never a dull moment at H.H.U.

Sipping her second cup of coffee, she resumed her reading
of the morning *Times*. There was an article about how little
information was being released on the recent death of an
H.H.U. student named Graham Fullerton. President Sunnydale, when interviewed, said that no doubt the young man's
demise would prove to be the result of some natural, if
tragic, event and that the university relied on the LSPD to
answer all questions, as they always did, the university and
the force having had friendly and trusting relations for many
years. An LSPD spokesman in the chief's office answered
all questions with a "no comment." H.H.U. Vice-President
Stanley urged reporters to respect the rights to privacy of the
grieving parents. All very discreet.

Except for Dr. Greta Marx. UNIVERSITY CLINIC DOC BE-
GINS AIDS CAMPAIGN, the headline read. *Oh boy,* Elena
thought, and read on. Evidently the doctor was flooding the
campus with posters, flyers, even E-mail on the necessity for
every sexually active student to be tested regularly for HIV.
When asked if she suspected an outbreak of AIDS at H.H.U.,
Dr. Marx referred the reporter to Meredith Corwin, the university public relations person, who said, "Our students are
exceptionally healthy and all looking forward to our next
concert featuring the newest rock sensation, Guano Lip."

Guano Lip? Where do they come up with those names?
Elena wondered. *And is the fact that I'd ask that question a
sign that I'm getting old and square?* She sighed, finished
her coffee, rinsed off her dishes, slotted them into the dish-
washer, and went off to brush her teeth. She and Leo would
begin the morning at Dr. Morton Conway's office, producing
a warrant to confiscate the red capsules.

Their appearance at nine o'clock caused confusion and
dismay among the staff and those patients who had come in
for treatment. Conway protested that he and his nurses had

found no signs of tampering and that the police were endangering a patient whose life depended on an uninterrupted course of medication.

Next, Elena studied the death certificates of patients who had died in the last five months, but she could find nothing that looked like poisoning. She sent copies to the medical examiner for evaluation. Finally, they questioned all employees as to who had been in the medication room and who had actually handled the red-capsule bottles. Each employee was asked not only about his or her activities relative to the case, but about anything they remembered concerning other employees.

By the last interview, Elena was aware of angry looks coming their way as well as those exchanged between employees, who evidently now suspected each other of making incriminating statements. "This office will never be the same," Elena murmured to Leo.

He shrugged. "They think they've got problems. They should try living with five babies. Little Sarah stood up yesterday. Now they're all either walking or on the verge."

Elena grinned. "So they're precocious. Be happy."

He grimaced. "I don't hear you offering to baby-sit again."

"I've got a new boyfriend," she said by way of reply and asked where Leo wanted to go for lunch.

"We're supposed to meet Mosconi and Sandoval on the Westside for Tex Mex," he replied, then mentioned as they left, "Evelyn Dietz told me she never went in that room, much less handled medication. No one I talked to saw her in there."

"I got the same answers," Elena agreed. "Maybe she's not the one."

They met at Tio Tico's and feasted on *tacos al carbon* with guacamole and refried beans, passing around copies of that morning's *Campus Enquirer*. The first item to catch Elena's attention was headlined NO APOLOGIES FROM US. In a by-lined, front-page article, the editor declared that the *Enquirer* had no intention of apologizing to the domestic staff. "If they think they have some right to hang out at the chapel instead of doing their jobs, they should work somewhere else,'' he declared. That would *not* go over well with Socorro Rascon and her union-minded fellow employees, Elena reasoned.

Another article declared that police harassment of Graham Fullerton's girlfriends in their time of grief was both unkind and ridiculous since the much-admired Graham had no doubt died of overexertion rather than any attempt on his life. Finally, Elena discovered in ''Willie's Whispers'' this question: Did our professorial Stud of the Month, Angus McGlenlevie, manage to knock up all those cute volleyball players who attacked him with canapés at yesterday's cocktail party in the Sacred Vestibule? If so, the man's fertility goes way beyond his creative imagination.

Elena pointed the column item out to Jaime Sandoval, who said, ''Someone threw more than food at him today.''

''Right,'' Mosconi agreed and went on to relay the news that around ten that morning someone had shot Angus McGlenlevie from the tower of the Administration building. ''We're supposed to find out who did it,'' said Mosconi.

''He's not dead, I take it?'' Elena thought back over the canapé attack. They'd have to get those pictures taken by the H.H.U. police developed immediately.

''Shot in the hand. He's gone to the hospital.''

''Hand?'' Leo grinned. ''Someone who doesn't like his poetry?''

''Or one of the coeds he's supposed to have knocked up got even?'' Elena suggested. ''Harry, why don't you follow him to the hospital and ask the names of the students who are or were carrying his children.''

''How many are there?'' Harry asked. ''And how come H.H.U. lets the professors screw the students?''

''Anything goes on that campus,'' said Elena gloomily. ''Leo and I will try to get Dr. Marx to tell us who's turned up pregnant. Jaime, you—''

''I'm chasing down the girls who left school.''

''O.K., then, Leo, you track down that columnist, Willie of 'Willie's Whispers,' and ask him for the names of the two pregnant coeds he knows about.''

"Who made you boss of this operation?" asked Leo. "You're not a sergeant yet."

Elena flushed, surprised that Leo would say something that mean, even if he did have five kids driving him crazy at home. "O.K.," she snapped. "How do you want to do it?"

"No wonder people are running around protesting fornication," muttered Mosconi. "Well, I'm on my way to the hospital."

"Right," said Jaime, "we'll let the children settle their spat between themselves." He picked up his bill and left as well.

Elena looked at her partner coolly. "So you'd rather talk to Greta Marx?"

"I'd rather take a shot to the head," he snarled. "Where do I find this Willie?"

"How should I know? You're a detective." Elena rose and stomped toward the cashier's stand, admitting to herself that she was being childish. Leo was usually pretty good-humored, even if he was a chauvinist pig, or at least liked to act that way. Was he really pissed off because she'd taken the initiative? Would he have said that to a man who suggested a division of labor?

The four detectives found themselves not an hour later in the president's office listening as Dr. Sunnydale said, "It's just like the University of Texas massacre, an unknown gunman shooting from the administration tower, wreaking—"

"He only winged one poet," said Elena soothingly.

"What are you saying?" Gus cried. He'd just returned from the hospital and come straight to the president's office to complain about Dr. Marx's treatment of him before the ambulance arrived. "It's my writing hand." He waved the bandaged appendage indignantly at Elena.

"So use a computer," she suggested.

"How insensitive. How heartless!" Gus cried. "My muse is in my heart and my fingertips, just as a lover—"

"Which you've been a few too many times, I'd say," she retorted. "If you don't want some furious coed shooting off the other hand—"

"Coed?" Dr. Sunnydale cut in, looking horrified. "None of our young ladies—I mean why would—"

"—you'd better tell us who's mad enough to shoot you," Elena finished up.

"A lover does not kiss and tell," said Gus loftily. Then he looked crestfallen. "But this mishap is going to ruin my next book of poetry."

"What's it called?" Elena asked. "*Impregnating the World?*"

"This shooting is going to ruin our reputation for peace and joyous youth," mourned President Sunnydale.

"And our hope to make this a record fundraising year for the Hobart Foundation," added Dr. Stanley. "Really, Professor McGlenlevie, I must protest your—your flagrant—"

"Protest, my ass," said Dr. Marx, who had just entered the room. "Someone ought to shoot the bastard."

"Someone did," Elena pointed out, "and you could probably tell us who if you wanted to." The doctor had refused to release medical information.

"Patient confidentiality," said Greta Marx smugly, then added, "Even if I gave you names, you wouldn't do anything about it." She glared at Elena accusingly, reminding her that she had yet to arrest Wayne Quarles.

"Did you have any luck, Leo?" Elena asked. She hadn't had a chance to ask whether the columnist had given him any information.

"He's protecting his sources," said Leo. "Gave me a lecture on freedom of the press. The scandal-mongering news toad."

"We've got the shells," said Jaime and mentioned what they had found that morning.

"We use those in the gun club," said Dr. Stanley, looking astounded.

Elena perked up. "So, Gus, are any of your girlfriends members of the gun club?"

Gus shifted uneasily in his chair. "I'm sure they aren't. My byword has always been 'Make love, not war.' "

"Tell it to whoever turned up pregnant," said Leo with a snort.

"Pregnant?" President Sunnydale frowned. "I'm not following this." He looked toward Harley Stanley.

"Nothing to worry about, sir."

"Do we have the gun?" Elena asked.

"Nope," said Jaime. "No gun. No shooter. Three shells. One hit."

"Dr. Stanley, we'll need the names of members of the club and the faculty sponsor," said Elena.

"That would be me," said the vice-president. "It's an arm of the Desert Adventure Club."

"This place is crazy," muttered Mosconi. "Shooting professors is a desert adventure? Is professors knocking up students a desert adventure, too?"

"I object to the term 'knocking up,' " declared Gus. "The natural desire for fatherhood—"

"Shut up, Angus," snapped Harley Stanley.

"I wonder if we might discuss the miracle I read about in the paper this morning?" suggested the president. "It seems that one of our maidservants . . ."

Elena was thinking that someone from L.S.A.R.I. might have shot Gus, who was a known fornicator. She wouldn't put it past Jerry Joe, that defender of chastity and the right to bear arms, probably the spray-painter of her house.

"I really must ask you to investigate the tears, Dr. Jarvis," the president concluded.

"I don't do Weeping Virgins," said Elena.

26

Friday, April 11, 3:45 P.M.

As the detectives left the president's office, Elena having refused to investigate the Virgin's tears, Sandoval flipped open his notebook and said, "O.K., here's what I found out. The two girls on class trips are in France for the semester. We won't be able to get to them personally until mid-May. They both cried when they heard Fullerton was dead; neither one was even in the country when he got killed or when he got the medication from Conway's office. I'd say they're clear. Not likely they snuck back from France to kill him.

"Of the two who actually left school, I got in touch with one at a Catholic girls' college where her folks sent her because they decided it was too immoral for her here. Her father made her get tested for AIDS because he had a private detective following her and discovered that she'd been 'unchaste.' She thought her old man's terminology was hilarious. Anyway, she's clean for HIV. When I told her Fullerton was dead, she said, 'So what?'

"She also said that at St. Ursula's College, where she is now, she spends the whole day in class or in study hall, and they're locked down in the dormitory after seven. I checked it out with the nun who runs the place. This girl couldn't have got out to kill him, and the Reverend Mother's willing to take an oath on the bones of St. Ursula. So, do you think the department would send me to Duluth to get the oath? I've never been up north. You and I could go, Harry."

"I personally got better things to do than freeze my ass off at some convent in the Arctic Circle."

"Duluth's not quite that far north," said Elena, grinning. "What about the last coed?"

"Amy Marquis," Jaime replied, looking disappointed at the failure of his trip plans. He flipped a page in his notebook. They were leaving the Administration building by then and faced a stiff, cold wind.

"Man, can you believe this weather?" muttered Harry, shoving his hands into the pockets of his sport coat.

"Marquis is the only virgin in his black book. He said—this is a quote—'It's a kick to get a virgin into bed, but from there on, it's all downhill. Makes you realize experience is all when it comes to sex.'" Jaime closed the notebook. "Not a very nice man," was his opinion.

Elena scowled. "She the one who left school for health reasons?"

Jaime nodded. "Fatigue, vomiting. That's according to her ex-roommate. Sounds bad, doesn't it?"

"Is there a date on his comments?"

"September. He met her at a get-acquainted mixer."

"Lucky her. Can AIDS hit that fast?" Elena looked around. No one knew. "I guess we could ask Dr. Conway."

"My guess is he doesn't want to talk to us anymore," said Leo dryly.

"So did you get in touch with Amy Marquis?" Elena asked Jaime.

"Not yet, and I don't want to."

She sighed. "I'll take it." Elena obtained the Albuquerque telephone number from Sandoval before her colleagues left to sign off their shifts at headquarters. Trekking over to Sarah's office to use the phone, she wondered how it was that she always ended up working the overtime, while Leo went home to his wife and quintuplets and Jaime to his mother and sisters, while Harry—well, she didn't know what Harry did. Called his ex-wife probably. "Get a life, Elena," she muttered to herself as she entered the Engineering building.

Sarah wasn't in her office, and Virginia Pargetter, the secretary from hell, wouldn't let Elena use the phone, so Elena went in search of Colin Stuart's office. He was on his way out and waved her to a chair. Although she could have used a public telephone, this wasn't a call she wanted to make in public.

Elena was told, when she reached the Marquis house in Albuquerque, that "Miss Amy" was out. Further questioning elicited the information that Miss Amy was in a clinic for treatment (which sounded ominous to Elena), that Mr. and Mrs. Marquis were out of the country (if their daughter was that sick, why were they traveling abroad? Elena wondered), and that Miss Amy's brother, Mr. Barton Marquis, was at his office at Marquis Properties. At that point the person at the Albuquerque end of the line said goodbye and hung up before Elena could get a telephone number for the brother. She had to call Information, then work her way through five receptionists and secretaries at Marquis Properties, which convinced her that the brother was a rich big shot.

Mr. Barton Marquis couldn't say when his sister would be home, wouldn't give out her location, said her medical diagnosis was none of Elena's business, and demanded for the fourth time the purpose of the call.

"An acquaintance of your sister's has been killed," said Elena.

"Killed how?"

"Murdered."

"When?"

"Last Tuesday."

"She was hospitalized then too, so if you're—"

"Has she been back to Los Santos since she dropped out of school?"

"She's too sick to go anywhere but to doctors' offices and hospitals," he replied angrily.

Amy Marquis must have full-blown AIDS and not be responding to medication, Elena thought. How terrible to lose your virginity to a scoundrel and then your life because of it.

"Who was killed?" the brother asked.

"A student named Graham Fullerton," Elena replied.

After a silence the brother said, "Good. But if you think my sister had anything to do with it, you're sadly mistaken." On that note, he hung up.

Elena sat in Colin Stuart's empty office and thought about the information she'd gathered. Amy Marquis was either dying or heading in that direction—probably. Fullerton was the killer—if she had AIDS, which must be the case. Otherwise, why had her brother said "Good" when he heard that Fullerton was dead. Would calling him back elicit any further information? Probably not. She needed to go to Albuquerque. At departmental expense. Where she could visit her own sister, as well, Maria being a medical student there.

Elena then called Leo to see if he was willing to fly to Albuquerque should the department authorize the expense.

"For Christ's sake," snapped Leo. "I try not to work weekends anymore. I'm a father. Remember? Anyway, Millard Fillmore Fong is coming here to interview us tomorrow, so I can't. Try one of the others."

Before she could call headquarters, she got a page from Onofre Calderon, who told her that the death certificates of Dr. Conway's patients looked like legitimate AIDS deaths to him. "All the usual causes. Pneumonia, Kaposi's. Doesn't look like any of them were murdered."

Elena thanked him, got off the phone, and called Manny Escobedo. He had gone home. She tried Lieutenant Beltran and got permission to make the trip.

"That's a nasty case," he agreed. "The quicker you can close it, the better. You think this girl could have killed him?"

"She had the best motive," Elena replied. "At least, I think so. If not her, maybe her brother."

"Make the reservations. Have the bill sent to the department."

Before Elena could call Southwest Airlines, she was paged again and told by Chief Clabb's office that a study of the gate logs didn't show any visits by Evelyn Dietz but did show visits by Wesley Hardin and Ora Mae Spotwood. The H.H.U. cop gave Elena the dates. That information would necessitate more interviews, she thought as she dialed Southwest and got two cheap round trips to Albuquerque.

Then she called Jaime Sandoval, thinking he might be glad to go to Albuquerque in lieu of Duluth. Jaime said that as long as he got back by 6:30, he'd love to go. He'd never been to Albuquerque.

Elena wondered whether he'd ever been anywhere. "Got a big date tomorrow?" she asked, laughing.

"No, Harry has," said Sandoval. "With my oldest sister. Of course, he's got to meet the family, so he's invited to dinner with Mama and the girls. Then if everyone approves . . ."

Poor Harry, Elena thought. She said, "You'll be back in time for the big blind date. I suppose you have to chaperone if he passes muster and they go out afterward?"

"Hey, what am I? A duenna? If Mama says he's O.K., my sister can go out without a chaperone. Gee, she is a widow and thirty-eight years old."

"Right," Elena agreed, grinning at the idea that a thirty-eight-year-old woman had to get her mother's approval before she could be fixed up by her brother. "See you tomorrow at seven-thirty."

By then it was after five, and Elena had a six o'clock date with Rafer Martin, two more interviews to do if she could get hold of the two L.S.A.R.I. people, and a trip to prepare for. She called Rafer, got him at his office, and explained her problem. Very disappointed, no doubt because he was hoping to get her back to his apartment for sex, or at least the preliminaries to it, he said reluctantly they could have an early dinner. Elena picked him up, ate Italian food with him at a place across from the mall, dropped him off at his apartment, wished he'd get a car to replace the one his wife had taken in the divorce, and drove off to pay Ora Mae Spotwood a surprise visit.

27
..

Ora Mae Spotwood and her husband were eating dinner when Elena arrived. "Detective?" The lady patted her formidably teased hair, a middle-aged version of the old beehive style. "Would you care to have a bite with us?"

Southern hospitality at its most reluctant, thought Elena as she entered the mini-plantation house with its Greek columns, desert landscaping, and one huge shade tree gracing the front yard. "I've eaten," said Elena, "but I'll sit down with you. You don't have to delay your dinner for my sake."

Ora Mae looked somewhat bewildered but led Elena to the dining room and introduced her to Mr. Spotwood, who said, by way of greeting, "Had my car stolen five years back. You people never found it or the thief."

Elena nodded. "Bad year for car thefts."

"Hear it's gettin' bad again." Mr. Spotwood was eating fried chicken with cream gravy, the latter a culinary mystery to Elena. Did the cook pour milk into the grease the chicken had cooked in? Yuck!

"Mrs. Spotwood, the H.H.U. logs show that you were on campus ten days ago. May I ask why?"

"Pregnancy counseling," said Ora Mae. "Are you sure you won't have something? How about some of these black-eyed peas?"

"No thanks. Where did you do this counseling?"

"We set up in the lobby of the dormitory, where we could

144

catch the young ladies coming and going." Ora Mae helped her husband to the black-eyed peas.

"Hard to believe what's goin' on over there," said Mr. Spotwood. "Bunch a sluts, you ask me. Still, the university's good for business."

"Mr. Spotwood owns Spotwood Trophy and Sports," said his wife proudly.

"Were you in any of the rooms?" Elena asked.

Mrs. Spotwood shook her head sadly. "No one invited us upstairs. In fact, our reception was not very friendly. Sinners tend to be defensive when it comes to changing their ways."

"Who is *we*?" Elena asked.

"The Reverend Wesley Hardin and myself," said Mrs. Spotwood.

"Hope you're watchin' out for him, Ora Mae," Mr. Spotwood cautioned. "Preachers tend to be a hot-blooded lot. I told you that."

"Yes you did, Orwin," his wife agreed, "but Reverend Hardin is only hot-blooded in pursuit of the Lord's work. Perhaps you'd care for a piece of peach pie, Detective? Made from peaches I froze last summer from our own tree. Good as fresh."

"Well, I—" Elena was tempted.

"I'll get you a slice right now."

Before Elena could protest, Ora Mae had disappeared into the kitchen. Mr. Spotwood said, pausing over a forkful of mashed potatoes dripping with cream gravy, "Why you as-kin' Ora Mae these questions? You folks goin' after the godly agin?"

"A male student was killed last—"

"I read about him," said Ora Mae, bustling in with the pie.

"God's judgment on a lecher," added Mr. Spotwood, helping himself to more potatoes and gravy.

Ora Mae nodded. "Fornication. It's rife in that evil place. No matter how many warnings we issue, no matter how sym-pathetic their president is to our—"

"Were you ever on the fifth floor of the dorm?" Elena interrupted. The pie was ambrosial, and she was beginning to feel that she shouldn't be suspecting any woman who could make crust like Ora Mae Spotwood's.

"You think I killed that horrible boy?" Ora Mae asked, aghast.

"How did you know he lived on the fifth floor?" Elena pounced on the admission immediately.

"Don't I get any pie?" asked Mr. Spotwood.

"I read the student newspaper, a disgusting gossip sheet, but just what you'd expect of a place like that," said Mrs. Spotwood, who then rushed out the swinging door to provide her husband with pie.

With no admissions of guilt forthcoming or any more slips of the tongue that couldn't be explained, Elena drove away and cornered the Reverend Wesley Hardin just coming out of a youth meeting at his church. As soon as he caught the gist of her questioning, he said he'd never been on the fifth floor, never got further than the dorm lobby, didn't feel that his antiabortion counseling had made much impression on the hardened sinners he encountered coming and going in that den of iniquity, and didn't plan to answer any more questions implying that he himself was guilty of terrible sins. Elena decided that on Monday or earlier, if Jaime and Harry agreed, she'd provide pictures of the two evangelists and get her fellow detectives to question fifth-floor residents as to whether they'd seen Spotwood or Hardin in the vicinity of Fullerton's room.

She was home by nine o'clock—in time to glance at the local section of the morning paper, while sipping a beer, and note that some AIDS support group had accused the Los Santos Police of trying to kill AIDS patients by interfering with their treatment. *Great!* she thought and picked up her ringing telephone.

It was Paul Resendez from the *Times*, asking about the police interfering with AIDS treatment. She told him that accusation was nonsense. He asked if the confiscation of AZT and other medications had any relation to her case at H.H.U. She said no interviews were being given on that case unless they went through the chief's office. He asked why the secrecy. She replied, laughing, that it was a secret. He asked if she was drunk. She said no.

"Tipsy?" he asked.

"On one beer?" she rejoined.

"Want to go out for another right now?" he asked.

"Trying to get information by getting me drunk?" she retorted.

"O.K., forget the beer, and we'll go straight to bed," he suggested.

Elena declined and hung up. The telephone rang again.

"You bitch," a female voice snarled when she picked up. "You'll be sorry if you don't back off." The caller hung up, and Elena stared at the telephone as if it had stung her.

Who was that? Someone from L.S.A.R.I.? Someone from the Evangelical Fountain of Faith Ministry? Someone who had shot Angus McGlenlevie? Her mind jumped from one possibility to the next as she flipped on her yard lights and stepped out to see if the graffiti-eradicating machine had visited her house to remove the message "W H O R E" from her walls. The machine had done its work, leaving a lighter version of the word where once the letters were red. Evidently the graffiti-eater devoured any kind of color, including the color in her adobe walls. Sighing, she went in and locked her door. She had to be up early tomorrow to catch a plane to Albuquerque. Jaime was picking her up.

28

VP Threatens Maids

According to employee spokesperson Socorro Rascon, Herbert Hobart University Vice-President Joel Smith has threatened to terminate the employment of any member of the housekeeping or gardening staff caught loitering in the university chapel.

"That's interfering with our religious freedom," said the H.H.U. maid. "We got a right to see the Weeping Virgin. Look what She done for Angel Guadaramma, kept her from miscarrying.

"Now they changed Angel's assignment and made her sign a paper saying if she miscarries, it ain't the university's fault. She oughta be able to clean the chapel like she always done. They're discriminating against Angel 'cause she's pregnant. We're gonna organize a union to protect our rights."

Los Santos *Times*, Saturday, April 12

Jaime accepted two packages of peanuts, a packet of peanut-butter-cheese crackers and a Coke from the Southwestern Airlines stewardess, passing the newspaper to Elena, who had the window seat. "Read the article on the maids," he advised.

"I have." Elena had already ripped open her peanuts and

was popping them into her mouth between sips of Bloody
Mary mix—without the vodka. "When I took her home, she
said they should organize a union. Gonna name it after the
Weeping Virgin."

Jaime took his newspaper back. "The poetry professor
getting shot is in here too," he remarked. Elena stared out
her window. They were flying over black-ridged mountains,
jagged and thrusting up from dun and brown plains, all mea-
gerly splotched with a green film that looked like dying
moss. White roads were scratched into the dust, above which
waterless white clouds streaked a blue horizon. The whole
terrain looked barren and uninhabited, as if it were never
seen by any eyes other than those of passengers flying over
in fragile metal shells.

"Can I have the window seat coming back?" Jaime asked,
craning to look over her shoulder.

She turned to her colleague. "Haven't you ever flown before?" she asked curiously.

Jaime looked embarrassed as he shook his head.

"Then you can have the window seat both ways," she
offered, standing up to switch. "Why didn't you say something?"

The flight to Albuquerque was short. Jaime had hardly
gotten his fill of staring out the window and experimenting
with the tray table and seat adjustment before he was asked
to put his seat into an upright position for landing, the
thought of which made him so nervous that Elena had to
help him refasten the seat belt. Then they both grabbed brief-
cases and filed off the plane to meet Detective Luis Quintela
of the Albuquerque P.D. As a courtesy, Quintela would drive
them around and participate in their case.

"Important family you're questionin' here," he said as
they pulled out of the airport lot in an unmarked car. "Lotsa
money, big real-estate holdin's."

"Are they the vengeful type?" Elena asked. She and Sandoval had already explained the case to Quintela, including
the motive the Marquis family might have had for murdering
Graham Fullerton.

"My experience, rich folks are vengeful. Someone gave

my sister AIDS, I'd be vengeful. But rich folks are more likely to hire a hit than do it themselves.''

"This one had a personal feel to it,'' Elena remarked.

In fifteen minutes they pulled up in front of an adobe mansion in the foothills of the Sandia Range. The house would have done credit to a pueblo tribe. A family retainer, a middle-aged Hispanic woman with a broad, expressionless face, eyed Leo and Elena with disfavor when she heard they were Los Santos cops. Speaking Spanish to Quintela, she protested that she was not at liberty to reveal Señorita Amy's whereabouts and didn't think they should disturb Señor Barton. Quintela insisted that the whereabouts of both should be revealed.

"They have done nothing wrong,'' said the woman.

"Then they have no reason to avoid these officers,'' Quintela retorted. He was becoming irritated, and Elena could see that the woman would turn stubborn as stone if he insulted her.

In Spanish Elena asked politely for the woman's name, which she was told, somewhat reluctantly, was Genoveva Cordero. Then Elena asked if Señora Cordero was, by any chance, from Trampas or thereabouts. The woman looked astonished. Elena mentioned her own family in Chimayo. The two found acquaintances in common. While they talked Sangre de Cristo genealogy, the two male detectives fidgeted. "I bring Señorita Amy good news,'' said Elena.

Señora Cordero sighed. "There can be no good news for that poor child.''

"The death of the one who made her sick.'' Elena smiled maliciously. The two detectives gaped at her. Señora Cordero said, "The Virgin has heard my prayers,'' and she provided the name of the private clinic where her young mistress lay ill.

"Pretty slick,'' said Quintela as they drove away. "You didn't tell me you were local.''

Elena shrugged. "Small-town girl from the mountains.''

"So how'd you end up in a hole like Los Santos?'' he asked.

"She married a Los Santos narc,'' said Jaime, "then

dumped him once she'd used him to get on the force."

"Yeah, right." Elena rolled her eyes. "Where'd you hear that, Sandoval?"

Jaime just grinned at her. "So it's not true?"

"Believe me, I didn't need Frank to get on the force. And, Quintela, Los Santos isn't a hole. O.K.? I like it."

"No accounting for taste," muttered the Albuquerque detective and pulled his car into the parking lot of La Vida Clinic. "Dumb name for a place that specializes in AIDS," he observed, leading the way to the front door. "Like anyone here has much life left."

"Our victim was symptom-free till someone spiked his meds with cyanide," said Elena. They introduced themselves to the admitting nurse, stated their reason for visiting in the vaguest terms, and were told as they were escorted through a maze of corridors that Miss Marquis had been in the clinic for over three weeks.

"Did she or could she have left during that time?" Leo asked.

The nurse shook her head. "I've never seen a case progress faster or resist treatment more stubbornly than hers. The poor girl can hardly get out of bed. She's just now able to breathe without oxygen. Pneumonia, you know."

Since they knew that Graham Fullerton had picked up the medication that killed him seventeen days ago, Amy Marquis, having been here seriously ill for over three weeks, could not have poisoned his red capsules or his AZT. The young woman, when they met her, looked weak and very sick, although the traces of a once-pretty girl showed through the ravages of the disease. The big surprise was that she was pregnant, the mound of the child swelling a nightgown from which protruded arms and legs like sticks.

When they told her that Fullerton was dead, she began to cry and said, "I killed him. That's why you're here, isn't it?" She wiped her eyes. "Because I killed him."

Sandoval gaped at her and started to speak, but Elena waved him to silence. "We'd appreciate your explanation of how you did that, Ms. Marquis," said Elena quietly. "Killed him, that is."

"I didn't tell him I had mono," the young woman whispered brokenly. "He was healthy when we ... were together. Now look at me." She closed her eyes. "Nothing works with me because of the mono. And the anorexia. My body wouldn't fight it off. The drugs don't help." She plucked a Kleenex from the bedside table and wiped away more tears. "And now you're going to tell me he's dead for the same reasons. Because I didn't warn him that I had mono."

Elena sat down abruptly on the hard visitor's chair. She gathered from the confession that Amy Marquis had gone directly from HIV infection to full-blown AIDS because her immune system was already compromised and her health poor. Still, she'd have to check that with a doctor, but it would explain Fullerton's own insistence on healthy food, his abstinence from liquor—except for the night he'd had two girls in his room and awakened with a hangover—and his exercise routine. He'd been trying to stay as healthy as possible to stave off the virus.

"Did Fullerton tell you that he was HIV-positive?" Elena asked.

Amy shook her head. "He probably didn't know then. Or maybe it was me. Maybe I gave it to him. Along with the mono. I'm sure he would have told me if he'd known. He was so careful with me." She sniffed. "It was my first time, and—"

"Then how could you have been infected with HIV before you were intimate with him?" Elena asked. "Had you had a blood transfusion or been an IV drug user?"

"No, of course not. But I just know he'd have told me if he knew, no matter what my doctor says."

"Ah." Amy Marquis was still in love with her only lover. In love and in denial, as well as obviously carrying Fullerton's child. Elena stared at the young woman thoughtfully.

Amy responded by defending Fullerton again. "The condom broke," she confessed. "He was so upset."

"I'll bet," muttered Jaime Sandoval.

Amy glanced at him questioningly. "He even gave me pills to take so I wouldn't get pregnant. He was so concerned, and I . . . I stopped taking them. They made me sick, so I threw them away, both the ones he gave me that night and the bottle he gave me the next day. He must have known what I did because he never called me again. He probably thought I wanted to get pregnant and trap him into marriage.''

''Did you ever tell him you were carrying his child?'' Elena asked.

Amy shook her head. ''I'd have been embarrassed to,'' she said earnestly, ''after he tried so hard to protect me. And anyway I didn't find out until I left school. I thought it was just the mono making me sick.''

''Could you describe the pills he gave you?'' Elena asked.

''What difference does it make?'' Amy replied sadly. ''I only took a couple. As you can see.'' She patted her swelling stomach. ''Not that I'm sad to be carrying his child. And I am going to stay alive long enough to have it.'' There was another spurt of tears. ''Especially now that I've killed him.''

''Miss Marquis—'' Jaime began. Again Elena silenced him.

''They can protect the baby from infection, you know,'' Amy explained. ''The AIDS drugs will protect her until she's born, and then they'll give me an IV drip during childbirth. She could be perfectly all right. I just have to stay alive long enough to have her. And hope I don't die before I know for sure that she's all right. It's six months before my antibodies stop showing up in the baby's blood and they'll know if she's HIV-negative. I just have to—''

''We wish you good luck,'' said Elena softly. The poor child. Fighting death so that she could give the world the offspring of the bastard who killed her.

''That's very kind of you considering that I killed my baby's father.''

Again Elena had to signal an enraged Jaime Sandoval to silence. ''For our records, Ms. Marquis, could you describe the pills Graham gave you?''

Amy Marquis curled on her side in the hospital bed. ''I . . .

I think they were white. With a blue stripe around the middle.''

"Capsules?" asked Elena.

"Umm."

He'd given her AZT, probably hoping to head off infection when the condom broke. Elena had heard about that preventive measure. A new kind of morning-after pill that had to be taken for however long. But Amy, feeling nauseated, either from the AZT or her own mono, hadn't taken the pills. And Graham Fullerton hadn't followed up to be sure she did. Hadn't told her why she had to take the blue and white capsules. He'd just gone on to the next lover, leaving Amy to her fate.

"Are you going to arrest me?" Amy asked pathetically. "It's not that I don't deserve to pay for deceiving him, but I have to think about our baby. She's all that's left of Graham now that I've killed him. In jail I might not get the kind of medical treatment—"

"Graham didn't die the way you think," said Elena. "Someone poisoned him."

Amy Marquis pushed herself up on one elbow and stared at Elena and at Jaime Sandoval standing behind Elena. "Poisoned him? Poisoned *Graham*?"

"Did you do that?" Elena asked. "Or anyone you know?"

"I *loved* him," the young woman cried. "I'd never hurt him. He was *murdered*?"

Elena nodded.

"He was my first," said Amy wistfully. "And he was very gentle and sweet. I'm so glad I got to be with him before this happened to me."

Remembering what Fullerton had said about Amy Marquis in his notebook, Elena had to grit her teeth to keep from badmouthing the late "gentle and sweet" Graham Fullerton—who deserved to die. This poor child didn't, but Elena wasn't about to disillusion her about her only lover. What good would it do? Still, Amy might have some idea who'd had reason to kill him. "Ms. Marquis—"

"You can call me Amy."

"All right, Amy. We wondered if you could give us the names of any other girls he dated, friends of yours maybe."

"Why?"

Good question. "Well," said Elena slowly, "he was HIV-positive, and we need to warn anyone he may have—ah—been intimate with. So they'll get tested."

Amy smiled sadly. "It's not really necessary. He told me he always protects his lovers. Always uses a condom."

"Still—"

"My brother said the same thing, so you don't have to worry. He called everyone I could think of. I felt bad about telling on Graham, especially since I didn't know then that he actually had—are you sure he had—*it*?"

"Yes. He was taking AZT and several other drugs to stave off full-blown AIDS. Someone poisoned his medication."

"How awful." Any wiped away more tears. "Were they working? The medications?"

"Evidently," said Elena. The two men with her had been silent throughout the conversation, Jaime having given up on trying to get a word in, Quintela leaving the investigation to them.

"Not for me," said Amy. "I'm going to die." Her voice was weak and breathy, as if she had not completely recovered from her bout with pneumonia. "And I don't want to—die. I want to live to take care of my baby." She thought a moment. "I hope you won't bother the girls my brother called."

"Could you give us their names?"

"No." Amy shook her head. "Don't you know they're frightened enough without having the police questioning them? Leave them alone. No one wants to die." Tears were sliding over her emaciated cheeks again.

Elena put her hand over the thin fingers. "I'm so sorry," she said. "We didn't want to cause you distress."

29

Saturday, April 12, 11:45 A.M.

"That poor girl," said Jaime once they had left of the clinic and were back in Quintela's departmental car. "Fullerton should have told her what the pills were for."

Elena sighed. "If she was in bad shape anyway, the AZT might not have helped." She fastened her seat belt and asked Quintela to take them to the brother's office. Then she turned to Jaime in the back seat. "But it sure looks like a coed could have killed him. If Barton Marquis called to warn them and one discovered she was positive for HIV, bingo. The best motive in the world."

"So why didn't you push her for the names of the girls her brother called?" Quintela demanded.

Elena replied shortly that they'd get them from Marquis. "Good luck there," said Quintela. And he knew his man. From the power of his huge office, which was decorated in heavy Spanish colonial, Barton Marquis denied making any calls. When they repeated what his sister had said, Marquis replied, "I told her I made them, but I didn't. Why advertise the fact that she's got AIDS?"

"We can get your phone records," said Jaime.

"You mean you can try."

"You been to Los Santos lately?" Jaime asked.

"You think *I* killed him? I wouldn't be much use to Amy if I were in jail, would I? And if her child lives, I'll probably be the one to raise it."

Remembering that that baby girl—the nurse had told them that Amy knew she was carrying a daughter—was Graham Fullerton's, Elena wondered what kind of guardian Barton Marquis would prove to be. Would he see his sister's killer every time he looked at his niece?

Marquis called his secretary on the intercom and asked her to bring in his activity logs. "Have I been out of town in the last few months?" he asked her.

"With the Simpson deal in the works? No, sir."

"Show them the logs."

Jaime and Elena read through his calendar for the preceding month. As claimed, every minute, even weekends, was tightly scheduled, including visits to Amy. After that the detectives were politely asked to leave; he was a busy man.

"Arrogant prick," muttered Quintela. "I'll get a warrant and fax you his phone records."

"He could have hired it done," Elena mused.

"Sure," Quintela agreed. "You can hire a hit in this town for a couple a thousand. That wouldn't count airfare."

"The hit man would have to get into the dorm or the doctor's office," said Sandoval, "and there are easier ways to kill a guy."

"Still, it could be done," said Elena thoughtfully. "And he was a very angry man. Not that I blame him. His sister's dying, and she won't even admit who's responsible. That could drive you right around the bend."

"Anywhere else you guys want to go?" asked Quintela.

"To the med school," said Elena. When he looked puzzled, she explained, "My sister's a student there."

"Is she pretty?" asked Sandoval. "Think she'd like to date a cop from Los Santos?"

Elena laughed. "You must like to fly."

"It really was cool," Jaime agreed, "but actually I can't afford a long-distance romance. I'm putting one of my sisters through college."

"So if you're not going to make a play for Detective Jarvis's sister, you can go with me to get the warrant," Quintela offered. "Then we'll have a beer and a good lunch. I'll show you what real Mexican food tastes like."

"I gotta be back in Los Santos by six-thirty," Jaime reminded Elena. "So I'll be there when Harry arrives to meet my sister Rosa."

Elena spent the afternoon with Maria, catching up on family news and asking questions about AIDS, mono, Amy's chances of delivering the child, and the child's chances of surviving HIV-free. The conversation was disheartening, so they switched to boyfriends—Rafer, Elena's new interest, and a fellow med student Maria was dating.

"It's kind of cozy," said Maria, "discussing gangrene excision over pizza and beer."

"That's disgusting!" Elena exclaimed, then noticed that her sister was laughing. Maria, the youngest, was the cut-up in the family.

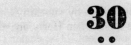

30

Saturday, April 12, 6:45 P.M.

Elena unlocked the door to her house and was greeted by the beep of her answering machine. Having had no dinner beyond the usual peanuts and a bag of bite-sized cookies provided by Southwest Airlines, she was tempted to eat before retrieving her messages, but a mixture of duty and curiosity overcame that impulse. Instead she put the kettle on for tea (herbal, provided by her mother) because the house was freezing, and depressed the message button, dropping onto the sofa and unbuttoning her coat as she listened.

The first message was from Monica Ibarra. While on patrol that morning, she had arrested the drug dealer who had been in Sinoloa for his mother's funeral.

Elena returned the call and got the following story: Caught with *roche* in the cuffs of his pants and a balloon of heroin in his mouth, Gustavo Palo was in no position to refuse to look at pictures of people who might have been his customers. In return for his identification of Wayne Quarles, Jr., the narcs were willing to let him go on the heroin and bust him only for the Rohypnol. Their cooperation was predicated on a dislike of Quarles's father, who had been the money launderer for a Juarez drug cartel.

According to Monica, Palo held Junior in the greatest contempt because Quarles hadn't even known the product was called *roche* and had been dumb enough to pay three times the going rate. "Palo said," Monica told Elena, "and this

159

is from my notes: 'You got some real cute chick to use this on?' Quarles said, according to Palo, 'Yeah, one who thinks she can date me without putting out.' The dealer said, 'So I tell the *pinche* bastard he must be pretty hard up for a lay, an' he tries to punch me, so I knock him on his *gringo* ass.' End of conversation. That what you're looking for?'' Monica asked.

''Absolutely,'' said Elena. ''You're going to make a bang-up detective.''

''Thanks. I gotta take the test first. Anyway, I passed this on to the detective in Sex Crimes today, and they talked to Quarles. He denies everything and says the dealer was just telling us what we wanted to hear.''

''Quarles is lying,'' said Elena.

The second call on her machine was from the latent fingerprint expert, who did his thing in the basement at headquarters. He told her that he'd matched a latent on the medication cabinet at Conway's office to the print card they had from one Evelyn Dietz. Elena stopped the run of messages, took a celebratory slug of hot tea, and called Leo to tell him that Evelyn, who claimed she'd never been in that room, had left a print behind and that Wayne Quarles, Jr., who said he hadn't given *roche* to Gretchen Farber, had bought some from a dealer working Paisano Drive downtown. The dealer had ID'ed Quarles for the buy. ''We could clear both cases tonight, Leo!'' she exclaimed.

''Get a life,'' said Leo. ''We can do it tomorrow just as well. They're both gonna be here. Tonight I got a crisis at home. Concepcion had a fight with Fong about bilingual education. Now she won't talk anything but Spanish to me and to the babies, and you know I'm not that great in Spanish. I can't even reason with her.''

''I told you to take a course.''

''Nobody likes that I-told-you-so shit,'' snapped Leo.

''What did Fong want?''

''Oh, some half-assed notion about using one language on the girls and the other on the boys, then see if they teach each other. I'm not sayin' Concepcion wasn't right; I just wish she wouldn't take it out on me.''

"So pick me up tomorrow, and we'll go after Quarles and Dietz." She hung up and played another message, this one from Gretchen Farber's roommate, who sounded frantic. She said that Wayne Quarles's sister Wendy had called Gretchen and threatened to blacken her name in court if she persisted in accusing Wayne of rape. "Gretchen's distraught, Detective. She should have police protection?"

Elena shook her head, surprised that Wendy Quarles Pickentide would want to get into something so ugly when she could hide out at the Galleria in Houston, shopping and having lunch with other wealthy young matrons. She punched the message button again and heard from H.H.U.'s Joel Smith asking her to return his call.

What was that about? she wondered, punching in the number and warming herself with another mouthful of hot tea.

"Dr. Jarvis, why has it taken you so long to return my call?" he demanded, sounding harried.

"I've been in Albuquerque. What's the problem?"

"The maids. They've formed a union, and they're threatening to strike."

Way to go, Socorro, Elena thought. "So what are they asking for?" she responded curiously.

"A raise of one dollar an hour, apologies from my office and from the student newspaper, Mexican food in their cafeteria, and free access to the Weeping Virgin. Have you ever heard a more ridiculous list of labor demands?"

"Sounds reasonable to me. Just give them what they want; the university can afford it."

"Even if we were amenable to such a loss of face, we can't accept their terms because they won't talk to us directly. They want an intermediary. In a word, you, Dr. Jarvis."

Elena stifled a snicker. "Well, I'm going to be busy arresting people tomorrow, but I'll see if I can fit you in on Monday."

"Monday will be quite soon enough," said the vice-president stiffly, "as long as you remember that you represent the university."

"You want me, I represent my own point of view," said

Elena. Two more messages. She pulled up the next, which was from Wendy. Elena called her collect in Houston. No reason to spend her own money when Wendy had plenty and undoubtedly nothing to say that Elena was interested in hearing.

"My brother did not rape anyone," said Wayne's sister. "He's a very attractive young man. Why would he—"

"Your 'attractive' brother has a rotten reputation with women," Elena retorted. "But then you must have heard that before. Your father used to buy off the girls Junior attacked."

"I don't know what you're talking about. And if his reputation is so bad, why did this Miss Farber go out with him?" Wendy demanded, triumphant in the logic of her query.

"Because she was armed with Mace and thought that would protect her. Unfortunately, she didn't realize just how desperate your brother is."

"People are supposed to be innocent until proven guilty," sniffed Wendy. "As a representative of the law—"

"I just catch 'em and send 'em on to the D.A. for prosecution. O.K.?"

"He's been arrested?" Wendy sounded alarmed.

"He will be," Elena assured her and went on to the last message, an invitation from Rafer to visit a comedy club on North Mesa if she got home from Albuquerque in time. Elena finished her tea and went to the kitchen to make a sandwich. She had to rebutton her coat because the house was so cold. Why the hell were the temperatures going down into the forties in mid-April? This was Los Santos, right on the Mexican border. The desert. It should be getting hot. Like it had been in March. She called Rafer from the kitchen to accept. The comedy club was bound to be heated.

Rafer was pleased. Once they got there, the show was raunchy and rowdy, making for a cheerful evening, something she needed after the sad visit to Amy Marquis. Afterward Elena allowed herself to be talked into returning to Rafer's place for brandy and microwave popcorn, a weird combination in her opinion, but what the heck! The apartment was toasty warm, so comfortable that she agreed to stay the night—on the living-room couch.

Rafer didn't argue. He was nice enough to be more worried about her freezing to death at home than about his own sexual satisfaction, although he made it clear that anytime she felt ready to go to bed with him, he'd be delighted to oblige. He even provided an old nightgown of Helen's, his ex, and fixed Elena pancakes and bacon for breakfast. You had to like a man that accommodating.

31
..

Sunday, April 13, 9:45 A.M.

The Sunday paper, which Elena read at Rafer's and in the lobby of the faculty apartment building while she waited for Leo to pick her up, had been full of surprises: an announcement of the engagement of Angus McGlenlevie, H.H.U. professor and poet, to Miss Linda Morell of Monterey, California, H.H.U. student and poetess (Was she pregnant, Elena wondered, and how would the other pregnant girls feel about Gus marrying one of their number?); a story about pilgrims walking all the way from Las Cruces to visit the Weeping Virgin at H.H.U.; and most interesting, an interview with the Reverend Wesley Hardin, who said that the police and the university were covering up the AIDS death of student Graham Fullerton by claiming poisoning. Now, how could he know that Graham was HIV positive unless Evelyn Dietz had told him? Good thing they were going after her today. Given Hardin's opinions on AIDS and how AIDS victims should be treated, he might be the poisoner himself. He'd been on campus; he might have snuck into Fullerton's room.

The detectives just missed Evelyn Dietz. A neighbor said she'd left for church minutes earlier. "Well, let's hope the judge comes through," Elena muttered. They were late getting to the Dietz house because they'd dragged a judge away from his morning coffee to ask for an arrest warrant on

Wayne Quarles, Jr. The judge had said he'd read their evidence, think about it, and make up his mind. His wife deplored these terrible times. "He drugged the poor girl? That's terrible. Would you care for a cup of decaf?"

"They don't need coffee, Margaret," said the judge. "They need to get about their business. If I decide to sign your warrant, you can collect it this afternoon, Detectives. Call me around noon."

Accordingly Leo had headed for the Dietz address, remarking that he'd taken note of Elena's request that he pick her up at the university rather than home. "Maybe you thought I missed that," he said, grinning. "So who were you staying with last night?"

"None of your business," she replied, trying to act cool. It wasn't as if she'd done anything but stay warm by sleeping on Rafer's couch. So why shouldn't she tell Leo? Before he dropped hints about her to their fellow detectives, remarks like, "Elena's got herself a new man, another damn professor would be my guess." She explained the situation.

"Oh, right," said Leo. "Like you couldn't have stayed with us if you didn't have enough heat at home."

"Really? Great." She'd fix him. "You're sure Concepcion wouldn't mind?"

"Well—"

"We can stop at my place as soon as we're through with Dietz so I can pick up some clothes." Elena concealed a smile because her partner looked flummoxed. Served him right. Then they discovered that Dietz had gone to church, where they followed her. Rather than drag her out in the middle of the service, Leo parked across the street, and he and Elena talked over the case while the sound of hymns floated on a cold wind. As soon as parishioners began to file out, stopping to shake hands with the Reverend Wesley Hardin, the detectives ambled to the church steps to watch for Evelyn Dietz.

She had just emerged and was complimenting the minister on his inspiring sermon when Leo and Elena appeared on either side and took her arms.

"Ma'am," said Leo politely, "if you don't mind, we'll

need to talk to you down at headquarters. Our car is right across the street.''

Evelyn Dietz turned pale and swayed in their grip. The preacher turned red and shouted, ''Take your hands off that good woman.''

''We wouldn't mind your coming along too, sir,'' said Leo, ''you being thick with this lady and making statements about our case that seem real suspicious.''

''What? What?'' the Reverend Hardin cried. Parishioners were gaping, coming back from the sidewalk and the parking lot to investigate the commotion.

''Well, sir,'' said Elena politely, ''you did recommend that AIDS victims be treated like lepers. Now a student is dead, murdered, and you're saying he died of AIDS.''

''But I—'' The minister backed away from them. ''You can't think I—''

''—poisoned his medication? Probably not,'' Elena murmured, ''but you sure might have talked this woman into doing it. She had access.''

''I t-told you I didn't,'' Evelyn Dietz stammered, glancing nervously at the people around them, who were edging closer, trying to hear. ''I told you I never even—''

''—went in the medication room? Too bad you lied about that,'' said Leo. ''Looks real bad. Now, come along, ma'am. You can talk to us willingly, or we can get a warrant for your arrest.''

''I demand that you—''

''Yours too, Reverend,'' Leo interrupted, ''unless you'd like to come along now.''

The preacher scowled furiously and strode back into the church, leaving his congregation to stare at Evelyn Dietz as Leo and Elena led her away. ''Didn't stick by you, did he?'' Elena remarked to the doctor's receptionist. ''If he talked you into doing something you shouldn't, you ought to give him up.''

''But I didn't do anything.''

''I'd call that abuse of power on his part,'' said Leo. ''A preacher telling an impressionable woman—''

''I am not an impressionable woman,'' Dietz protested.

"Thought it up all on your own, did you?" Elena assisted her into the car.

"I didn't do anything," Dietz wailed.

"Then why lie?" Leo asked as he fastened his seat belt and started the motor.

They put a terrified Evelyn Dietz into a small interrogation room, large enough only for the three of them, and, sitting knee to knee, asked her over and over again how her fingerprint came to be on the medicine cabinet in a room where she claimed never to go. She had no answer beyond the theory that someone might have sent her in there and she'd forgotten about it.

"The medical personnel send you after medication, do they, Mrs. Dietz?" asked Leo.

She started to say yes, sometimes, but was reminded by Elena that her answer could be checked at the doctor's office. Then she fell silent. Questions about the fingerprint were alternated with questions on how she felt about AIDS patients in general and Graham Fullerton in particular. Her initial answers were that she felt sorry for anyone with a fatal disease and that she didn't particularly remember Fullerton.

"But you must have seen him every time he came in," Elena insisted. "And he was a very good-looking young man."

"Sinners are not good-looking," snapped Evelyn Dietz.

"Ah, sinners. You feel sorry for sinners?"

"Yes."

"Your minister doesn't. He thinks they should be locked away or branded so that everyone will know what they are."

"That's for the protection of the public," said the woman defensively.

"So you agree that, for the protection of the public, AIDS victims should be segregated?"

"I didn't say that."

"It seems to me that the best protection for the public would be for them to die," suggested Leo.

Evelyn Dietz said nothing.

"Is that what the preacher thinks?"

"I don't know."

"But you think that."

"I didn't say—"

"So why are you working for a doctor who's trying to save people who'll just turn around and infect others?"

They hammered away on that theme until she burst into tears and said, "I needed the job."

"Ah, so you needed the job, but you hate the patients."

"I—I—"

"—think it would be better if they were all dead? Isn't that what you think?" Leo asked. "Better for the public, better for them."

"Well, it would," she cried. "It's a horrible death."

"So you tried to help some of them along by—"

"No! I swear. I never touched that medication. I—"

"Evie!" A rotund, middle-aged man with a halo of gray hair in a half circle around a gleaming bald head burst into the cubicle, then backed out when he realized there was no room for him. "Don't say anything to them, Evie," he admonished. "I've brought you a lawyer."

Elena leaned back in her chair. Evelyn Dietz had not once thought to ask for a lawyer. Behind the chubby fellow, who was evidently the suspect's husband, was another, slightly taller chubby fellow. Fred Bob Rush demanded that his client be allowed to have a drink of water and be seated in a larger room where the detectives wouldn't hover over her so threateningly.

"Oh, thank God," cried Evelyn Dietz and fell weeping into her husband's arms. "They think I poisoned someone."

The husband looked at Leo and Elena with absolute astonishment. "Poisoned?" he managed to say weakly.

"Nonsense," said the lawyer. "I've known Evelyn for years. She doesn't know anything about poison."

"Not even about rat poison?" Elena asked blandly. They had moved into the large interrogation room and provided the weeping Mrs. Dietz with a glass of water.

"Got some in the garage," said Mr. Dietz.

"For heaven's sake, Earl," said Fred Bob Rush. "You don't have to be helpin' the police out."

"I'm not," said the husband indignantly. "That stuff is for rats, not folks. Evelyn knows that. Don't you, Evelyn?"

Evelyn nodded.

"We think your wife was lured into the murder by Reverend Wesley Hardin, Mr. Dietz," said Elena.

Mr. Dietz seemed to find that an amazing idea. "Well, she thinks highly of him. Both of us do, but—"

"Earl, would you stop talkin'?" said Fred Bob Rush. "An' you too, Evelyn." The couple nodded humbly. "Now, you pay me to make you a will an' to handle the closin' on your house, an' when I tell you how to do it, you listen. Right?" Husband and wife nodded. "So you just listen to me now. 'Pears to me that this is all some big mistake. Ordinary folks like you don't go around poisonin' other folks."

"Right," Earl Dietz agreed.

"So stands to reason all we got to do is convince these two officers of that, an' Evelyn can go home. Right?" He turned to Leo and Elena.

Since Mrs. Dietz could have insisted on going home at any time during the interrogation, neither detective disagreed.

"So what we'll do here is we'll just have Evelyn take a lie-detector test." Fred Bob looked triumphant at having come up with such a technologically astute idea.

"I thought they wasn't any good in court," said Earl Dietz.

"Don't argue, Earl," said his wife. "That's just what I want to do. Take a lie-detector test."

"I gotta pay for that?" asked Dietz suspiciously.

"Not if you're willing to have our expert administer it," said Elena.

"Well, there you go," said Fred Bob Rush, pleased. "Gets you set free, Evelyn, an' it won't cost you a dime, Earl."

"How much you costin' me, Fred Bob?" asked the husband.

"Same as always," said the lawyer. "Might even give you a discount on my hourly rate since I don't know anything about criminal law. Not that it doesn't seem easy enough in this case. Take a test. Get off. Nothin' to it.''

When they were gone, the test having been scheduled, Elena said to Leo, "So, you think she's a pathological liar and knows she can pass? Or is she innocent?"

"Beats the hell out of me," said Leo. "She never did explain how her fingerprint got on that cabinet. Even if she passes the test, I'd say she's still a suspect."

"Right. None of them seemed to realize that, though. Be interesting to see how her test turns out."

32

Sunday, April 13, 2:05 P.M.

Leo needed to get home; it was, after all, Sunday, he pointed out. Mosconi didn't answer his telephone, making Elena wonder how his date with Jaime Sandoval's sister Rosa had gone. If Mosconi was shacked up with Rosa, Jaime would not be pleased.

Still needing someone to accompany her to the arrest of Wayne Quarles, Jr., for whom the judge had agreed to sign the arrest warrant, Elena called Sandoval, who was delighted to meet her at headquarters, and still appalled that any man would drug a young woman and rape her. On a happier note, he was convinced that it had been love at first sight between Harry and Rosa, and why not? Rosa was beautiful and a terrific cook; she'd prepared the *pescado bandera* for the introductory family dinner last night, and it was *muy sabrosa*. *Pescado bandera* meant banner fish or a fish prepared with sauce in the colors of the Mexican flag, he explained earnestly.

Elena told Jaime that she knew what *pescado bandera* was, but Jaime was irrepressibly enthusiastic and went right on to say that Mosconi had had three helpings of Rosa's tasty fish and six of "Mama's empanadas; you haven't tasted empanadas until you've sampled her apple or pineapple—"

"Enough, Jaime," Elena interrupted. "If we don't pick up the warrant and head for the dorm, Quarles will have

171

skipped town. His sister's been calling around threatening
people, so they know he's in trouble.''

"O.K.," Jaime replied cheerfully, "but I want you to
know that Rosa liked Harry, too. In fact, she invited him to
church, so we all sat together at Mass this morning.''

Well, that answered Elena's speculation that Mosconi
hadn't answered his phone because he was shacked up with
Sandoval's sister. He'd been at Mass with the lady. Maybe
Mosconi's ex was about to be cut out of the on-again-off-
again game she'd been playing with him since the divorce.

When Jaime and Elena drove up to the gate at Herbert Hobart University, it was getting dark, They'd had to track the
judge down on a golf course. Although, as promised, he'd
left the warrant with his wife, he'd forgotten to sign. Outside
the wall they found a crowd of twenty windblown people
carrying a banner that said EVANGELICAL CATHOLICS OF LAS
CRUCES. Each person, some of them very young teenagers,
others evidently in their late sixties, carried a backpack with
sleeping bag and various camping and hiking appurtenances
dangling from belts and straps. They looked weary but triumphant and were arguing with the security guard at the
gate, claiming to be pilgrims who had made a long, slow,
overnight trek from New Mexico to see the Weeping Virgin.

Elena rolled her eyes at Jaime, who was driving slowly
through the crowd. By the time they had been admitted and
were entering the campus, Elena spotted Chief Clabb and his
minions hurrying toward the confrontation. Poor man. This
sort of thing upset him. And if the administration was to be
believed, the window did not depict the Virgin. The crowd
of pilgrims from Las Cruces had walked all this way,
camped in some roadside park on the interstate through a
bitterly cold night and all for the sight of some pagan fertility
goddess, which they might not be allowed to see, anyway.

When the detectives knocked at Quarles's door, one of his
roommates answered and said that he was not in.

"When do you expect him back?" Jaime asked, anxious
to apprehend the sinister Wayne Quarles, Jr., who, as Jaime
had explained to Elena, was a danger to decent women

everywhere, women like his sisters, especially Cipriana, the sister he was putting through college, an innocent and beautiful girl who, without doing anything but being her own sweet self, aroused lustful thoughts in young men, who had to be watched closely by Jaime.

Poor Cipriana, Elena had thought. *Having such a doting and protective brother must put quite a crimp in her social life.*

"How would *I* know, man." said the roommate in an answer to the question about when Quarles was expected back. "He and this girl went hiking."

"What girl?" Elena asked with a sense of foreboding; it was getting dark.

"Gretchen Farber. Don't know why he'd go out with her again. She called him a pig yesterday in the dining room, and everyone knows she's a crack shot." He grinned. "Maybe she's out somewhere shooting him." The roommate laughed uproariously at his own joke. "Wayne affects girls that way. She's already Maced him."

"Did she have a gun?" Jaime asked, obviously astounded by these revelations. "Where did she learn to shoot?"

"Where everyone does. At the university's shooting range, and I was just kidding. No one carries guns around."

You'd be surprised, Elena thought. "Where were they planning to hike?" she asked urgently.

"I don't know. The desert. The mountain. He's local. He likes that sort of shit. Said when he was a kid he used to go out and do drugs sitting on some rock looking out over the desert. Christ, you can do drugs without getting out there among the snakes and lizards and that shit."

"Did he say he would be staying out overnight?"

"Hey, he doesn't check in with me. Who are you, anyway, lady? His mother?"

"Detective Elena Jarvis." She showed him her ID.

The young man looked chagrined. "Listen, I didn't mean anything about drugs. I mean he doesn't do them anymore. I was just—"

"How long has he been missing?" asked Jaime.

"Who said he was missing? Even if he doesn't come back

tonight, I wouldn't figure he was missing. I'd figure they were keeping each other warm in a tent somewhere. Right?"

"He took a tent?" Jaime asked.

"Beats me."

"What time did he leave?" Elena demanded.

"Nine. Ten. I don't know. We're not on the clock here. He wants to go hiking with some babe, it's none of my—"

"Has anyone seen Gretchen since they left?" Elena broke in.

"I don't know." The roommate had begun to look worried as well as put upon.

"What about the third man in your suite? Does he know anything?" asked Jaime.

"He's out of town. Left Thursday."

"We'd better look for Farber," said Elena. Good grief. What if Gretchen had gone out on the mountain with Quarles and pushed him off a cliff? She certainly had the motive, since she didn't know that Elena had enough information now to send her rapist to jail, maybe even without her testimony. But that was the whole thing, of course. Gretchen didn't want to testify. And if Quarles was dead, she wouldn't have to. Maybe they were both dead.

"Hey," said Jaime. "Don't look like that. We don't know anything's happened."

"No? Why would she go with him if she wasn't planning something?"

"Let's find her before we jump to any conclusions."

They found Gretchen easily enough. She was taking a shower and had to be fetched by her roommate. When she came into the sitting room, toweling her wet hair, and saw who it was, she said, "Why don't you just forget the whole thing? I'm going to get therapy so I can."

Elena studied her. "You went hiking with him."

Gretchen looked surprised and somewhat uneasy. "That's right," she admitted.

"Where is he?"

"I—I don't know. Around, I guess."

"You went out with him. You came back. He didn't."

The coed turned pale. "Well, I don't know where he is. And I don't care either."

"What did you do to him?"

"Nothing. I didn't do anything to him."

"So why didn't you come back together? Maybe more to the point, why would you go out with him, go somewhere you'd be alone with him?"

"I—" Gretchen Farber dropped onto the sofa. "I was going to kill him," she said in a tired voice.

"How?" Just what Elena had feared.

"With a gun."

"Where did you get it?"

"From the Gun Club. I checked it out on the range and never returned it."

"Where is it?"

"I threw it away."

"Where?"

"Up—up on Transmountain. I never fired it. I promise."

"So why did you change your mind about killing him?" Jaime asked after the long series of staccato questions from Elena.

Gretchen wiped tears away from her cheeks. "If I tell you the whole story, will you leave me alone?"

"We can't promise you that, but you'd better tell us, anyway," said Elena. She sat down beside the student. "What happened up there?"

"He had this tea in a Thermos. We were both supposed to drink some of it. I said, 'No way.' He said it wasn't *roche*; it was just this herbal tea, and he was going crazy because, with the police watching him, he couldn't do any drugs, so he'd got this stuff from someone. He said it was great; I'd love it." The story came tumbling out of her in a rush of confession.

"What was it?" Elena asked.

"I don't know. A hallucinogen, I guess. He said it would make the desert seem like a wonderland, every twig like a flower, stuff like that. He used to trip out on it when he was a kid, and he wanted to make up to me for what he'd done. He said he was sorry, and he wanted to share the stuff with

me. Can you imagine? Like I'd ever take anything he handed
me. But the thing is, I suddenly wondered what I was doing
there. Why I wanted to ruin my life by killing such a pathetic
loser. So I said I was going home.

"Then he got sort of nasty and said, how was I going to
get home when he had the keys and the car."

"And you got home how?" Jaime asked.

Elena was wondering where Quarles's car was. In a student parking lot if Gretchen was lying and had used it to get
back once she'd disposed of her rapist. If she wasn't lying,
it could be anywhere, including up on Transmountain.

"I walked back to the road and hitched a ride home."
Gretchen sniffed and swiped at her wet eyes again. "I was
lucky. A woman picked me up and brought me all the way."

"I don't suppose you know her name," said Elena dryly.

"Penny Penasco. She works at White Sands. She was
really nice, gave me a lecture, but she brought me all the
way back to campus."

"And the gun?"

"I threw it into the brush on the trail as soon as I got out
of sight of Wayne."

"Where did you leave him?"

Gretchen described the spot as best she could, a trail leading up the mountain from a parking lot and scenic overlook
on Transmountain Drive. She thought they'd hiked maybe
three-quarters of a mile before he offered her the tea and she
backed away. She thought she'd thrown the gun down
maybe a half mile from the road.

"What time did you get back here?" Elena asked.

"A little after seven."

The roommate, Nita, whose run-in with Quarles had
started the whole disastrous chain of events, confirmed the
time of Gretchen's return while giving them angry looks
when she saw her friend's tears. Having been unaware that
Gretchen planned to go with Quarles, Nita burst into tears
herself when she heard. "That's so dangerous, Gretch," she
cried.

Nita didn't know just how dangerous, Elena thought, particularly if Gretchen Farber had killed him.

First Jaime and Elena had the campus parking lots and the streets in the immediate vicinity searched for Quarles's vehicle, while sheriff's deputies were asked to check for his car on Transmountain. It was found in the parking lot, just where Gretchen had told them to look. Then Jaime called out the mountain rescue team to search for the missing rapist, who had been gone more than twelve hours. Temperatures were predicted to fall below freezing up on the mountainside tonight, not, as Jaime said, that it would make any difference if Gretchen Farber had shot and killed the bastard.

Elena called Dr. Harley Stanley for a check of the gun inventory belonging to the gun club. By the time they had finished the count at just before ten, Wayne Quarles had not been found, but one pistol, checked out to Gretchen Farber, was missing and one rifle.

Maybe that was the rifle used to shoot at Gus, Elena thought. Between the Quarles and Fullerton cases, she'd almost forgotten about Gus and his wounded hand and his pregnant lovers. She looked at the list of people who had used the rifle range the day the rifle disappeared. Two women. One Kimberly Sweet, whose name rang no bells, another Estelle Grant.

"Mama's going to be mad I missed dinner," said Jaime. "How long you gonna stare at that list?"

"Go on home," Elena replied, her mind puzzling over the name Estelle.

"How are you going to get home?"

"My truck is here," she replied. "Leo picked me up this morning."

"Here?" Jaime looked puzzled.

"No heat at my house. I stayed with a friend."

He looked astounded. "Look, if you need a place for tonight, I'm sure Mama could—"

Elena laughed and thanked him. "Hey, if the Las Cruces pilgrims can sleep out overnight, I guess I can throw a sleeping bag on the bed at home and do just fine."

Again the name Estelle caught her eye and nudged her memory. "Estie!" Elena recalled the girl swinging a tennis racket at Gus in the hall of the English Department. "Does

Estie sound like a reasonable nickname for Estelle?'' she
asked Sandoval.

''I guess.''

''Then maybe Kimberly and Estelle are our shooters.''

''Which shooters?''

''Of Angus McGlenlevie.''

''The professor who knocked up all his students? I thought
he didn't want to prosecute even if we found them.''

''Yeah, well—'' The *Enquirer* had said Gus impregnated
two volleyball players. ''Wonder if Kimberly and Estelle
play volleyball?'' Elena mused.

She folded the list and tucked it in her shoulder bag. ''We
might have all these cases solved by tomorrow,'' she told
Jaime exuberantly.

''Great. Let's stop for pizza and a beer. I'm not used to
going this long without my dinner.''

''Isn't your mother expecting you home?'' Elena asked.

33

Elena and Jaime finished a beer each and split a large pepperoni pizza at Pizza Academmia near the university while Jaime speculated on the relationship between Mosconi and his sister: Would Harry ask her out again? Would Harry make her as good a husband as her late husband, the plumber? Elena remarked that Rosa would be looking at a drop in husbandly income if she married a detective.

Jaime disagreed. Refugio hadn't been a very good plumber, just a fine and loving husband. While Jaime enlarged on the virtues of his late brother-in-law, Elena thought about the shooting of Gus McGlenlevie and the telephone calls she'd made in an attempt to follow up on that shooting before they left the campus. Estelle, or Estie, the impregnated tennis-racket wielder, had been out of town. Kimberly, to whom the missing rifle had actually been issued, had been out on a date. Dr. Greta Marx was at home but refused to release the names of any girls who might have had abortions recently. That pretty much stymied the McGlenlevie investigation for the time being.

"I remember Refugio bouncing my nephew Timoteo on his knee. He didn't bat an eye when the baby threw up on him. Refugio would have made a wonderful dad, but he injured himself in a plumbing accident and couldn't father a child. Rosa was very disappointed." Jaime looked thought-

179

ful, then asked, "What about Harry? You think he'd like to have a few kids?"

Before Elena could point out that Harry and his first wife had two, which might be enough to satisfy Mosconi, Paul Resendez from the *Times* slid into the booth beside Elena and lit a cigarette.

"This is the No Smoking section," she pointed out.

"If you don't complain, they won't say anything," said Resendez. "Listen, you're just the person I wanted to see. You read the quote from that preacher this morning? He said your victim died of AIDS. That true?"

"No," said Elena shortly. "He died of cyanide poisoning, just like the chief's office said."

"Right. Well, did he have AIDS?"

"No," she replied. And that was true. He'd been HIV positive, but he hadn't been showing symptoms.

"So how come the preacher—"

"He's got AIDS on the brain." She took Paul's cigarette from his hand and stubbed it out on her pizza plate. Maybe that would encourage him to go away. It didn't. He lit another.

"This is Detective Jaime Sandoval," she said. "If you're looking for a date, he's got beautiful sisters." That ought to distract Resendez.

Sandoval looked displeased. "My sisters don't date smokers," he said.

"Mosconi smokes," Elena pointed out.

"He does?" Sandoval looked worried. "Rosa doesn't know that." He thought about it. "Maybe he's planning to quit for her sake."

"So what's the AIDS connection with this case?" Resendez prodded.

"If there was one, we couldn't tell you," said Elena, "so stop asking. O.K.?"

"Aha!" Resendez looked pleased with himself. "He was infected, but you can't say so. Why not? Because he could sue you. But he's dead. So his family could—"

"Oh, shut up," snapped Elena.

"So what happened? Did Fullerton pass the virus on to

some girl, and this is a revenge killing? That makes sense since everyone at that school is screwing everyone else.'' Resendez grinned.

Elena scowled. Jaime narrowed his eyes. "You think that's funny?" he demanded. "There've already been cases go to court where the guy didn't warn his partner and got charged with attempted murder. In my opinion, people who are HIV positive should be required to notify partners. There should be a law just about that. You read about that guy in New York infected all those girls? That's criminal. In my opinion.''

"Won't make any difference where Fullerton's concerned," said Resendez. "He's dead, so no one's going to be taking him to court.''

"Who said he was infected?" Elena retorted, trying defuse a possible disaster. "Neither one of us did, Paul, so don't go printing—"

"Tell it to the preacher," said Resendez. "He's the one who's spreading rumors.''

Jaime had dropped Elena off at headquarters, where she picked up her truck and drove home. Walking from the truck to the door and from the front hall to her bedroom, she'd had this eerie feeling, a crawling sensation up her spine. As if she was being watched. It made her check the place, room by room. It made her uneasy as she changed into heavy sweats in an attempt to keep warm in the cold house. It kept her from locking her Glock in the kitchen drawer as she usually did. It made her glance over her shoulder while she was making herself a cup of tea in the kitchen.

Finally disgusted with herself and worrying that she might be having some recurrence of posttraumatic stress, she called Sam Parsley, the psychologist who had treated her after the mountain-lion incident.

Sam wasn't any help at all. He said, "Maybe it's your natural cop instincts kicking in.''

"What's that mean?" she demanded.

"Lock your doors.''

"Oh, for Pete's sake.'' She decided they were both paranoid, said good night to Sam, and marched into the living room with her tea, sprawling out on the sofa to see if there was anything on late-night TV. On her way home she'd listened to the local news and heard Socorro Rascon announcing a maid's strike at H.H.U., a strike that Elena would be expected to mediate, the thought of which made her grin.

She was still grinning when the living room turned into a mini-war zone. Two shots rang out, accompanied by the sound of breaking glass and the explosion of a prized pot on the end table beside her. She quickly rolled off onto the floor, feeling the pain of pottery shards cutting into her arm through the thick sweatshirt. Wishing she hadn't left the Glock in the kitchen, she pulled the plug on the table lamp and crawled across the room to turn off the TV so that the shooter couldn't see to take aim at her. Then she got a handle on her shock, and fury exploded in her mind.

Whoever it was had just destroyed the best thing in her house—well, maybe not. The best things were those fabrics her mother had woven for her sofa and draperies, but that pot was a treasure. Harmony's friend at the Taos Pueblo had given it to Harmony as a gift, and Harmony had given it to Elena. Enraged, Elena scrambled into the hall and burst out the front door, determined to catch the person who had put a bullet in her pot.

"Went that way," called Omar Ashkenazi. He pointed toward the side of the house. The retired rug dealer from across the street was evidently intent on giving chase with his dog Sheena, Queen of the Jungle.

"He's got a gun," Elena called back. Damn, hers was still in the kitchen.

"So do I," called Gloria Ledesma, hobbling from her house with a rifle. She was wearing a quilted ski jacket over her nightgown.

"Is it loaded?" asked Elena.

"Of course not."

Ben and Amy Fogel and their cocker spaniel twins, Spanky and Spinney, joined the crowd, all of whom were stumbling through Elena's side yard in slow pursuit of the

shooter, dogs barking, senior citizens determined in spite of
their aches and pains.

"I've got a bullet in my gun," said Dimitra Potemkin.
"Kept it under my pillow ever since God struck down
Boris."

Elena was opening the gate to the alley, figuring the sniper
must have gone that way. "Don't shoot anyone, Dimitra,"
she called over her shoulder. "You might hit a neighbor."
Elena got a glimpse of a slender figure in black jumping into
a dark car. Before she could catch up, the engine fired, and
the car roared out of the alley onto the cross street and turned
left, still without lights.

The dogs, let loose by their owners, bounded down the
alley and out into the street, barking, but to no avail. The
shooter was gone. Elena closed her eyes and reconstructed
what she had seen in the backyard security lights next door.
A figure—slim, black clothes. Not much to go on. Could
have been male or female, young or old. Who would want
to shoot at me? she wondered. Jerry Joe from L.S.A.R.I.?
Evelyn Dietz's husband? He hadn't seemed the type. Anyway, he was chubby. Wesley Hardin? Wayne Quarles, Jr.?
Maybe he wasn't lost or dead up on the mountain, after all.
Maybe he wanted people to think that, so he could sneak
over to Sierra Negra and shoot the woman who had arrested
his father, then threatened to arrest him.

She heard the sirens and walked back around the house
with her neighbors, all of whom had found the incident very
stimulating, except for Gloria Ledesma, who complained that
she'd get in bed late again because someone was always after
Elena. "I haven't forgotten the mountain lion someone put
in your house," she said darkly.

As if I have, Elena thought.

Two police cars had drawn up in front of her house.
"Drive-by?" asked one of the uniforms.

Elena shook her head. "Someone outside the window. Hit
a pot on the table beside me, then ran around the house,
through the backyard, and into the alley, where they drove
off in a car."

"Description," said the second officer, pencil poised over a little notebook.

Elena shrugged. "It was dark and the shooter wore dark clothing. Five-six and slender is about all I saw."

"What about the car? Stop that!" Spanky and Spinney were leaping up, long ears flopping, trying to lick the patrolman's hands.

"Don't do that, you bad dogs," cried Amy Fogel.

"Anyone else see anything?" The officer looked from one wrinkled face to the next.

"No, but we chased him," said Omar.

"So it was a guy?"

"Of course," said Gloria Ledesma. "Women don't go around shooting people through windows."

"I beg to differ, Gloria," said Ben Fogel. "I can think of one woman who walked right in and put the gun to a man's head."

"God inspired that," said Dimitra Potemkin, recognizing the description of her husband's death, even if she had never accepted the explanation.

Maybe God did, thought Elena. Boris had been a mean and violent old man, but Elena doubted that tonight's shooting had been inspired by God. More likely the inspiration was fear of arrest. Although shooting a cop was pretty stupid. So they were looking for a five-six, slender, stupid shooter. That didn't narrow the field much.

"You got ID & R coming?" she asked the patrolman. "I expect they can dig the bullet out of my wall." Elena had no idea what that pot was worth. Could be a lot, but she'd have to prove that to get any money from the insurance company, and then they'd probably raise her rates, and she still wouldn't have the pot, which had been a beauty.

The patrolman was gaping at her, so she produced her department ID. "Crimes Against Persons," she said.

"So why do you need us?" asked the second patrolman. "You can investigate this yourself."

"Don't be a smart-ass," she replied.

34

AIDS at H.H.U.?
by Paul Resendez

Evidence mounts that the student murdered on the
H.H.U. campus infected a number of coeds with the
HIV virus. The Reverend Wesley Hardin, although he
refuses to reveal his source, claims that Fullerton
actually died of AIDS.

Mrs. Evelyn Dietz, a member of his congregation
and receptionist at the office of infectious-disease
specialist Dr. Morton Conway, was taken to police
headquarters and questioned by detectives after a
conversation in front of the Evangelical Fountain of
Faith Church. Parishioners say the police indicated that
both the lady and the minister are suspected of killing
Fullerton because he had AIDS.

Yesterday in an interview with Elena Jarvis and
Jaime Sandoval, two of the detectives investigating the
Fullerton death, Sandoval stated heatedly that infected
men who give the virus to unsuspecting partners
should be charged with attempted murder.

How much more evidence do we need that the most
sexually active campus west of the Mississippi has a
bigger problem than its latest murder?

Los Santos *Times*, Monday, April 14

Elena had known trouble was coming their way as soon as she read Resendez's article, and Lieutenant Beltran, furious, had the four investigators on the carpet as soon as they signed in for their eight o'clock shifts. Harley Stanley at H.H.U. had been on the line to Chief Gaitan, who had then telephoned Beltran, complaining that confidentiality had not been maintained. "Why the hell were you making speeches to a reporter?" Beltran demanded of Sandoval, "And why didn't you shut him up?" he shouted, turning on Elena.

"Neither one of us said Fullerton had AIDS," Elena retorted. She'd thought Jaime was stupid for talking the way he had to Resendez, but he hadn't breached confidentiality. "Resendez was talking about AIDS. Sandoval complained about people who spread it. He said it was akin to murder. Which it is. Resendez is just blowing smoke in that article, so if H.H.U. has a problem, they should complain to him. Or to his editor." *There goes my chance of making sergeant,* she thought.

"You people were told not to discuss the case, especially with the press. So don't."

Jaime looked abject. Leo shrugged and said, "When I see a reporter, I'd rather kick his ass than talk to him."

Mosconi scowled and muttered, "Jaime's got a right to his opinion," but he didn't say it loud enough for the lieutenant to hear. Still, Elena figured Mosconi must like Rosa or he wouldn't be sticking up for her brother.

When she got back to her desk, she called Resendez at home. "Nice going, Paul," she said. "You just put one and one and one together and got five."

He laughed. "Caused a little stir down at headquarters, did I?"

"Yeah," she agreed. "We're not allowed to talk to you anymore. About anything."

"I guess that means if I ask you out, you're not going to go," he retorted cheerfully.

"I guess that means if you ask me the time of day, I'm not going to answer," she snapped back and hung up. She'd been told not to trust reporters; she should have listened. Resendez wouldn't have gotten Sandoval in trouble if she hadn't been thick with Resendez. End of press-police co-operation. If Paul didn't see it now, he'd find out next time he tried to talk to her.

Among the messages on her desk when she calmed down and started looking at them was one telling her to check with Greta Marx at the university Health and Reproductive Services Center. Now Elena sat in the waiting room while the doctor saw students. The clinic was more crowded than Elena had ever seen it. Two-thirds of those waiting were coeds, many recognizable as former girlfriends of the late Graham Fullerton. Were they all here to get tested for AIDS after reading in the paper that they might have been infected? They looked remarkably cheerful as they sat chatting with one another and ignoring her.

But then, when you were twenty you didn't think that death could be knocking at your door, no matter how ill-advised your behavior patterns. Several of the girls were staring out the windows at the demonstrators on the sidewalk, L.S.A.R.I. picketers carrying signs that broadcast messages such as: Victims of Angus McGlenlevie, Do Not Abort your Babies! H.H.U. is a Den of Sexual Depravity. God is Watching You. Avoid Fornication, Avoid AIDS. AIDS is a Punishment from God. And so forth.

The campus was jumping. Photographers from the local newspaper and TV stations were circulating among the picketers. H.H.U. police were out in force to protect coeds or anyone else who wanted to visit the clinic. Devout Catholics were crowding the chapel. *Memorable days*, thought Elena dryly. Several reporters had tried to question her about her progress on the Fullerton case and the McGlenlevie shooting. She snarled at them.

One asked if it was true that Wayne Quarles's son was missing. She shrugged off that question, too. As far as she knew, he hadn't been found, which she considered ominous. She could hear the sound of helicopters circling the mountain, no doubt trying to spot him or his corpse.

To take her mind off the possibility of having to arrest Gretchen Farber for murder, Elena picked up a copy of the

Campus Enquirer. The front-page headline screamed that a student petition was being circulated demanding that everyone on campus (students, faculty, and staff) be tested for AIDS, whether they wanted to be or not, and the results posted in public places.

There was an ad from Happy Hobart's safe-sex dating service (Happy was the nephew of the founder and a graduate in last year's class) advising students to sign up by calling the 800 number or contacting the company web site: safesex@hhu.edu.

On the editorial page, Dr. Marx had provided the guest editorial, the gist of which was that a student's only protection from death due to promiscuity was Greta Marx and the Herbert Hobart Health and Reproductives Services Center. So much for Dr. Stanley's desire to keep the whole AIDS problem quiet by harassing the police. The cat was out of the bag.

A piece by the editor announced that the *Enquirer* would not apologize to the maids. "Let them go out on strike," said the editor. Well, they already had, Elena thought. This morning's *Times* had announced that various Hispanic organizations were supporting the strike of domestic and service workers at the university and planned to attend the meeting of strikers in the basement of San Isidro del Valle that morning. Good. The university couldn't recruit Elena to mediate if the maids were congregating in the Lower Valley.

Willie of "Willie's Whispers" said that rumor had Graham Fullerton dying of poisoned vitamins. Willie thought it was a sad day for the country when a man had to keep his vitamins under lock and key. He suggested that the university chef might have poisoned the vitamins because Graham had complained repeatedly about the high fat content of the gourmet meals.

The sports page announced a banquet honoring the girls' volleyball team. How many of them would arrive in designer maternity clothes? Elena wondered and reminded herself that she needed to check out Kimberly Sweet and Estelle Grant, who had been at the gun club the day a rifle went missing, a rifle that could have been used to wing Angus Mc-Glenlevie.

Putting down the student paper, Elena picked up the morning *Times*, which she hadn't been able to finish before leaving the house, and noted that Father Conrad Bratslowski was demanding a scientific investigation of the weeping "Virgin" at Herbert Hobart University, which he felt was some sort of sacrilegious hoax perpetrated by Godless Protestants or unbelievers. An investigation wouldn't be a bad idea, in Elena's opinion, or at least an announcement of who the window really depicted, if it wasn't the Virgin.

"The doctor will see you now," said the receptionist as a coed exited the examining room and met her lavender-uniformed police escort.

"Why don't you shoot those freaky people?" she asked the campus cop as she peeked out the window at the L.S.A.R.I. picketers.

"My gun doesn't have bullets," he replied, embarrassed, and opened the door for her.

Elena trotted down the hall to the doctor's office, where she learned that Dr. Marx had received three threatening telephone calls the previous night, the first at 1:15, the next one at 3:45 and another at 4:42. "I have Caller ID," said the doctor and handed Elena a slip of paper with telephone numbers written beside the relevant times. "After the first call, I put a whistle around my neck and blew it in the ears of the other two callers. If you follow up these numbers and find a deaf anti-free-choicer, you'll have the criminals dead to rights."

Elena nodded. "We'll do that," she promised, although she didn't plan to follow up personally. Harassing phone calls paled beside murder and assault.

"One of them threatened to burn my house down if I performed any abortions, not realizing that I live in the faculty apartment house, I suppose."

That would be a disaster, Elena thought. If someone set fire to the faculty tower, the authorities wouldn't be sure if the arson was aimed at Gus or Dr. Marx. With that possibility in mind, Elena called headquarters to warn the police arson investigators that a threat of arson had been made, giving them all three numbers, and specifying which belonged to the prospective arsonist.

In Elena's opinion, things were getting really scary.

35

Monday, April 14, 9:30 A.M.

Leo joined Elena at nine-thirty, but he had no news about the search for Wayne Quarles, Jr. "They're still up on the mountain," he said. "Did you know Maggie Daguerre belongs to the mountain rescue squad?"

Elena nodded. Daguerre might be the department's computer guru, but she was also a hiker, climber, canoer, and general outdoorsperson, which was nice for the men of the rescue squad. Or maybe not. Elena supposed you could get killed scrambling around on a mountain when you were distracted by the presence of a six-foot beauty with the figure of a Las Vegas chorus girl. "What did you find out about Kimberly and Estie?"

"They're both on McGlenlevie's volleyball team," said Leo. "I've got the names of all the members." He pulled a computer printout from the pocket of his heavy jacket. "Bitch of a day. Wish it would warm up."

"I don't know why you're complaining," Elena muttered. "You've got refrigerated air and gas heat and can have either whenever you want."

"You could have stayed with us last night. You just didn't want to spend the night in a house full of howling kids."

"Still teething?"

"Only some of them. The rest are crying because the teethers woke them up. And me. I'm crying too. But I'm getting ear plugs."

"Is that some privilege reserved for fathers while the mothers have to stay awake?"

"Don't start that feminist crap with me, Elena," said Leo. "On no sleep, I don't want to hear it. If we hurry, we can catch both coeds coming out of a class in the Fine Arts building: Sculpture for Novices. What the hell does that mean?"

"I don't know. Maybe they get to stand around looking at naked statues and identifying the parts on quizzes."

As it turned out, the class was busily patting clay into unrecognizable reproductions of a naked man posed on a platform in front of the classroom.

"Wonder what he gets paid?" Leo mused.

Elena laughed. "You thinking of volunteering?"

The "artist in residence" approached and asked them what they were doing in his classroom. "We don't allow visitors in to ogle the models," he said loftily.

Both detectives flashed their badges and pulled the two coeds out of class. Elena took Estelle Grant; Leo, Kimberly Sweet. "So we meet again, Estie," said Elena.

"I don't know you," said Estie.

"I was there when you smacked Professor McGlenlevie with your tennis racket and accused him of getting you pregnant."

"I'm not pregnant."

"You said you were."

"I was mistaken."

"O.K., so you'll give permission for us to look at your medical records, right?"

Estelle Grant pouted. "O.K., so I had an abortion."

"How'd you make it through the picketers?"

Estie giggled. "I stuck my nose in this old coot's face and yelled, 'I've got terrible cramps! Menstrual cramps! I've been through two tampons and three pads in an hour. If you don't get out of my way, I'll probably start bleeding on your *foot*.' The old bastard couldn't back up fast enough. Then some lady with big hair bustled over and took me to the door herself. That's how I got through."

"And was that before or after you shot Gus McGlenlevie

from the tower of the Administration building?''

"How come you think *I* shot him?''

"You and Kimberly Sweet were the only two girls who signed in on the rifle range the day a rifle went missing.''

"That doesn't mean I took one.''

"Who else?''

"There were lots of guys there that—''

"Why would lots of guys want to shoot McGlenlevie with a stolen rifle?''

"How do you know he was shot with that rifle?''

"Ballistics,'' said Elena. Since they didn't have the rifle, they only had half of a ballistics test, but this kid probably didn't know that. "I'll bet the rifle's in your room.''

"It is not.''

"Well, then it's in Kimberly's.''

"I don't know any Kimberly.''

"You play volleyball on the same team, eye naked men in the same class, go to the shooting range on the same day at the same time, and you don't know her?''

"I didn't shoot him. It was probably—''

"Who? Is someone else with a rifle pregnant?''

"I'm not.''

"But you were.''

"It was probably his wife.''

"He's not married.''

"I mean his ex-wife. I've heard she hates him.''

"I know her. She couldn't hit the broad side of a barn with a cannon. What kind of shot are you?''

"Leave me alone.''

Leo's interview with Kimberly Sweet was about as productive as Elena's with Estie Grant. "I think they did it,'' said Elena. "We need to find out from Harley Stanley what kind of shots they are. And we need to find the rifle. Also we should get McGlenlevie to admit he impregnated both of them.''

"Jeez, I hate to talk to him,'' Leo groaned. "He's such a dickhead. Concepcion is still pissed off about him horning in on her delivery and writing that tacky poem about our kids.''

Dr. Stanley, when questioned, refused to reveal the shooting records of the two students. "That's privileged information," he said.

"Under what law?" Elena demanded.

"The bylaws of the university."

"Those don't count."

"We don't keep records."

"Why not?"

"It destroys the self-confidence of those students who do poorly, and after all, this is a club, not a class. It's a leisure activity, meant to provide relaxation and pleasure—"

"—and the expertise to shoot one's professor," Elena finished for him. "We'll get a warrant."

Then she and Leo walked toward the Humanities building, where they were waylaid by Marilyn Fone, one of the young women in Graham Fullerton's book of lovers. "Do you remember me?" she asked Elena. "Marilyn Fone? You interviewed me."

Elena remembered her, the one with a sexually boring fiancé who liked Graham for mid-week sex and multiple orgasms. She nodded to the young woman, hoping that Marilyn wouldn't describe her sex life for Leo. He wouldn't be amused.

"I heard—" Fone was very pale. "People are saying—he had—you know. Did he?" Marilyn Fone's eyes filled with tears. Leo looked uncomfortable.

Elena said, "I can't say one way or another."

Marilyn burst into tears and threw her arms around Elena's neck, which was awkward since the young woman was a good deal taller and had to hunch to cry on Elena's shoulder. Elena glanced desperately toward Leo, who grinned. Big help, he was. She patted the girl's shoulder. "If you're worried about these—ah—rumors, the best thing to do is get tested."

"But I can't bear to know," Marilyn cried.

"If you don't know, you can't get treated," Elena pointed out. "Maybe till it's too late."

"If I know and I am, then I'd have to tell my fiancé, and he'd have to get tested, and he'd be furious and tell my parents. They'll probably cut off my allowance—or—or take away my car.''

"Gee," said Elena, "surely not." That's what the kid was worried about? "You could get tested and then decide what to do," Elena suggested.

Marilyn Fone stopped crying and considered that idea. She evidently liked it. "That's just what I'll do. I don't have to make up my mind about anything today, do I?" She hugged Elena. "Thank you. Thank you. My mama always said, when you don't know where you are, ask a policeman." She fluttered her fingers at them and danced off toward the Student Union.

Elena and Leo, after exchanging glances, continued to the Humanities building, where they called on Angus Mc-Glenlevie, who protested, "Even if you know who shot at me, I wouldn't dream of pressing charges."

"Harley Stanley get to you?" Elena asked wearily.

"At this joyous time in my life, I put all vengeful thoughts behind me."

"Someone—probably Estie Grant and Kimberly Sweet— tried to kill you, Gus," snapped Elena.

"They could try again," said Leo.

"Why would they? They are no longer pregnant. Much as I weep for those little seeds of my love, now no more, I can still look forward to marriage to a lovely girl."

"Is she pregnant, too?" asked Elena.

"Yes indeed, and she assures me that no one will try to do me harm now that she has taken me under her loving wing, my little bird, my sweet poetic—"

"How does she know more girls won't turn up pregnant?" asked Leo.

"Even I, Detective, am not that potent," said Gus. "And now, if you'll excuse me, I feel the muse stirring."

Angus McGlenlevie ushered them out of his office which, unlike other professors' offices Elena had visited, had no books on the shelves, no piles of student papers, only copies of Gus's poetry collections and one notebook, in which he would have written a poem, presumably, had his writing hand not been disabled by rifle fire. There was also a tape recorder with a microphone, and a picture of the poet himself receiving an award.

"You realize," said Elena, once they were in the hall outside Gus's office, "that we're going to have to interview the whole girls' volleyball team."

Leo groaned.

36

Monday, April 14, 12:30 P.M.

"You were shot at last night?" asked Leo, looking shocked. They were having lunch on North Mesa, fried chicken and cole slaw, anything to get away from H.H.U. and the interviews with female volleyball players.

Jaime and Mosconi had been temporarily reassigned by Manny Escobedo, their sergeant, to a bar killing on Alameda. "Till Beltran calms down about the *Times* story," Manny had confided to Elena privately.

"I was shot at," Elena confirmed. She put down a crispy chicken leg and wiped her mouth. "You should have seen the uproar, all my ancient neighbors, half of them armed, and their dogs, heading for my yard. The shooter must have thought he was being attacked by a chapter of A.A.R.P. But it wasn't funny. The son of a bitch shot this really great pueblo pot my mother gave me."

"Better the pot than you." Leo looked at her half-finished chicken leg. "Are you going to eat that?"

"Yes."

He sighed. "Don't you know that ladies are supposed to leave half their food so the male can eat it?"

"Why?"

"So he'll have the strength to go out and bring down a saber-toothed tiger for dinner."

"Well, number one, I'm not some finicky lady; I'm your partner. Number two, you're not a hunter, and if you were, you'd be hunting for your wife and kids, not me. And number three, I don't think I'd want to eat a saber-toothed tiger. They probably taste gross.'' Elena lifted her chicken leg and took an appreciative bite.

"No sense of history or gender propriety," Leo muttered. "So who do you think took the shot at you?"

"If I knew, I'd have him in cuffs and booked."

They finished their chicken, wiped their fingers on paper napkins, and returned to campus to interview the last four members of Gus McGlenlevie's volleyball team. With Millie Quitman they hit pay dirt.

"Of course I know who he was screwing," she said. "Estie and Kimberly. Like they're better in bed than me! Much he knows. Anyway, I wouldn't have him on a bet. Like he's getting everyone pregnant. Who needs that? I'd—"

"So about Estie and Kimberly," prodded Elena.

"Oh yeah, they were so proud of themselves, because he picked them for this semester. Big deal. All they got was morning sickness. They were really mad about *that*. Got the whole team to throw hors d'oeuvres at him. But not me. Why should I make a fool of myself at a funeral?"

"So the attack at Fullerton's memorial service was their idea?"

"Absolutely. And then they weren't satisfied. They said the team should have poured drinks down his pants and ripped up that aviator's scarf he wears with his leather jacket. I mean, isn't that cool? He looks so adorable. Not that I'm interested in him."

"Right," Elena agreed. "So did they plan anything else to get even?"

"I saw them whispering with Bonnie the next day. Not that they told *me* anything. Everyone said I was a traitor for not supporting them, but I don't see why I should. If they get pregnant, they know what to do. It's not like that doctor at the clinic won't take care of you."

"So Kimberly was pregnant too?" Leo broke in.

"Absolutely. She was furious. He wanted to marry her. Can you imagine? She'd make him a really rotten wife. That's what I think. She was madder about the proposal than being pregnant. I bet she was the one who shot him."

"Why do you say that?" Elena tried to look casual.

"Because she's a crack shot. She's the Virginia fox-hunting type. Big deal. You put on a funny-looking hat and jodhpurs and chase some poor, ratty fox around."

"Kimberly's a good shot?" Elena seized on that.

"Absolutely. I heard her say she could shoot the balls off a rabbit at four hundred yards. But why would she want to? That's what I'd like to know."

"What about Estie? Is she a good shot?" Leo asked.

"I don't know. She belongs to the gun club, but I think she joined because there's a guy she likes who's a member."

"Did you hear any other rumors about who shot at your coach?"

"Sure. Everyone he ever got it on with, and if you're thinking I shot him, no way. I wouldn't sleep with him if he asked me. I mean he's *old*. Even if everyone says he's great in bed, I wouldn't want to. He's probably wrinkled or something. He probably has a wrinkled butt. Wouldn't that be gross? No way. I had no reason to shoot him."

"So what do you think?" Leo asked once they left Millie Quitman. "Is she a reliable source or just jealous?"

"Both would be my guess," said Elena. She was looking at her pager. "That's headquarters." She called the number and got her friend Maggie Daguerre.

"Thought you'd want to know right away," said Maggie. "The helicopter spotted him, and we found him. Way the hell off the trail."

"Is he O.K.?" Elena asked, more concerned for Gretchen than for Quarles.

"Hell, no. He's dead."

"What did he die of?" Elena asked, expecting to hear that he'd been shot.

"Have to wait for the autopsy on that," said Maggie, "but the medic said he looked really dehydrated and probably had convulsions. He was banged up, like he fell down a lot, but not enough to kill him. Neri, the medic, said he'd have guessed Quarles died of thirst, but he wasn't out there that long. Maybe exposure. It was pretty cold last night."

Dehydration? Elena recalled a story she'd read in the paper several years back. Some kid who drank jimsonweed tea wandered off into the desert and died of dehydration. Loco weed, some people called it. That death hadn't been Elena's case. But had jimsonweed tea been what Quarles was trying to sell Gretchen on? "Did he have a Thermos with him?" Elena asked.

"If he had, he wouldn't have been dehydrated," said Maggie.

"Anyone *see* a Thermos—or a canteen?"

"Not that I know of."

"Anyone find a gun on the trail?"

"Yeah, a revolver in a bush, and before you ask, it hadn't been fired, and he hadn't been shot."

Elena called the coroner's office and told them the tea story, mentioning jimsonweed. Wilkerson promised to keep it in mind and make a note on the samples he sent out for toxicology. Then Elena called Marialita, her mother's *curandera* friend, to ask about symptoms and sources for jimsonweed.

"He din' get eet from me," said the *curandera*, "but sure, eef he drink eet or eat the seeds or any part of the plant an' go off een the desert by heemself, I be surprised eef he make eet back. Eet's poisonous."

"He didn't make it back," said Elena. "Where might he have got it? Could he just pick it and make his own?"

"Could. Wilted leaves are dangerous. But he haf to know what he ees lookeeng for, an' the flowers don' bloom until the fall. He could buy eet. Call—ah—Jean Rockingham, the herbalist."

Leo had talked to Dr. Norris Minor, the university's botanist, who said someone had called asking about jimsonweed. "Minor told him it was dangerous and hung up. Me, he didn't hang up on. He had to tell me everything about the damn stuff including the Latin name."

"Did he mention symptoms?"

"Yeah." Leo consulted his notebook. "Hot skin, thirst, dizziness, delirium, convulsions, coma, death. Those are some."

"Well, if that's what he took, and he didn't get it from the botanist, I've got the name of an herbalist." Elena started to dial.

"Just happened to have an herbalist's number in your little black book?" Leo asked, grinning. "Or did you call your mother in Chimayo?"

"I called my mother's *curandera* here in Los Santos. Hello? Is this Jean Rockingham?" Elena introduced herself and explained her problem.

"It's not illegal to sell jimsonweed," said the woman sharply, "but I wouldn't sell it to just anyone."

"Have you sold some?"

"Yes."

"To whom?"

"Some young fellow. He bought a number of herbs he said his girlfriend wanted. She evidently had an old family recipe called for four or five herbs and a dash of jimson. Sounded dangerous to me, but he said she wanted to make it in a chemistry lab and test it for toxicity because people in her family drank it in the old days. That's true enough; people did, but they died of it, too. I told him, at best, the jimson would ruin the flavor of the tea; at worst it would kill."

"Did he mention hallucinogenic properties?"

The herbalist laughed. "He did, but I told him a hallucination followed by death wouldn't be much of a kick, not unless you're suicidal."

Had Quarles been suicidal? And what about the story of the girlfriend's family? "Could you describe him?" Elena asked.

The description sounded suspiciously like the late Wayne Quarles, Jr.

"Have you heard of people using jimsonweed to get high?" Elena asked.

"I've heard of people using spray shoe polish to get high. Jimsonweed certainly wouldn't be the herb of choice," said Jean Rockingham. "Heavens, if you want to get high, there are hundreds of things available on the street. You don't go to an herbalist."

"Maybe you do if the street's closed and you're really hard up to trip," said Elena. She thanked the woman for the information, hung up, and turned to Leo. "Ten to one they find jimsonweed in his toxicology. He died because he wanted to see twigs flower."

Leo shrugged. "Well, no one ever said he was a rocket scientist or even a nice guy. Did Maggie know whether they found the gun Gretchen took up there?"

"Yeah, but it wasn't fired. The herbalist told me Wayne claimed his girlfriend wanted him to get the weed."

"Farber?"

"Rockingham didn't have a name."

"O.K. So say Farber asked him to get the weed, encouraged him to drink the tea, then left him there."

"Maybe, but Gretchen Farber isn't from around here. How would she know about jimsonweed tea? Maybe Quarles told Rockingham that to cover his ass in case his experiment went wrong. He evidently figured to try it out on Gretchen first, and his motto was always: Blame someone else."

They called Penny Penasco at White Sands, who confirmed picking Gretchen Farber up on Transmountain Road late Saturday afternoon and taking her as far as the gates at H.H.U. "Gretchen said it took her a while to get a ride," Elena mused aloud. "But she could have been out on the trail waiting for him to trip out before she beat it."

"The autopsy will make or break her story," Leo suggested.

Elena glanced at her watch. "Will you sign me out at headquarters? I got a date with Rafer."

"Again? You've had a date with him every night."

"Not last night. I was home getting shot at. Anyway, he just bought a motorcycle."

"What for?"

"Because his wife got his car in the divorce, not to mention his money and everything else."

"Well, don't you ride it. Motorcycles are killers."

"Jeez, Leo. You're getting to be a real fuddy-duddy. We're riding up to Las Cruces for dinner."

"I'll tell you what. I'll pay for some life insurance if you'll make me the beneficiary."

37
⁚

Elena wrote reports on her cases with one part of her mind while the other relived the exhilaration of speeding along Interstate 10 with the wind in her face, Rafer's ponytail against her cheek, and his tall, leather-clad body to hang onto. They'd stuffed themselves with shrimp *rellenos* and other spicy seafood dishes at a restaurant near New Mexico State, attended a rock concert at the Pan-American Center on the campus, and roared back at ten-thirty. A thoroughly delightful evening, in Elena's opinion. It would have been even better on a weekend, but big-time rock groups scheduled more lucrative venues than Los Santos and Las Cruces on weekends.

When her telephone rang, she picked up while continuing to type with one hand. Reports were such a pain. Of course, hers should have been written last night, but she'd had more entertaining things to do. "Jarvis."

"It's Wilkerson at the morgue. Your corpse went into a coma and died between ten and twelve Sunday night, give or take a few hours. Could very well have been datura."

"What?"

"Jimsonweed."

"If it was, when would he have taken it?" Elena asked.

"Seven or eight."

Sundown, Elena thought. Quarles had been looking to make the desert a wonderland. Hell, you didn't need to die

203

to do that, not at sunset. She wondered if he'd seen twigs flowering before his latest venture into tripping out killed him. And if he'd drunk his tea at sunset, he hadn't done it with Gretchen Farber because she'd been back home by then. Her roommate had said so. Of course, the roommate had been victimized by Quarles, too. She might lie. But why would Penny Penasco, the White Sands computer scientist who'd picked Gretchen up?

"I'll fax you the autopsy report," said Wilkerson.

"Thanks." One down, she thought. Probable suicide. Now they just had to find out who poisoned Fullerton and who shot Gus McGlenlevie. Elena went to find Leo to tell him the news. He was having coffee in the lunchroom with two detectives from Sex Crimes, who took an interest in the Quarles death, having heard about the rape from Monica Ibarra.

"Why didn't you hand it over to us?" asked Glenda Karltoff. "I wouldn't mind solving one of the university's cases and getting an honorary doctorate."

"Yeah, you'd love it," Elena agreed. "The sprinkler system and landscaping blew up when I got mine. Anyway, the girl wouldn't press charges."

"You sure she's in the clear?"

"Looks like it. When he drank the stuff, Farber was either back at the university or on her way, riding with a stranger who picked her up."

"She was hitchhiking?" Karltoff scowled. "Wonder she didn't get raped a second time."

"A female computer scientist picked her up, Glenda. Does that sound like a sex-attack scenario?"

"Hey, I could tell you stories—"

"Don't," said Leo, whose pager sounded before the Sex-Crimes detective could subject him to the horror stories of her trade. "Gotta go," he muttered. "Elena, you better come, too. We got an H.H.U. exchange here."

Elena rose with alacrity and followed him back to Crimes Against Persons. The call was from a man who identified himself as H.H.U.'s waste-disposal expert. He was reporting the discovery of a rifle in the toxic-waste bin at the university health facility. "That's an improper disposal," he informed them testily. "People just don't seem to realize that the EPA has its eye on us. We could be cited. But do people listen? Never. Students throw their dead batteries into wastebaskets; diabetics toss syringes into aluminum-can bins; no one wants to recycle at all, much less properly. I'm always finding newspaper among the plastics, cans in the newspaper bins—"

"Hang onto the rifle," said Elena, who was patched in on Leo's call, "and don't touch it."

"How do you think I got it out of the toxic-waste unit? Of course I was wearing latex gloves—"

"Bless you," said Elena.

"—because safety procedures call for—"

"We're on our way," said Leo, and they both hung up and headed for the garage to check out an unmarked car for the trip to H.H.U. By noon, fingerprints had been lifted from the rifle, its serial number had been matched to the rifle missing from the gun club, and Ballistics matched it to the bullet that clipped Gus McGlenlevie's hand. Having secured a warrant to get prints from Estelle Grant and Kimberly Sweet, Leo and Elena went off to catch the two girls exiting the dining room after a lunch consisting of gazpacho, lobster salad, tiny croissants, fresh tropical fruit sorbet, and almond macaroons.

"And we ate at McDonald's," Leo grumbled. "You think if we'd showed up at the housemother's table, she'd have invited us to lunch?"

"Doubt it," said Elena. "You want to talk here"—she waved at the lobby—"or up in your rooms?" she asked the girls.

"My room's all messy," said Estie. "The maids have suddenly stopped doing their jobs."

"No one showed up to do my underwear this morning," said Kimberly, "much less make my bed or change my towels."

"They're on strike," said Elena.

Both girls looked at her with horror.

"So your room, Kimberly? Leo can talk to Estie down here."

"We don't have any secrets from each other," said Estie.

"Not yet," murmured Leo and escorted his assigned volleyball player toward a couch in the lobby. Elena guided Kimberly to the elevator.

Once they were seated in Kimberly's sitting room, Elena said baldly, "We found the rifle."

"What rifle?" Kimberly asked.

"The one used to shoot Angus McGlenlevie."

"So?"

"So you forgot to wipe the fingerprints off, and I've got a warrant to take your prints so we can match them to those on the gun, yours and Estie's."

"You're going to get my fingers all inky?" Kimberly looked at her pink fingernails, then turned her palms up as if she expected to see ink on her fingertips already. "If I confess, can we skip the fingerprints?"

Elena sighed. The stupidity, or was it arrogance, of these students never failed to astonish her. "Do you want a lawyer?"

"What? Right now?"

"You don't have to have one to confess, but you have a right to a lawyer."

"Oh, for heaven's sake. I shot at him. All right? He got me pregnant. I shot at him. It's only fair, after all."

"You fired all the shots."

"No, Estie fired one."

"Did you hit him?"

"I have no idea."

"Kimberly, one of you hit him. Which one?"

"I don't know. Estie will tell you the same thing."

"You've worked that out between you?"

"Why do you care?"

"As I understand it, you're the crack shot."

Kimberly looked pleased. "I am good."

"So you're probably the one who hit him, right?"

"Estie's not bad. She could have been the one."

"So you're saying, because you two didn't manage to kill him, it was probably Estie's bullet that—"

"Who said anything about killing anyone. We didn't kill him. We didn't even mean to. It's like his wife—"

"Ex-wife," Elena corrected. She had a good idea what was coming.

"She blew up a snail on his plate, but she didn't kill him."

"We don't know that she blew up the snail." Sarah, the ex in question, had been Elena's friend ever since that incident, but Elena still didn't know the real story on the exploding snail. "It may have blown up on its own," said Elena.

"Whatever. He wasn't hurt much, and she wasn't arrested." Kimberly smiled, pleased with her logic. "Well, he wasn't hurt much this time either. But he shouldn't go around getting girls pregnant, should he? Now he won't do it anymore. And you don't know—"

Elena stood up. "You'd better hope he doesn't press charges, or you'll both be arrested for assault," said Elena.

Estie, although it took her a little longer to confess to Leo, told him approximately the same story. "I know damn well they could say which one hit him," Leo grumbled.

"Right," Elena agreed, "but they're not going to tell us, and we can't figure it out for ourselves because we can't be sure what they meant to do."

"Huh?" Leo was frowning at her.

"If they meant to kill him, it was probably Estie's bullet that didn't hit him in the head. If they meant to wing him, Kimberly, the good shot, did it."

"But if they meant to kill him, why didn't Kimberly do it?" Leo asked.

"Oh, hell, you're right. I hate these H.H.U. cases. Let's see if McGlenlevie wants to file charges. You'd think he'd be pissed off about this. They got rid of his offspring and then shot at him, injuring his writing hand, or vice versa. Maybe they carried the rifle into the clinic when they got their abortions and dumped it into the toxic-waste bin then."

"Well, we're not going to find out from Greta Marx," Leo predicted.

Elena agreed, but she was thinking about the shot that hit McGlenlevie's hand. "In fact, that was a terrific shot if you wanted to disable a poet," she mused. "Maybe it *was* Kimberly."

"Give it up, Elena," said Leo. "We'll just get him to accuse both of them of assault." But they didn't. Angus McGlenlevie was out of town, giving a poetry reading in Cincinnati.

That being the case, Elena finished the afternoon talking to Gretchen Farber, who caught her coming out of the dorm and cried, "Why didn't you tell me he was dead?"

"I guess you mean Wayne."

"I didn't kill him."

"Datura killed him."

"What?"

"The tea he offered you."

"He wanted to kill me?" Gretchen shoved her hands into the pockets of her suede jacket, which looked more decorative than warm in the unseasonably cold April wind. "He was an even worse person than anyone knew, wasn't he? First he raped me. Then he tried to kill me."

"Look Gretchen, he probably just wanted to get high, and druggies like company."

"But I never get high." Her face was white with anger. "I'm glad he's dead. He deserves to be dead. Dr. Marx was right. It was all his fault, not mine. Even if I did plan to spray him with Mace, I didn't deserve to be raped. I hope he's already in hell. I hope the devil cuts off his penis. I hope—" She stopped abruptly. "But I didn't kill him."

Elena patted her on the shoulder. "I don't think you did, Gretchen. Maybe it was a sort of—higher justice."

"You mean like God. If God gets into stuff like this, why didn't he stop Wayne *before* he doctored my Coke? Maybe I ought to ask Dr. Sunnydale that."

"Good idea," Elena agreed. Gretchen seemed to be recovering. No doubt Dr. Marx would consider Gretchen's fantasy about the rapist's genitalia being lopped off in hell a sign of improving mental health.

"He's always blathering on about God watching over every student on campus. Where was God when Wayne Quarles drugged me? I'm going over to the Administration building right now and ask the president that."

Poor President Sunnydale, Elena thought. Gretchen was striding away with fire in her eye. The death of a rapist seemed to do wonders for his victim, but Elena was going to be embarrassed if evidence turned up to link Gretchen to Quarles's death. Like Penny Penasco was her cousin, and they planned the whole thing between them with the room-mate's complicity.

Elena shook her head and started toward the Physical Sciences building. Her shift was over, and she had date with Rafer—all-you-can-eat Italian, her treat, and a ride up Scenic Drive on his motorcycle.

38

Tuesday, April 15, 9:15 P.M.

Rafer and Elena stood at the stone wall that marked the
boundary between Scenic Drive and the small park that jut-
ted out high up on the mountain. The night was cold with a
light wind tossing loose strands of Elena's hair and stars
piercing the blue-back sky with clear, bright pinpricks of fire.
Rafer had his arm around her, and they were companionably
silent as they gazed out across the lights of the city, warm
and mutely golden.

Beyond Los Santos was the dark, meandering strip that
marked the passage of the river as it swept in a great curve
around the tip of the mountain. Beyond the river the greenish
glow of sodium-vapor lights pinpointed Juarez, where a mil-
lion and a quarter people dwelled unseen in the night, many
in cardboard shacks on dirt roads where they burned refuse
to keep warm and bought their water from trucks because
the water lines didn't extend into the *colonias*. But then it
was the same here in the poor neighborhoods surrounding
Los Santos.

Elena shook away those thoughts and breathed deeply. For
once, there was no pollution, only the smell of mountain
stone and desert sand and the prickling, aromatic scent of
the hardy, gnarled, spare plants that grow where little rain
falls. "It's beautiful," she said.

"I thought so the moment I saw it," Rafer agreed. "Day
or night."

210

"Although night masks some of the less lovely sights," Elena added, laughing.

Rafer kissed her and tightened his arm on her shoulders. "If it weren't a school night," he said regretfully.

"In the middle of a big case," she added.

They turned toward the motorcycle, pulling on their helmets. Rafer was wearing his leathers. Elena thought he looked as sexy in them as the city looked beautiful in its dark cloak. The only other car at the lookout point started its motor and pulled out, heading down the other side of Scenic Drive toward the old neighborhoods, in one of which Elena lived. They took their time in following, both loath to end a very pleasant evening. Elena buttoned up her jacket. She was wearing jeans and flat-heeled boots.

"If we're going to keep doing this," said Rafer, smiling down at her, "you ought to have your own leathers."

"Since I don't," she replied, "I'll just have to trust you to drive carefully." She climbed on behind and felt the vibration of the motor as he revved it. Then they pulled out onto the two-lane road and picked up speed as the twisting curves of the pavement flew under their wheels.

Elena tipped her head back, exhilaration bringing laughter to her throat. In the next second the bike jolted, then slued, hurtling them toward the sheer stone cliff rising above the other side of the road. Rafer was cursing, fighting the skid, and Elena hung onto him frantically, panicked into breathlessness, her heart pounding. She felt a sharp pain in her knee as it hit stone, a searing flash along her thigh as denim and skin were scraped away.

Then they careened across the road toward the drop-off, the bike leaning, leaning, bumping, slamming into the ground. Dimly, through the pain, Elena expected free fall or a long, bruising tumble down the mountainside, but she came to rest abruptly with thorns piercing her upper right arm, head aching from glancing contact with a rock, a dead weight resting across her body. She couldn't drag air into her lungs. The gasping wheeze was hers, she thought dimly, and every part of her hurt. That meant she wasn't dead, but she couldn't breathe and was afraid to move and make the pain worse or discover how bad things were with her.

And through this she heard noises from the road, screeching tires, the thud and crunch of metal, the frantic ululation of a car alarm and the blare of a horn, continuous and importunate. Doors slamming, footsteps stumbling, cursing, a voice saying, "Are you all right? Miss?"

Elena dragged in air at last.

"What happened?" asked the voice.

"Blowout." That was Rafer.

"Us too," said the voice.

"EMS," Elena whispered.

"What?"

"Ambulance."

Footsteps, laborious and departing. She tried to move away from the cactus thorns and tore her arm. Stopped trying.

"Elena?"

"Alive," she replied to Rafer.

"Me too," he said.

"Two blowouts?" Even through the pain, which, she thought, might have eased a bit, her mind was puzzling over the coincidence of two almost simultaneous blowouts on two vehicles, one following the other on a narrow road. "Someone's trying to kill me," she said.

Rafer laughed weakly. "Just like a homicide cop to think that."

Elena resented being laughed at. He probably hurt a good deal less than she did. He had protective clothing, and he'd landed on top of her. She'd been bruised and peeled and pierced and probably had multiple broken bones, and he was saying she was paranoid. "Shot at. Last night."

"What?" He sounded so surprised that she opened her eyes to find him kneeling beside her. Proof positive he wasn't as badly hurt as she.

"At home. Shot my mom's pot. Through the window."

"Pot?" he repeated, bemused.

She could hear the siren coming. The driver who'd bounced his car off the cliff had gotten help. Good man. She hoped that EMS had painkillers on board. Lots and lots of painkillers.

39

Wednesday, April 16, 6:45 A.M.

Elena had been at Thomason General most of the night for X-rays and patching. She had no broken bones, which was a miracle, but her knee was swollen, and she limped. She had more scrapes and bruises than she cared to count, and the cactus against which she had landed had attacked her upper arm viciously. The emergency room doctor had seemed more worried about these puncture wounds made by thorns, some of which had to be dug out, than about the other injuries.

All in all, she'd had a miserable night and no sleep. Rafer, whose treatment had taken less time, had waited and escorted her home in a taxi, the expense of which worried her now that she had forgiven him for doubting her analysis of the accident. Tacks had indeed been found liberally scattered on the road. Of course, it could have been kids playing an ugly and dangerous trick, but given the fact that someone had already taken a shot at her and before that spray-painted *whore* on her house, the police were taking the accident seriously. Two C.A.P. detectives were assigned to look into all three incidents.

Unfortunately, she couldn't remember anything about the car at the other end of the parking lot on Scenic Drive, the one that had left just before they did. Not that that driver had necessarily been the culprit with the tacks but since that car had driven down the hill safely, either its driver had

spread the tacks, or there had been someone lurking in the
area, waiting until she and Rafer made a move to leave. It
was all speculation on Elena's part, not anything the detectives could follow up when she had no descriptions to give
them. Rafer was even less help. He hadn't noticed the car at
all.

She had arrived home in time to wash those places on her
body that the hospital hadn't scrubbed and disinfected and
to limp around the kitchen getting breakfast, facing another
day on the job. Or should she call in sick?

If someone was out to get her, she might be safer fully
conscious, in company, and working. At home in bed,
knocked out by painkillers, she'd be more comfortable but
also more vulnerable to the stalker, and she'd be damned if
she'd ask the department for protection. Wouldn't that look
great? She could see the headline, her so-called friend Paul
Resendez's by-line underneath: HOMICIDE DETECTIVE NEEDS
POLICE PROTECTION FROM TACK-WIELDER.

She put off a decision on what to do with the rest of her
day by sitting at her kitchen table in a brightly painted yel-
low and green chair, eating egg-and-bacon burritos, drinking
coffee, and reading stories in the Los Santos *Times*. The first
detailed the ACLU's offer to protect the rights of students
at H.H.U. who did not want to be tested for AIDS, much
less have their names and results posted conspicuously
around campus. "A gross invasion of privacy," the American Civil Liberties Union called the proposal, which had
garnered three hundred signatures from those students who
didn't want to be infected by fellow collegians.

Wincing at the pain caused by moving her arm, Elena set
her coffee cup down, forked up another bite of burrito, and
read doggedly on. A second story covered the administration's refusal to let Dr. Marx test indiscriminately or even
run education sessions at the health services center. Elena
wondered when the parents, with their high-powered lawyers, would get in on the controversy. Soon, she imagined.

She poured herself a second cup of coffee, then rose,
groaning, to answer the telephone and receive instructions

from Lieutenant Beltran. "The administration at H.H.U. has sent out an S.O.S.," he informed her.

"Don't tell me," she responded. "Someone else has been poisoned."

"There's going to be a big conference in the lobby of the Administration building on the maids' strike. They want you there."

Elena couldn't believe it. He wanted her to rise from her bed of pain, metaphorically speaking—she was actually leaning heavily on the kitchen counter to take the weight off her knee. But still he was suggesting that an injured officer volunteer to negotiate a labor dispute. "Why me?" she said plaintively.

"I was told you'd agreed to intervene for them."

Elena then remembered that she had said, sarcastically, that she might get to their problem at some future date, when she wasn't so involved with their murders, shootings, suicides, etc. "Lieutenant, maybe you haven't heard, but I was injured last night in a motorcycle accident, one that was probably staged to get me."

"You taking medical leave?" he asked brusquely.

Well, there it was. Did she want to drop off this case and stay home sick? If she did, maybe the stalker would leave her alone. But that would mean he'd driven her off the case. "No," she said angrily. "But what about the Fullerton investigation?"

"We've got three other detectives on it. They ought to be able to get along without you for a couple of hours. Sunnydale will be expecting you in the administration lobby by eight-fifteen."

Elena groaned to herself. Sunnydale? The president was getting into the act? As she hung up, drank the last of her coffee, and headed, limping, toward her bedroom to dress, she was hoping that they'd provide her with a comfortable chair at H.H.U. Maybe a footstool. A couple of hours off the knee might induce the swelling to subside. She decided to take an ice pack with her.

●   ●   ●   ●

Elena arrived at the lobby of the Administration building, having parked in a slot for the handicapped and demanded that a nervous H.H.U. police officer put a permission slip on the dashboard of her truck saying she had a right to be there. When he demurred, she made him look at her knee, which was both colorful and swollen. She even rolled her loose slacks high enough to give him a glimpse of the bandage that covered her badly scraped thigh. Then she insisted that he help her inside.

When she arrived in the lobby on the arm of the reluctant, lavender-clad cop, various members of the administration rushed to accommodate her injury. Chief Clabb sent the officer to drag over a comfy chair from a lounge area at the end of the huge room. Other participants were seated in uncomfortable-looking folding chairs placed in rows on the pink marble floor. A second officer was dispatched to bring a matching ottoman so that she could elevate her leg, and Dr. Marx was summoned to supervise the proper leg placement. Dr. Sunnydale's secretary rushed off to bring a bowl of ice in case Elena's ice pack liquefied during the heat of the discussion to follow.

While all this protective hovering was going on, Elena took the time to look over the participants: the president and two vice-presidents of the university; Meredith Corwin of Public Relations, carrying tastefully designed handouts that stated the university's position; the majority of the H.H.U. security force; Bishop Chavira of the Roman Catholic Diocese; Professor Apulonia, expert on religious sects; large delegations of maids, gardeners, and students; Alope Randall, the labor lawyer; Dr. Greta Marx of the H.H.U. Heath and Reproductive Services Center; and various representatives of the media, who no doubt hoped to record something scandalous and/or acrimonious for the six o'clock news and the next morning's paper. Paul Resendez was in attendance, but Elena refused to speak to him.

Once she was comfortable in her chair (foot and leg propped up on an ottoman whose pillowed top was so soft that her injured leg might have been floating in a cloud, knee iced to the point of numbness, a microphone pinned to the lapel of her blazer), Harley Stanley informed her that she was to moderate the discussion. "You are the only person both sides trust," he explained, "although, of course, we know whose side you're on, don't we, *Dr.* Jarvis?"

Elena was not pleased. That Dr. Jarvis thing was a reminder that she'd been given an honorary doctorate, for which she was now expected to show gratitude. As if she had wanted the damn thing! If Chief Gaitan hadn't insisted, she'd have refused.

And why did the maids trust her? she wondered. She found out immediately when Socorro Rascon leaned down to whisper in her ear that the "H.H.U. honchos don' know you was the first one to encourage our Union de la Virgin, but we know you're on our side." Socorro said this in Spanish, a sure if disturbing sign that she now trusted Elena, while Elena didn't even want to be mixed up in this confrontation.

"What am I supposed to do?" she asked grumpily.

"Just run it like a town meeting or a debate," said Vice-President Joel Smith.

Socorro glared at him. "You're tryin' to intimidate us. We don't know nuthin' about town meetin's or debates."

Me either, thought Elena gloomily and called the meeting to order, since that seemed to be a likely opening move. "Who wants to talk first?" she asked.

No big surprise to anyone, Dr. Sunnydale appropriated a microphone and launched into a paean of good will and family feeling. "First I would like to invite our employees to an interdenominational worship service."

"We're Catholics," muttered Socorro Rascon, loud enough to be heard by many of those seated in the rows of folding chairs.

The president beamed at her. "Indeed," he said. "A fine old church, the Roman Catholic Church. In fact, I would like to point out that all Christian churches are more or less descended from the Roman Catholic Church and that some of my best friends are Roman Catholics."

Elena rolled her eyes.

"Dear Bishop Chavira, for instance." He beamed at the bishop, who did not return the friendly look.

Dr. Sunnydale seemed disconcerted. Perhaps he didn't remember that the bishop had left his office, highly peeved and without accepting an offer of California Chardonnay. "Be that as it may," President Sunnydale resumed, "we at H.H.U. think of our employees as family. For instance, they eat the food prepared by our superb university chef, and they have the services of our excellent Health and Reproductive Services Center."

"O.K.," said Socorro Rascon. "My turn." She had risen, looking belligerent. Sunnydale was obviously nonplussed to be interrupted by a member of his "family."

Elena reasoned that this was how a debate went. One side said something; then the other side answered. Therefore, she nodded to the maid, who flipped her long hair back and grabbed a second microphone.

"My family don't eat the kind of garbage they feed us here. It would give 'em the trots, just like it does us maids. An' if we're family, how come our johns got these rolls of stuff that feels like crepe paper on your butt, an' the students, they got this real soft toilet paper with flowers all over it?

"An' if we're family, how come we got a separate waitin' room at the clinic, an' that doctor's always tryin' to give us condoms an' birth-control pills an' lectures on not havin' babies. She made Angel Guadaramma cry by askin' if she wanted an abortion."

During the last part of Socorro's diatribe the bishop had been looking more and more appalled. He rose majestically, patted the maid on the shoulder, and took the microphone from her. Being a good Catholic, she gave it up, although clearly she had not finished her remarks.

"It becomes more apparent with every word spoken that this university is not only discriminating against its Catholic employees by seeking to bar them from the site of a possible miracle, but that an attempt is being made to lead them into sin. The Church's position on birth control and abortion is perfectly clear. For the university's medical personnel to attempt to—"

He was unable to finish because Greta Marx had leapt from her chair, grabbing a microphone and howling, "Position! The Church's position is immoral! *Unconscionable!*"

The bishop turned to stare at her, crossing himself as if to ward off evil influences.

"If the bishop or his boss, the Pope, had to carry an unwanted child to term, you can be sure there'd be a pretty rapid change in the Church's so-called position," declared Dr. Marx.

Elena had lost her ice pack at the start of the argument and leaned forward to try to fish it off the floor as the debate heated up.

"Dr. Jarvis," hissed Harley Stanley. "You're the moderator. You're supposed to—"

Finally successful, Elena laid the bag gently over her knee and shouted, "Knock it off," into her microphone. The combatants turned to her in mute surprise; however, the hush was only momentary.

Into the lull, Castor Apulonia cried, "May I address the bishop's suggestion of a miracle?"

"No," said the bishop.

"Do forgive me, dear sir," the professor continued blithely, "but I have been studying the weeping lady in question, and I do not believe that she is the Virgin Mary, mother of Jesus of Nazareth. She may indeed be a Middle-Eastern deity, but the likelihood is that she is a goddess of fertility rather than—"

"That's hardly evidence that she is not the Virgin," called someone from the audience. "Christ's mother was certainly Middle-Eastern."

"Who are you?" asked Elena. She didn't think they needed any more debaters than they already had.

"Abraham Rubenstein, Professor of Hebrew Studies. As I was saying, Mary was Middle-Eastern. A clear-sighted study of Catholic doctrine and history convinces us that Mary is certainly a fertility goddess."

"She is not!" cried the bishop.

"With all respect, sir," said Professor Rubenstein, "she

is venerated because of her motherhood, her fecundity in other words.''

"Her virginity," snapped the bishop.

"If I may interrupt," said Harley Stanley. "It should be noted that Professor Rubenstein is supposed to be on sabbatical in the Holy Land, his classes having failed to make for lack of student interest."

"Is that my notice that I'm not to be granted tenure?" Rubenstein demanded. "Do I detect the stench of anti-Semitism?"

Socorro Rascon then stated that either the maids' demands were met or they would continue on strike.

"We're with you," said Collie Reed. "The Feminist Coalition stands behind the rights of women to a decent wage and no discrimination in matters of diet and health care. It's well known that for years medical research was done only on men. We members of the Feminist Coalition are ready to make our own beds and wash our own underwear until these ladies' demands are met."

"Oh yeah," snarled Socorro Rascon. "You gonna clean your own toilets?"

"They're on your side," Elena told her.

"We've agreed to the raise in pay," said Vice-President Joel Smith, "and I'm sure the clinic and—er—toilet tissue problems can be worked out."

"Not from my point of view," said Dr. Marx.

"We shall take you to court, madam, for interfering with freedom of religious belief," said the bishop.

"I'm afraid the chef refuses to cook Mexican food," said Mrs. Poleby, who had been sitting unnoticed in the audience and now rose to address the issues under discussion, "but we can certainly put the same bathroom tissue in the domestics' retiring room that the students have."

"What about us?" asked one of the gardeners.

Chief Clabb was wringing his hands. "The chapel is a problem," he said, addressing Vice-President Joel Smith. "The fire marshal has informed us that too many people are trying to crowd into the chapel—"

"That's it," cried Socorro. "We're gone." The strikers,

probably bored to tears with arguments of no interest to them, walked out.

"I'm very disappointed in you, Dr. Jarvis," said Harley Stanley. "We expected you to resolve matters, not show favoritism to the opposition."

"Can I get back to my case now?" she retorted irritably.

40
##

Wednesday, April 16, 1:05 P.M.

After the unsuccessful labor-management meeting, Elena
shanghaied another campus cop to help her to the car, go
along to the student dormitory, provide another Handicapped
permit, and help her into the lobby, where she settled into a
chair, her leg propped up on a coffee table, with the ice pack,
replenished by the president's secretary, on the injured knee.
She thought she detected improvement there. However, her
abraded thigh and cactus-punctured upper arm hurt as much
as ever, so she took a pain pill, water provided by the helpful
cop, and devoted herself to reading the *Campus Enquirer*
while she waited for her colleagues to reappear. Now that
Graham Fullerton's health problems had been revealed in the
newspapers, the three other detectives were upstairs quizzing
all the young women they had interviewed before about what
they had or hadn't known about Graham's health, and when.

The *Enquirer* was, as usual, filled with a wonderful array
of pseudo-news and outrageous opinion. For instance, an
obituary for the late Wayne Quarles, Jr. described him as a
"known cokehead who ODed on some exotic local vegetation . . . A for originality, Wayne," was the closing line.

In a letter to the editor, Collie Reed of the Feminist Coalition belabored the paper for failing to support the maids'
strike. "But then what can you expect from a newspaper so
blatantly sexist? Nine out of ten staffers are male, not to

mention chauvinist pigs.'' Willie of ''Willie's Whispers''
complained that he was getting threatening calls in the middle of the night from females who disapproved of his stand
against the maids. ''You'd think my fellow students would
resent not having their beds made,'' wrote Willie. ''By next
week the campus will be uninhabitable. We'll all have to go
home. Or hire new maids. Which seems the most sensible
solution.''

''My God!'' exclaimed Leo. ''What happened to you?''

Elena looked up to find three C.A.P. detectives staring at
her with dismay. Evidently she looked worse than she'd
thought, she decided as she explained the motorcycle accident.

''Told you motorcycles were dangerous,'' said Leo.

''Not as dangerous as people who spread tacks on the road
in front of your tires,'' she snapped. Her colleagues got lunch
from the dorm food machines, replenished the ice in her ice
bag, and discussed the answers they had received from coeds, all of whom denied knowing that the sexually talented
Graham had been HIV positive, many of whom burst into
tears at the idea that they too might now be infected. Those
were the ones who hadn't been reading the newspaper and
hadn't visited the clinic to be tested.

Elena listened and devoured a ham salad sandwich accompanied by a Seven-Up and topped off with an eclair. Too
bad they didn't have eclair machines at headquarters, she
thought. ''Leo, I think we should go have a talk with Angus
McGlenlevie. The fingerprint matches came back on the gun
that shot him. They belong to Estie and Kimberly from the
rifle range and one more girl, Renee Winter, the one Jaime
turned up. I guess the other two covered for this Renee when
we talked to them, but now we've got three probable shooters. If he wants to prosecute—''

''O.K., O.K.,'' Leo muttered ''but if he quotes any of his
disgusting poetry to me, I'm going to arrest him for lewd—''

''—literature?'' Elena suggested and giggled.

''You're sure in a good mood for someone who almost
got killed on a motorcycle.''

''The eclair raised my endorphin level.''

"Whatever that means." Leo helped Elena to her truck, and they drove to the Humanities building, where he walked her into the English Department. Dropping into a visitor's chair, she asked the redhead in the departmental office to buzz McGlenlevie. Because Leo was staring at the woman's overlapping teeth, Elena elbowed her partner in the ribs.

"What?" he asked, looking surprised.

"Don't be rude," she mouthed as the secretary checked a departmental register.

"He has an appointment at the vice-president's office."

"Maybe his sins are catching up with him," Leo commented as they set out for the truck and the Administration building, hoping to catch Gus at the end of the meeting.

"All this walking around isn't doing my knee any good," Elena complained. "And if Harley Stanley hears what we're up to, he'll try to stop us. He's not going to want any students arrested. The coeds could shoot Stanley himself, and I expect he'd try to hush it up for fear it might affect contributions to the Hobart Foundation."

Harley Stanley's secretary mistakenly assumed that Leo and Elena were to be participants in the meeting and ushered them into the conference room, where they were greeted with some surprise by the vice-president. "Detectives," he said, recovering his aplomb, "you'll be happy to know that we are here resolving a knotty problem that you yourselves have been involved in."

"Cover-up," Elena murmured to Leo. She noted the occupants of the comfy conference chairs: Gus (looking pleased with himself); a pretty, dark-haired girl sitting beside him (one of the impregnated?); Joel Smith, VP for business; Harley Stanley himself; a stenographer, and a man Elena had never seen before.

"I believe you know Professor McGlenlevie and Vice-President Smith," said Harley Stanley. "But let me introduce Miss Linda Morell, the bride-to-be, and James Merry Covington, the university's lawyer."

"Miss Morell?" Elena studied the girl with interest, then nodded to the lawyer.

"Yes." Harley Stanley beamed paternally. "We're here

to finalize plans for the happy event and work out the prenuptial agreement.''

''Ah.'' Elena nodded. ''Well, we're here to tell Professor
McGlenlevie that the attack on him the other day was carried
out by Estelle Grant, Kimberly Sweet, and Renee Winter,
using a rifle pilfered from your gun club, Dr. Stanley. You
may want to press charges, too.''

Dr. Stanley gaped.

''Estie, Kimberly, and Renee?'' Gus looked saddened.
''The girls who aborted my—''

The vice-president cleared his throat. ''I really doubt that
any of our students would—''

''They did,'' Elena assured him. ''We found the rifle with
their prints on it. They'd thrown it into the toxic-waste bin
at the health-services center.''

''Greta Marx!'' cried Gus. ''She must have put them up
to it.''

''The shooting or the abortions?'' asked Elena. ''Did the
doctor say anything to you indicating—''

''She treated me most shabbily, belittling my natural desire to be a father, accusing me of—of—'' Gus composed
himself, tossing his white silk scarf over his shoulder, patting
his new Van Dyke beard to be sure that it was neat. ''Perhaps I should press charges against all four of them.''

''Mr. Covington,'' said Linda Morell, ''my prenup will
have to say that Gussie can't press charges against anyone.''
She had a high, little-girl voice, straight black hair blunt-cut
at her shoulders and in bangs that brushed her eyebrows, and
wore an outfit featuring a fabric printed with tiny flowers
and a ruffled hem on the long skirt.

To Elena the garment looked like a nightgown, or perhaps
something a pioneer woman trudging over the plains beside
a covered wagon might have worn. At any rate, both the
prospective bride and the bridegroom, in his World War I
aviator togs, obviously liked to play dress-up. Maybe the
marriage would be a success.

''But Linda, my love,'' cried Gus, ''these young women
tried to kill me. Me, your true love, the father of your child,
the husband of your dreams.''

"If you love me, Gussie, you won't care about any babies but ours."

"Well, of course not, but—"

"And I *am* marrying you, so I think you should do this itsy bitsy thing for me."

Gus considered her demand. "Well, my love, a man can't help but feel somewhat protective of the seed of his loins, no matter what womb it resides in. And Dr. Marx is my enemy. If she's behind the attack on me ... well, you wouldn't want some antisex female orchestrating an attack on *your* writing hand, would you, my love? Naturally, I, as a *famous* poet, am very protective of the hand that produces best-selling verse." He laid his uninjured appendage over his bandaged hand as if another attack might be imminent.

"You may be a famous poet, Gussie, and I love you for it," said Linda, "but now you have me, and I'll write everything down for you. Your least poetic word."

"I appreciate that," said Gus.

"Good. Now, about the other provisions. You have to promise to be faithful."

"But of course, love. How can you think—"

"And if you're not, the copyrights and royalties from *Erotica in Reeboks* and *Rapture on the Rapids* revert to me. I think that's only fair."

"Well really, Linda, I wrote those before I ever met you. I don't see—"

"I suggest you agree, Angus," said the vice-president for Financial Affairs. "If you get into a messy divorce, she'll take you for everything you've got anyway, so you might as well have it all settled ahead of time."

"What happened to the mutual trust and affection of those who share the nuptial couch?" asked Gus plaintively.

"And I want half the royalties of *Scattering Seeds of Love* and *The Sensual Parent*," said Linda.

"I haven't even written *The Sensual Parent*," Gus complained.

"But you will, and I'm the one who's bearing the child, so it's only fair that, as your muse, I get my half of *Scattering Seeds of Love*—You did say I was your muse?"

·

"Well yes, but—"

"And half of *The Sensual Parent* is fair because I'll be the other sensual parent. Write that down, Mr. Covington."

The lawyer cleared his throat. "I don't take down the provisions personally, Miss Morell. Miss Garza does." He nodded toward the stenographer. "Once we have the agreement ironed out, she'll type up the document."

"Well, at least she's homely. Now that Gussie has promised to be faithful, I don't see any sense in tempting him to stray. After all"—Miss Morell beamed at her fiancé—"it wouldn't be to your financial advantage, would it, Gussie?" She ignored Miss Garza's baleful stare.

"Gussie" didn't look too happy either, although Elena thought the whole situation hilarious and wouldn't have left for anything. Leo, on the other hand, was frowning and muttering under his breath, anxious, no doubt, to get back to the Fullerton case now that it seemed the McGlenlevie shooting would never come to trial. Unless Gus backed out of the marriage.

"Do you have a problem with the agreement so far, love?" Linda asked sharply.

"Yes, I do," said Gus.

"No, you don't," said Dr. Stanley. "Much as we'd hate to lose a poet of your fame, Angus, the administration's official position is that you should marry. Four different women have tried to kill you, not to mention one enraged husband. Scandals of this sort are embarrassing to the university. We feel that you should settle down."

"Who's *we*?" Gus demanded.

"*I* am we," said Harley Stanley. "The man who holds your hopes of tenure in his hands."

"Any university would be delighted to employ me," said Gus loftily.

"Are you saying that you don't want to marry me?" Linda demanded. "I'm carrying your *baby*!"

"Of course I want to marry you, my love, but you're asking me to—"

"—be faithful."

"I've already promised to do that."

"And I'm seeing that it's worth your while. Having a baby is not fun, Gussie. I talked it over with Dr. Marx. I'll get big and fat, my hormones may prevent me from continuing to write poetry myself, and then I have to go through excruciating pain, so if you can't make a few little sacrifices for me, fine. I'll get an abortion——''

"Linda!" McGlenlevie looked horrified.

"And then I'll have my daddy sue you and hound you to the ends of the earth for seducing his little girl."

"My advice, sir," said the lawyer, "is take the deal. I've met her father."

"Oh, very well," Gus grumbled.

"Good, good, good," declared Harley Stanley, rubbing his hands together. "Now that we're all agreed on the provisions of the prenuptial agreement——''

"I have one more little matter," said Linda Morell. Gus looked alarmed, but Linda now had her sweet, steely gaze on Vice-President Stanley. "What about my degree? I would have graduated in a year or so. But if I'm going to have this baby and be a mother and all that, I'll never have time for classes. On the other hand, Daddy will be very disappointed if I don't get my degree, so . . .''

Dr. Stanley sighed. "How many hours would we have to waive so that you can graduate, Miss Morell?"

"Oh, I don't know," she said airily. "I'm a little behind on my degree program, but I *have* learned ever so much, especially from Gussie."

Harley Stanley's secretary popped her head in the door and announced, "Dr. Sarah Tolland is here to see you, sir. Was she invited to this meeting?"

Sarah followed close on the secretary's heels, noted the people around the conference table, and muttered, "Good grief, what have you done now, Gus? I've been hearing rumors about you."

"Well, if you'd agreed to bear my child," Gus began resentfully, "none of this——''

"Gus!" cried Linda. "You asked her first?"

"Don't give it a thought," said Sarah. "I had no interest whatever."

"I have another provision for the prenuptial," said Linda.

"Are you marrying Gus?" asked Sarah with interest.

"Yes, and I'm not allowing him to be unfaithful."

"Good for you, and best of luck enforcing that," said Sarah.

"I resent your insinuation, Sarah," snapped Gus.

"Dr. Stanley, there is no heat in my building." Sarah had turned to the vice-president.

"See Buildings and Grounds," he retorted. "I don't take care of heat."

"And the finals schedule that just came to my desk is a disaster. You've got some of our upperclassmen scheduled to take three finals simultaneously."

"*Hello*?" Linda interrupted. "I believe we were discussing my prenuptial agreement. I want it written in that Gus is to have nothing to do with his ex-wife."

"I'll sign off on that," said Sarah fervently.

"You don't have to be insulting!" Gus exclaimed.

"If there's nothing else," said the lawyer, "let's get this typed up. Miss Garza?" The stenographer rose.

"What about the wedding plans?" asked Linda, looking imperiously toward Miss Garza.

The stenographer sat down again, hand poised once more over her notebook.

"I want the ceremony in the chapel," said Linda, "the president officiating, and I don't want *her* there." She stared hard at Sarah.

Sarah beamed at her and responded, "You've made me very happy, young lady. I'll send you a wedding present and leave town on the day you're married." She noticed Elena and asked, "Are the police overseeing this wedding? A sort of official shotgun affair?"

Elena grinned. "No, Leo and I were here to find out if Gus wanted to press charges against the women who shot him."

"If he does, let me know. I'll contribute to their defense fund." Then Sarah turned to Dr. Stanley. "The finals schedule—see that it's changed or I'll hack into the system and do it myself."

"Once the prenuptial agreement is typed, all present except the principals can sign as witnesses," said the lawyer. "Miss Garza, why aren't you typing?"

"I'd be delighted to act as a witness," Sarah agreed jauntily.

"I don't want her name on my prenup." Linda was looking sulky.

"Your wish is my command," Sarah agreed promptly. "I'm leaving."

"I thought you were still in love with him," said Linda. "Why aren't you?"

"That's for me to know and you to find out," Sarah murmured as she swept out of the room.

"Am I supposed to be typing up the contract or taking notes on the wedding?" asked Miss Garza.

41
..

Wednesday, April 16, 3:30 P.M.

"I think the great poet-lover has met his match," said Elena as she and Leo left the Administration building. They found Sandoval and Mosconi drinking coffee at the table facing the quadrangle where they had met before. "We're tapped out," Elena told them. "McGlenlevie's fiancé won't let him prosecute."

"Man, I wouldn't want three trigger-happy coeds running loose, gunning for me," said Harry.

"Although you can't blame them too much," Jaime added. "I mean, he did get them pregnant."

"Anything from your interviews?" Elena asked. She and Leo were sitting on a salmon and turquoise brocade sofa, Elena's leg resting atop a satin turquoise pillow on the coffee table.

"Not one girl knew Fullerton was HIV positive to hear them tell it," said Mosconi. "No fingerprints but his in his john. This case is going nowhere."

Elena's pager beeped, and she fished it out of her shoulder bag, wincing at the necessary arm movement. "Headquarters," she muttered and asked Leo to pass her the telephone on the end table beside him.

"You get the hot motorcycle dates," he complained, "and I gotta fetch and carry when you're injured."

Elena laughed. "You don't even have to get up, Leo," she retorted as she took the salmon-colored telephone from him and tapped in the numbers on her pager screen. "Who knows. Maybe this is the lead we've been looking for." She identified herself and listened to the police lie-detector expert, who said Evelyn Dietz's polygraph result showed that she had been telling the truth when she said she hadn't tampered with AIDS medication, but lying when she said she had never been in the medication room.

"Well, another suspect just bit the dust," Elena announced, hanging up. "The charming Evelyn Dietz didn't kill our victim. Or else she's a pathological liar and fooled the machine."

"So we've got nothing," said Leo.

"Which means we've gotta talk to every damn student in this dorm in case anyone knows anything." Mosconi scowled.

Elena was thinking, *So who took that shot at me? And who threw tacks in the road last night?* The questions made her realize that with Quarles dead, she really had believed her assailant was someone egged on by the Reverend Hardin in order to protect Evelyn Dietz. And he could still be behind the attacks, she supposed, just not on Evelyn's behalf. She glanced around nervously. Could it have been a student? Perhaps lurking behind some Art Deco sofa, waiting for the opportunity to attack again? She shivered.

"Think you guys could send my share of the interviewees down here? The ice and the leg propping are definitely helping my knee," she said. "Walking around doesn't." And getting down to business would take her mind off her fears.

Elena had made a six-thirty date to meet Rafer in the lobby of the faculty apartment building when he paged her to find out how she was doing after last night's accident. At the time of the call, she was feeling a lot better, having taken two painkillers provided by the emergency room doctor. A half hour after ingesting the pills, however, she was falling asleep during her interviews. When the other detectives left at four, she considered begging off the date and going straight home to bed.

Two considerations convinced her not to: she'd make

Rafer feel guilty about the accident if she canceled, and if she was going to take a nap, she reasoned that she'd be safer here in the lobby of the student dorm than at home, where she had already been attacked. Maybe she'd even stay at Rafer's tonight. No one had yet attacked her on campus.

Accordingly, she said goodbye to her colleagues, asked the lobby clerk to awaken her at 6:20, leaned her head back against the soft cushions of the Art Deco sofa, and fell into a deep sleep, leg still elevated, knee still iced.

She was awakened at 6:35, fifteen minutes late, with a wet spot on her slacks where the ice bag had been and a knee that was stiff but pain-free and hardly swollen at all. Nothing like common-sense home remedies and pain pills, she told herself and decided to walk to the faculty apartments. Dusk was falling when she limped down the steps in front of the dorm, clinging to the railings. Stairs were harder than flat, carpeted lobbies.

Still, she had the cane the hospital had given her, and she could take the shortcut through a corridor of bushes that, in less than a month, would be covered with flowers. Right now they cast sparse, wavering shadows on the path as she headed toward the faculty apartments, watching the ground and setting her feet and cane carefully to avoid a fall. Maybe this hadn't been such a great idea. For one thing, dusk among the bushes was sort of creepy. *Come on,* she told herself. *Get a grip. So someone shot at you. They missed. And you were in a little motorcycle accident. You survived.*

Now she was glancing nervously from the ground to the walls of shrubbery, keeping a lookout. What she didn't need was another bout of post-traumatic stress—or a fall. She was still keeping her eyes open when a woman in a tatty raincoat stepped out from between the bushes. Her face was obscured by sunglasses and a head scarf pulled forward.

Sunglasses in the evening? Elena almost laughed because the woman looked like a badly costumed actress playing the part of a female spy. The laugh, however, never got past her lips because she saw the gun coming out of the woman's raincoat pocket and threw herself to the side, lashing out with the cane. They both went down as a shot rang out.

Elena's knee hurt enough to make her think the bullet might
have connected. A short wrestling match ensued for possession of the gun, and it discharged a second time. Elena's
assailant quivered beneath her.

"You shot me!" she exclaimed in a weak voice.

"Wasn't that what you had in mind for me?" Elena, who
now had the gun, tossed it into the shrubbery and rolled the
woman over on her face. Kneeling on her assailant, knee
aching furiously, she grabbed handcuffs from her shoulder
bag, and cuffed the woman. "What the hell are you shooting
at me for?" Elena demanded.

"Because you're a bitch and a whore," the woman
snarled.

The graffiti on Elena's house came to mind, and she rolled
her prisoner over roughly, bringing groans and sobs. The
silly sunglasses were askew, and Elena plucked them off.
Then, her aching knee on the woman's midriff, she fished
in her bag for a flashlight and shone it into the face of her
attacker to be sure she wasn't wrong about the identity.

"Helen? Helen Martin?"

Helen tried to bite her hand as Elena pulled the scarf away.
"Quit that. I thought you'd left town."

"And that excuses your stealing my husband?"

"Damn it, Helen, I never went out with Rafer until the
divorce was final, and I sure wasn't the cause of your divorce." She stopped talking and listened for a minute.
"Shit," she muttered, for she heard Rafer's voice calling
her, Rafer and others. Campus cops probably, in response to
the two gunshots, although she wasn't sure members of the
campus police force would recognize a gunshot if they heard
one.

Then Rafer was kneeling beside them on the path. "Helen?" he asked incredulously. "What happened?"

"She shot me," said Helen.

"Correction," retorted Elena angrily. "You got shot trying to kill me, and I suppose when we do ballistics on your
gun, they'll match the bullets fired at my house."

"She's lying. I was never at her house. And now she's
letting me bleed to death."

Elena glanced up at a lavender uniform coming along the path. "Get an ambulance and a police unit," she instructed.

"Why police?" Rafer asked.

"Because she tried to kill me, Rafer," said Elena with what little patience she could muster. "If she's the one who put the tacks on the road last night, she could have killed you too."

"I'd never kill Rafer," protested Helen. "He was protected by his leathers."

"Not if he fell off the mountain," snapped Elena. "Anyway, you're going to jail for assault on a police officer."

"You can't arrest my—my ex-wife."

"See," Helen crowed triumphantly. "Now that he has to choose, he chooses me."

"I don't care who the hell he chooses," Elena retorted. "You're going to jail as soon as they patch you up."

"Couldn't she just—just go into treatment?" asked Rafer. "Have a heart, Elena. She's stressed out because of the divorce. And she always hated it here."

The sound of approaching sirens was making conversation more and more difficult. Besides that, Elena had started to shake. Delayed reaction, and she hated it. It made her twice as mad. And her knee hurt so much she had to grab Rafer's arm to pull herself up. He tried to evade her hand.

"You don't get to shoot a cop because you don't like where you're living, Rafer," she said through gritted teeth. What the hell was he up to, anyway? He'd never had anything good to say about Helen, which was understandable. Elena rarely met anyone as offensive as Rafer Martin's ex, although Elena's circle of acquaintance included some very nasty criminals.

She noted with relief that the real cops had arrived, reassuring blue uniforms instead of silly lavender ones. "Hi, Vince." Elena nodded to Sergeant Vincent de la Rosa of the Westside Command, relieved to see someone who could understand that cops didn't like to be attacked. "Since this woman took a shot at me, maybe you could get another C.A.P. detective to investigate. It'll probably turn out this is the second or third time she's tried to kill me, and we've got bullets from the first time. Also they need to check her house for tacks."

"What did you do to her?" de la Rosa asked.

"Don't start with me."

"So it was just a random shooting? Or two random shootings?" He grinned.

"I dated her ex." Elena scowled at Rafer. "That's him."

"Officer," said Rafer stiffly, "I'd like to be allowed to ride in the ambulance with my—with Helen."

De la Rosa squatted beside Helen Martin as the medics came down the path with their equipment. "You'll live," he said after a brief inspection of her upper arm. "As for you, sir." He rose and faced Rafer. "We take trying to shoot a police officer very seriously. This woman will be transported to a hospital in the company of my men, not you."

"But she said Elena tried to shoot *her*," Rafer protested.

"And you believe her?" Elena was incensed. "The gun's in that bush, Vince."

The sergeant sent a patrolman to fish it out. Then they all stared at it. "No cop would be caught dead with a weapon like that," said Vincent de la Rosa. "Where'd you get that, ma'am? In a Cracker Jack box?"

"It can shoot a bullet through a window," snapped Helen, "and I'll thank you to show me a little respect. My family—"

"What window?" asked Rafer. "What window, Helen?"

"My window," Elena told him. "I hope someone's taking notes on what the suspect just said."

"Oh, my God," gaped Rafer. "I thought you said that just a pot was—"

"Well, you know I love you," said Helen defensively. "How could you look at another woman? Especially one like her. Some Hispanic—"

The police and the medics, even the campus cop in his lavender uniform, scowled at her, and she shut up.

Elena told the sergeant that she'd go to headquarters later in the evening, or better yet the next day, to give a statement.

"But what about Helen?" Rafer asked.

She ignored him. "Arrest her," Elena said to De la Rosa. "I'm—ah—going to visit a friend."

"You O.K.?" asked the sergeant. Elena shrugged and limped toward the faculty apartment house. She was going to see Sam Parsley, her therapist and buddy, the person she had come to think of first when she felt shaky.

In front of the doors to the lobby were L.S.A.R.I. pickets carrying signs decrying the immorality of faculty and students at H.H.U. Making her way through the demonstrators, Elena came upon Jerry Joe, who shouted into her face, "Cease your sinful ways. You should be a leader of youth, not a corrupter."

"I'm a cop, not a professor," she barked. "So get out of my face." She planted her cane on his toe.

Jerry Joe stumbled back, with a frightened expression. *I must look half crazy and dangerous to boot,* Elena thought as she entered the lobby and pressed the elevator button. Within minutes, she was being admitted to Sam's apartment, where she made a fool of herself by crying on his shoulder.

"I'm tired of being shot at and bombed and jumped by mountain lions and—"

Sam interrupted calmly with a suggestion. "Maybe you should ask for a desk job, Elena. If you make sergeant, you'll—"

"A desk job?" Elena wiped her eyes while she considered that prospect. "It sounds awful."

"But much less stressful," he pointed out.

"But boring," she complained.

"Then maybe you need to decide what it is you want."

Anyone else who said that to her would have sounded sarcastic; Sam Parsley sounded friendly and supportive. Elena put her head back on his shoulder, feeling thoroughly miserable, even in the comforting circle of his arms.

The man was actually muscular, she noted with surprise. She had always thought of him as a big, soft cuddly-bear type. On the heels of this revelation came another, greater surprise when Sam tipped her head up and kissed her.

Because she was so astounded, although not in an unpleasant way, Elena didn't even close her eyes.

Sam grinned at her and murmured, "Not very professional, I'm afraid, but that's the way it goes. Want something to eat?"

She wouldn't have minded another kiss, but on the other hand, she *was* hungry. "What have you got?" she asked.

"Barbecue and coleslaw. I ordered in a lot."

"I'll bet," said Elena. Sam Parsley ate more than any man Elena had ever known, and he did it constantly, not only at regular mealtimes, but during therapy, while he was teaching classes and advising students, driving, walking. She wouldn't be surprised to hear he ate in his sleep, not that she'd be sleeping with him in order to find out.

Then as he dished up barbecue and coleslaw onto paper plates, Elena glanced at him speculatively. She'd never thought of sleeping with Sam. He was her friend. But he *was* a good kisser.

Somehow she didn't feel as hurt as she might have by Rafer's defection, even if she had given him a whole week of attention. What was a week, after all? She'd known Sam lots longer.

42

Thursday, April 17, 8:35 A.M.

Elena was in a ladies' room at headquarters with her slacks rolled up so that she could refasten the clip on the Ace bandage wrapped around her knee. She had just returned from a very mean-spirited and pleasurable interrogation of Helen Martin at the jail. Helen was still maintaining that Elena had attacked her the evening before at H.H.U. The nerve of the woman!

Rafer's ex also insisted that she'd never admitted to shooting a gun through Elena's window and destroying a valuable pueblo pot, much less spray-painting *whore* on the walls or scattering tacks on Scenic Drive in front of Rafer's motorcycle. She even claimed that pathetic little midnight special belonged to Elena and that Elena had attacked her with a cane before jumping on top of her and shooting her with the gun.

The whole thing made Elena so mad she could have spit. Especially since Rafer had hired a lawyer, who was saying that Helen was either innocent or insane. Well, he had that half right; Helen was crazy—crazy mean! Even so, the department wasn't going to let her get away with stalking a police detective. The C.A.P. guys who had taken Elena's statement assured her that they and the A.D.A. on the case planned to put Helen away for a lot of years. Unfortunately, that meant that she'd be out on parole before the cactus scars had disappeared from Elena's arm.

"Hey, Jarvis." A detective from the other C.A.P. squad stuck his head around the door to the ladies' john. "You got a long-distance call." He eyed her knee and the two inches of thigh exposed above it. "Need any help there?"

"Need to have your nose broken?" she retorted, waving her cane.

"Touchy females," he said, grinning, and withdrew to safety.

Elena rolled down her slacks and limped back to her desk.

"Reckon you folks must work bankers' hours down there on the border," said a voice, as yet unidentified, on her telephone.

"I've been on the job since seven, not that it's any of your business," she retorted. "Who is this?"

"Your Albuquerque connection. We got those phone numbers for you."

Elena dropped into her blue-gray tweed chair and propped her leg up on an open desk drawer. The Amy Marquis angle. "Barton Marquis made calls to Los Santos?"

"Sure did. All the same exchange, but four different numbers. No calls after your victim died. Wanna take down the numbers?"

Now they'd get somewhere with the Fullerton murder, she thought with elation. Three lesser cases closed or at least solved, McGlenlevie, Quarles, and Helen Martin, stalker, but the important one had been hanging fire. Elena grabbed a note pad and a pen from a chile mug on her desk. "O.K.," she said and took down the four numbers, reading them back to Quintela to be sure she had them right. "How come it took you so long?"

"Marquis's got a lot of pull in this town. Had to find the right judge. Maybe you didn't need the numbers. Got your case solved? You coulda called me."

"No, no, Quintela. I'm much obliged for the information, and I'll let you know how it turns out."

"No skin off my nose either way," he replied.

"O.K. Well, if you're ever in Los Santos—"

"Not if I can help it."

This was a hard man to thank. ''—we'll buy you a beer, or help you run down a suspect. Whatever.''

"I'll keep that in mind. More likely I'd need your connections up in the Sangre de Cristo. We get maggots who try to hide out up there.''

"So I'll call my father for you.'' Proper appreciation expressed, she now wanted to get off the phone so she could find Leo.

The Fullerton task force reassembled that morning in Sergeant Manny Escobedo's office—Leo, disgruntled because, having been scheduled to work the weekend, he was supposed to have Thursday off; Elena, who hadn't appreciated his unenthusiastic response to the news from Albuquerque; Jaime Sandoval, who reported that the testing of the medication from Dr. Conway's office and drugstores around town had been completed with no more poisoned capsules, AZT or otherwise, turning up; and Harry Mosconi, who had dropped in on the lie-detector technician who administered Evelyn Dietz's test.

"He said there was no question she was telling the truth about not poisoning medication, but just as clearly she lied about never being in the drug room. When I confronted her with the test results this morning at the doctor's office, it turns out she's got herself a little tranquilizer and painkiller habit left over from an automobile accident, and she's been helping herself to samples left by drug salesmen.

"Of course I told the doc, and he fired her. Then she shouted in front of a waiting room full of patients that she hated being around sinners and sodomites, anyway. That went over real good with the gays. Anyway, she seems to be clear in the Fullerton murder, just like we figured yesterday.''

"So we're looking at someone from the university,'' Manny concluded. "Probably someone he infected.''

"I've got a call in. They're supposed to let me know who these numbers belong to,'' said Elena, waving the notes she'd taken from Quintela.

"What numbers?'' asked Mosconi, who had arrived late.

"The ones Amy Marquis's brother called. Amy, who's pregnant and probably dying of AIDS after a date with our victim, told us her brother had warned other girls she knew who'd been out with Fullerton. A girl who'd been warned that he was HIV positive and who'd slept with him would have a good motive to kill him."

"Especially if *she's* HIV positive, too," Jaime agreed. "Too bad Dr. Marx won't cooperate. She probably knows who's infected."

"Not necessarily," Elena pointed out. "She didn't know about Fullerton because he was diagnosed in Chicago and treated across town. The girlfriends wouldn't necessarily go to the university clinic either."

Manny's telephone rang. He spoke briefly, then passed it to Elena. Nodding, she wrote down four names, then hung up and read them aloud: "Cathy Zimmer, Minette LaFaure, Genevieve Hessick, and Barbara Chalmers."

The four detectives flipped through their casebooks, reading from notes on the four young women. Not surprisingly, all four coeds had denied being in Fullerton's room during the month before his death or knowing that he was contagious.

"Chalmers wept all over me," said Elena. "Pretended she thought he'd killed himself because he had a brain tumor and that she hadn't been sexy enough to get screwed twice by the great lover. I actually felt sorry for her."

"Well, don't beat yourself up over it," Mosconi advised. "Women are devious."

"My sister Rosa isn't," Sandoval objected. "Did she strike you as devious?"

"No, man," said Mosconi. "Your sister's a doll, but when I asked her out a second time she said no."

"That's 'cause the Ladies' Altar-Cloth Society was meeting," said Sandoval. "She likes you, Harry."

"Yeah? Did she—"

"Fellas," Manny interrupted. "We got a case here."

Elena had been thinking about Barbara Chalmers. "She had to have known Fullerton was infected. Marquis called her, so she knew, and that whole bit about 'Was he sick?

Did he have a brain tumor? Boo-hoo'—that was so much crap."

"I still can't get used to women cursing. I guess because my mom never let my sisters," said Sandoval.

"I noticed that about Rosa, very ladylike," Mosconi agreed. "Did she say she wanted to go out with me again?"

"All four of them must have been friends of Amy's," Elena reasoned, ignoring Sandoval's implied criticism of her language. "So not only are they scared for themselves, but they knew after Christmas that Amy was pregnant and dying because of Fullerton."

"You remember that note we found in his room? From the Ménage à Trois Sisters?" Leo asked. "Didn't Mayhew and Carswell, his roommates, say he'd had two girls with him the Saturday night before he died?"

"Right," said Elena, studying her notes again. "That would have been a good time to fix his meds. One girl keeps him busy while the other one packs cyanide into his capsules."

"So you need handwriting samples from the four suspects to compare to the note," said Manny. "Will the university cooperate?"

"Can I use your phone?" Elena asked. With his permission, she called Chief Clabb and told him they were closing in on the poisoners.

"Not a student, I hope," he said anxiously.

" 'Fraid so. What I want you to do is fax me something with the signatures of these four girls."

"Rosa said you were a real gentleman," Sandoval told Mosconi in an undertone.

Chief Clabb asked, "Where would I get—"

"Don't they have to apply to you for parking permits?" Elena interrupted.

"Yes, but Dr. Stanley—"

"—will want this case closed as quickly and quietly as possible. Look at all the newspaper coverage. We need to end it. We'll find the killers, arrest them, and that will shut down all the bad press."

"Yeah, Jaime, but did she say she wants to go out with

me again?'' Mosconi persisted. ''Maybe she meant I was boring when she said I was a real gentleman.''

''Sure she wants to date you again,'' Jaime said reassuringly.

''For Pete's sake, you two, you sound like a couple of high-school kids,'' murmured Elena, hand over the mouthpiece.

Chief Clabb sighed in Elena's ear. ''I suppose you're right about putting an end to the newspaper stories. Shall I fax the application forms?''

''Please.'' Elena gave him the four names and the fax number of the handwriting expert downstairs.

''I'll give her a call tonight,'' said Mosconi.

''It's a long shot,'' Elena told Manny. ''The note looked like someone trying to disguise their writing.''

''That doesn't always work,'' said Leo. ''Let's each take one of the girls. Then they won't get a chance to synchronize their stories.''

''If they haven't already,'' said Elena grimly. ''I'll take Barbara.''

''Rosa will be real glad to hear from you, Harry,'' Sandoval assured his partner.

''Could you guys stop arranging your social calendars,'' said Manny. ''And Jarvis, no roughing the girl up. Just because she lied to you—''

''Everyone lies to me,'' snapped Elena. ''What really gripes me is that I put my arm around her. I felt sorry for her, and it was all a con.''

''If she's got AIDS,'' said Jaime somberly, ''she had reason to cry, even if she fooled you about what the tears were for.''

43

Thursday, April 17, 10:15 A.M.

"Yes, Amy's brother called me," said Barbara Chalmers, showing no sign of alarm when Leo and Elena confronted her with the question outside a classroom in the Humanities building.

"And he said?" Elena prodded.

"He told me that Amy was pregnant, and I should watch out for Fullerton if I was still dating him." Chalmers looked embarrassed. "Not that it mattered. Graham wasn't interested in seeing me again."

"How did you feel about his having got Amy pregnant?" Leo asked.

Chalmers shrugged. "If it were me, I'd have an abortion, but poor Amy's the sentimental type. According to her brother, she wants the baby."

"So you knew Amy pretty well?" Elena asked.

"She was a friend of mine."

"What else did her brother tell you?"

Chalmers looked confused. "Nothing that I remember."

"He didn't tell you that Fullerton was HIV positive?"

"No, he didn't. I only heard that recently."

"What about you? Have you been tested?"

Chalmers shrugged again. "I guess I'll go in next week." She thought a moment. "You're not saying Amy—" She looked alarmed. "You don't mean—"

Elena would have believed her if she hadn't proved such

a convincing actress and liar during the previous interview. Since Amy's infection was Amy's business, Elena diverted Barbara Chalmers by asking, "What's your major, by the way?"

Chalmers smiled. "Theater arts," she replied.

Leo and Elena exchanged glances. Then they went in search of Minette LaFaure after Elena had read her notes on the young woman.

"You told us you stopped going out with Fullerton when you found out he was dating other girls," Elena said to her once they caught up with LaFaure in the Student Union.

"That's right."

"That would have been about the time Amy Marquis's brother called you."

"Right. Did you know the bastard got her pregnant? Poor Amy was such an innocent. Graham was probably so excited about seducing a virgin, he forgot to use protection. And she's too soft-hearted to get rid of the baby. Her brother told me she thinks she's in love with Fullerton." LaFaure seemed perfectly at ease talking about the call from Marquis as she sipped a cup of something piled with whipped cream and sprinkled with cinnamon.

"Did you call her to tell her Fullerton is dead?" Leo asked, fishing.

"Why do that? She'd just be upset. It's not like she was holding out any hope Graham was going to marry her. Amy's not *that* naive."

"But she was a friend of yours?"

"Sure. Everyone loved Amy. She was really popular among the girls on our floor. No bitchy qualities, you know?"

Elena nodded. Amy Marquis had certainly exhibited no *bitchy qualities*. "So when her brother told you Fullerton was HIV positive, you dumped him and got tested?"

"What?"

"When her brother told you—"

"Amy's brother didn't say anything about Graham being infected. Is that why you were fishing around when you talked to me before? I told you then I was clean, so you don't have to worry."

"I know what you told me, but—"

"And if you want to pay for another test, I can prove it. What's this about, anyway?"

"It's about what Barton Marquis told you," said Leo.

"He told me Amy was pregnant. Period."

And that was all they got from Minette LaFaure, who said her major was French history and literature (not something that would give her expertise in poisons and lying) and that socially she was "playing the field." She also said that she had never been in Graham Fullerton's bathroom and would be happy to take a polygraph on the subject if her lawyer agreed. Did they really think she'd poisoned him?

At lunch the detectives compared notes over *tacos al carbon* with guacamole and *pico de gallo*. Sandoval and Mosconi had interviewed Genevieve Hessick and Cathy Zimmer, both of whom told the same story. Barton Marquis had called to tell them about Amy's pregnancy. Cathy was thinking of flying a group of Amy's friends up to Albuquerque for a baby shower.

If they really didn't know that Amy had AIDS, they were in for a real shock, Elena remarked when Jaime mentioned the proposed shower.

"She's real sick?" asked Mosconi, spooning spicy green sauce onto his taco.

"She looks like walking death," Elena replied.

"What happens to the baby?"

"They're medicating the mother, and they'll continue to do so right through delivery," Elena replied. "Then maybe the baby won't turn up positive. Or maybe it will. They won't even know for a couple of months, by which time Amy might well be dead and her brother stuck with bringing up the kid."

"That's really sad," said Leo, probably thinking of his own babies. "That's awful."

"Yeah," Elena agreed.

"Hessick's a chemistry major, so she could have got the cyanide," said Mosconi, "but the professor she's taking

chemistry from this semester says there's no way they could
tell if a little potassium cyanide is missing from the store-
room. The chairman says the same thing.''

"And Zimmer's a diabetic," Sandoval offered. "If the
capsules had been injected with poison, she could have provided the syringes.''

"But they weren't injected," said Elena. "Neither of your
interviews admitted to being told by Marquis that Fullerton
was HIV positive?''

"Nope. Just that his sister was pregnant.''

"I don't believe it," said Elena. She laid a half-eaten taco
on her plate. "Why would he call to tell them that, which
wasn't any of their business, when Fullerton's infection was
the thing that would be important to them. And Amy said
he'd warned them. Add to that, they're all telling the same
story. Isn't *that* convenient?''

"Aren't you going to eat the rest of that taco?'' Leo asked.

"Yes, Leo, I am.'' Elena took another bite to prove it.
"Let's get a warrant to look at their phone records,'' she
suggested. "Maybe when he found out that his own records
had been subpoenaed, Marquis called again to warn them.
Maybe Marquis made the next round of calls from some
other phone. We want to see if any of those four coeds got
calls from Albuquerque yesterday or today.''

"I'll go after the warrant,'' Sandoval offered. "Talking to
all these girls is depressing.''

"Why? What did they say about being infected themselves?'' Leo asked.

"Oh, they denied it,'' Mosconi replied. "But who knows
whether they're telling the truth.''

"You know, everyone seems to have liked Amy,'' said
Elena. "This could be some campus-wide conspiracy to
avenge her.''

"Don't say that,'' Leo groaned.

"Well, we need to catch one or all of these four in a lie,''
said Elena, "so let's start asking around about whether anyone saw any of them going into Fullerton's rooms in the two
weeks before his death, and about people who were Amy's
friends. Particularly, let's ask the girls who admitted being

in Fullerton's john during the target period whether they're friends of Amy.''

"You're pretty smart for a newcomer, Sandoval," said Leo. "I wish I'd offered to go get the warrant."

They all reached into the straw basket for *sopaipillas* and doused them with wild honey to fortify themselves for the afternoon ahead.

44
..

Thursday, April 17, 1:00 P.M.

The detectives started on the floor where Amy Marquis had lived before she left school, exchanging information as they passed in the hall. Sandoval, who partnered with Harry, accumulated more because he seemed to have a special rapport with the young women, who thought he was cute. Elena and Leo got some interesting hits, too. Jennifer Newton said, "I heard there's an actual organization called Friends of Amy. I don't know why I wasn't asked to join. I was a friend of Amy's."

"And what do the Friends of Amy do?" asked Elena with interest.

"How would I know? I don't belong," said the resentful Jennifer. "Big secret-society stuff—that's what I think. I heard she's pregnant. Maybe they're going to get together and support the baby, although I don't know why they'd do that. Amy's family has money. 'Course maybe they threw Amy out. If I got pregnant, my mother'd probably throw me out. She thinks I'm a virgin, you know."

"You told us," said Elena.

Jaime and Sandoval were picking up rumors about a group called the Friends of Amy too, but they had yet to find anyone who was actually a member or knew what the object of the group was, how many members there were, or who belonged.

Bitty Cinderhalt told Leo and Elena that Cathy Zimmer

had been organizing a baby shower for Amy. Everyone was
going to fly up to Albuquerque for the shower, then continue
on for "a tour of all these cute little mission churches in the
mountains between Santa Fe and Taos."

Elena scowled because her family lived near one of those
cute little mission churches, where the tourists and pilgrims
who arrived to sightsee or seek miracles were often a pain.

"So when's the shower going to be?" she asked, wondering if anyone had told poor Amy about this good-hearted
plan to welcome her baby to the world and study mission
churches in one, worthwhile trip.

"Well, actually it's probably not going to come off at all.
Cathy wanted the shower to be a surprise, so she called
Amy's brother. He's a big real-estate mogul in Albuquerque.
Of course, how big could you be in a little place like Al-
buquerque?"

Again Elena scowled at her. "In northern New Mexico,"
she said, "Albuquerque is thought of as the big city."

"Well, it's no New York or San Francisco," Bitty retorted.

"So Cathy called Amy's brother. Then what happened?"
Leo prodded.

"He threatened to get his lawyers on her," Elena suggested, remembering how uncooperative Barton Marquis had
been when she and Sandoval visited his office with Detective
Quintela.

Leo glared and kicked her ankle, which happened to be
the ankle below her bad knee. "Yeow!" Elena doubled over
and rubbed the bruise.

"*What*?" said Bitty. "Are you sick or something?"

"Just tell us about the phone call," Elena gasped.

"Oh. Well, Amy's brother said, no shower; it would be
too embarrassing for the family. I mean, that's pretty mean,
don't you think? Just 'cause she's not married doesn't mean
she doesn't deserve a shower. Cathy said they ought to go
right ahead and plan it, but Barbara and Minette said if the
family didn't want one, forget it."

"Did they?" Now that was interesting, thought Elena.
Barbara and Minette wanted to distance themselves from the

Marquises. Maybe when Cathy called Barton Marquis, he'd told her that his telephone records had been subpoenaed. Maybe that's how the four girls got together on their stories.

She suggested this to Leo once they got out in the hall, but he said, "It's all speculation."

When they had finished the floor, the detectives huddled in the social area at the end of the hall, Elena muttering that she now needed ice for her ankle, Leo ignoring her.

"Lotta people have the idea there's something called the Friends of Amy, but some just say, "We're all friends of Amy," offered Mosconi. "Minette LaFaure said that."

"She would," said Elena. "Cathy Zimmer said that."

"So did Genevieve Hessick," said Mosconi.

"What about Chalmers?" asked Leo. "Who talked to her?"

"She wasn't in her room," Jaime admitted.

"Good grief, I hope she hasn't skipped town." Elena was still rubbing her ankle. "The kind of money these kids have, she could be in Hong Kong or Brazil by now."

Jamie shook his head. "Her roommate, who has this awful frizzy hair, said Chalmers is out playing golf."

Elena nodded. Chalmers had been out playing golf before their first interview—a con job by a theater-arts major. The memory of it still rankled.

"Gretchen Farber said, 'I'm not going to press charges. For Pete's sake, Quarles is dead,' " Mosconi volunteered. "She thought we were back about the rape."

"I wish she'd get counseling," murmured Elena. "Did Farber know of any friends of Amy?"

"She said she was one."

"A member of an organized group?"

"No, just a friend. She showed me a Christmas card she'd got from Amy, about the least cheery Christmas card I ever saw in my life."

They then proceeded to Graham Fullerton's floor to repeat their questions about who might have been seen coming in or out of Fullerton's room. "Be sure to ask about the Saturday night before he died," Elena reminded her colleagues.

"Playing sergeant again?" Leo asked sarcastically.

"Leo, you're getting to be a real pain," she retorted. "Do I have to talk the university into providing nighttime baby-sitting so you can get some sleep and get off my back?"

"No squabbling, children," said Mosconi. "We've got a case to solve," and they went about their business, tracking down students in their rooms and then all over campus. The four detectives finally split up to follow the last of the male students on that floor. Elena caught up with a kid named Norman Massengale V. He had a plume of bright red hair and was shooting pool in the Student Union, evidently for high stakes because he didn't want to interrupt his game to talk to her.

Her knee was aching again, and she wasn't about to take any guff from another snot-nosed H.H.U. millionaire's kid. "Gambling's against the law. I can bust you and take you down to headquarters. Maybe you'd rather talk to me there."

The kid slammed the butt of his pool cue down on the floor and said, "All right, but if you ruin my game, I'll—"

"You'll what?" she snarled right back and slammed the tip of her cane beside the butt of his pool cue.

"I'll nothing," he mumbled. "I thought you cops were supposed to give special consideration to the rich."

"Only the cooperative rich," Elena retorted. "Now, I want to talk to you about anyone you may have seen going in or out of Graham Fullerton's rooms in the two weeks before he died."

"Some Hispanic guy or Italian guy already asked me that."

"Right, and you said you didn't remember."

"Right, so why are you asking me again?"

"I'm going to show you a list of names. I want you to look at them all and tell me if you recognize any of them, and I don't mean because you've been out with them or you've slept with them. I mean because you saw them with Fullerton. Particularly near his room. Or in his room."

"I didn't hang out in Fullerton's room. Who needs that kind of competition?"

Elena could understand that. Norman V was not the handsomest kid she'd ever seen. "So look at the list." She shoved it under his nose.

Sulkily, he plopped onto a sofa, swinging his legs up so that she couldn't sit down herself except on the far arm; then he studied the list. "No . . . no . . . no . . . um, no . . . yes, but I think that was last fall . . . no . . . no . . . hey, maybe." He put his thumb on one name.

"Who?" asked Elena.

"Minette."

Her heart gave a little skip as Massengale's eyes continued to slide down the page. "Oh yeah, Chalmers."

"What about Chalmers?" asked Elena. She had to restrain herself from jumping up and dragging him off the sofa so that she could question him nose to nose.

"I remember now. Minette and Barbara. The three of them went into his room one night. Yeah. I thought, 'Lucky bastard. Gets two girls in the same night when I'm doing good to have one.' "

"What time did they go in?"

"I don't know. After midnight."

"Were his roommates there?"

Massengale scratched his head, displacing some of the red hair. "Beats me."

"What night was it?"

"I don't know. For Pete's sake, until I saw the list, I didn't remember anything."

"Well, think about it. What were you doing when you saw them? Was it a school night? Were you coming back from the library?"

"You gotta be kidding. I don't go to the library."

"O.K. Were you coming back from a date? Where had you been? You were obviously outside your room. Were you coming out of your room or going in?"

"Going in," he said. "I had my key in the lock when I saw them."

"Uh-huh. Where had you been?"

"To—ah—I remember now. I'd been to a strip joint in Juarez with some of the guys."

"O.K., so what night was it?"

"It was the night that lawyer got shot at a stoplight on Juarez Avenue."

Elena thought back. She knew what he was talking about. Part of the drug wars after the local kingpin got iced during plastic surgery. "So was it a Saturday night?"

"Could have been. Could have been Friday night. I don't know. I remember the strippers, though. Chunky. I mean you expect big tits on a stripper, but these girls were just— chunky. Peasant types. It was really weird."

Elena didn't care about his opinion of Juarez strippers. "Listen, you have to think about this. Ask the guys you went with if they remember what night it was. Better yet, give me their names."

"They're not going to thank me for getting them mixed up with the cops."

"You want an obstruction-of-justice charge?"

"So O.K." He gave her three names. All of them lived on a different floor, so they wouldn't have seen Chalmers and LaFaure going into Fullerton's room, but they might remember what night they had gone to the strip clubs with Massengale. Most important, she was getting somewhere, because both Minette LaFaure and Barbara Chalmers had denied being in Fullerton's room before his death. Chalmers said she'd never been there.

"Can I get back to my pool game?" Massengale asked.

"Sure, sure. Go." She thought a minute, then headed for the telephone and called the *Times*. "Hey, Resendez," she said when she got her party, "you want to get back in my good graces?"

"I don't know," Paul answered. "Obviously you want something from me."

"Obviously I do. You remember when that car pulled up beside that Juarez lawyer at a stoplight and someone shot him through the window?"

"Yeah, I remember."

"I need to know the date."

"Hang on." He put her on hold, and she lifted her leg to rest it on a coffee table while she waited. It wasn't bad enough she'd hurt her knee and thigh in a motorcycle accident; she now had a bruise from being kicked by her own partner.

"O.K., Jarvis, don't say I never did anything for you," said Resendez, and he gave her the date of the attack.

"Bingo." It was just what she'd been hoping, the Saturday before Fullerton's death.

"So am I square with you?" Resendez asked.

"With me, yeah. With Sandoval, who knows?" She hung up, paged the other detectives, and told them to meet her at the Student Union ASAP.

45

Thursday, April 17, 4:05 P.M.

Leo arrived first at the Student Union and slid into a booth across from Elena, a black and white marble table between them. "I ordered coffee for everyone," she said, pushing a cup toward him.

"Great. So what's the big hurry?"

"Let's wait till the others get here," she temporized, wanting to keep the delicious news to herself. She figured that Massengale's testimony should give them enough to arrest at least Chalmers and LaFaure for Fullerton's murder. Leo shrugged and put three teaspoons of sugar into his coffee before taking the first sip.

"What's with you?" Leo asked when he saw Jaime Sandoval striding toward them, a big grin on his face.

"Nothing much." Jaime slid into the booth beside Elena, trying to look casual as he took a sip of coffee. Then his grin widened. "Nothing except I got 'em."

Elena frowned at him. "What's that supposed to mean? *I* got them."

Leo, who had been sprawled out across the black leather seat of the booth, long legs extended into the aisle, said, "Maybe at least one of you'd like to tell me just what it is you've got. Elena's been sitting here looking like the cat that swallowed the canary and refusing to—"

"I just said we should wait till the others arrived," she protested.

"Yeah, well you still got feathers hanging out of your mouth, Miss Cat, an' now Sandoval looks like he's been eating birdies too."

Sandoval set his cup down carefully and pulled a sheet of pages from his pocket. "Got the phone records on the four girls," he said smugly.

"Move your legs, Weizell," said Mosconi, joining the group. He dropped onto the seat and pulled the last cup across the table. "Man, am I sick of this case."

"Well, you're in luck, Harry," said Sandoval, obviously elated, " 'cause all four girls got calls from Albuquerque the night Quintela got the warrant for Barton Marquis's phone records. If that isn't enough for an arrest warrant, I don't know what—"

"Wouldn't it help to put them at the scene of the crime?" asked Elena sweetly. "Motive's nice, but—"

"Can't have everything," said Sandoval jauntily.

"It's a good start," Mosconi agreed. "No matter what those girls say, we know Marquis told them Fullerton had AIDS—"

"Not AIDS," Elena objected. "HIV."

"Whatever. They knew he'd put them at risk. They knew Amy was sick because she'd been with him. Then they knew we knew, so they had to get together on a lie about what Barton Marquis told them. The D.A. can subpoena Marquis and bring him before a grand jury."   .

"Yeah, yeah, yeah." Elena grinned. "But I can put two of them, Chalmers and La Faure, at the scene of the crime." Leo, Sandoval, and Mosconi turned to stare at her. "I found a guy who saw them going into Fullerton's room with him."

"When?" Leo demanded.

"After midnight the Saturday before he died."

"The Ménage à Trois sisters?"

Elena grinned. "Stands to reason."

"I always liked them for the job, but we didn't know who they were," said Leo.

"Yes, we do," said Harry. "ID & R paged me about fifteen minutes ago. They're ninety-percent sure that cute little Minette wrote the note we found in Fullerton's suite."

"And they both said they hadn't been there, right?" said Sandoval.

"Right," said Elena. "Not lately anyway. Not at all for Chalmers, the great actress."

"You know"—Sandoval looked at his notebook—"I heard from four different people that there's a secret society called Friends of Amy. Big buzz 'cause no one knows what it's about."

"Except maybe the four girls Barton Marquis called," said Leo.

"That's the next thing we have to decide," said Elena thoughtfully. "We've got a good case for murder against the two who went into Fullerton's room. Less so for the other two, Hessick and the diabetic."

"Cathy Zimmer," Sandoval interjected helpfully.

"Right. So do we go for two arrest warrants or four?"

"Hessick's the chem major," said Leo. "They had to get the poison somewhere."

"How about murder one for the first two and conspiracy to commit for Hessick and Zimmer?" suggested Mosconi. "Can't hurt to try for warrants on all four, and who knows? You get four spoiled, rich college girls in jail, one of 'em's bound to break and roll over on the rest."

Elena nodded. "We play them off against each other."

"That is unless you got a date or something, Elena," said Sandoval, glancing at his watch. "Wouldn't want to screw up your social life with the biker."

"Physicist," Elena corrected, "and he's toast."

"No kidding." Sandoval looked pleased. "Listen, I got a cousin—"

"Forget it," said Elena brusquely. "Let's get those warrants."

It took two hours to secure the four warrants, and the judge, irritated at being delayed in chambers past his usual time of departure, was not easy to convince on the matter of Cathy Zimmer and Genevieve Hessick. "Your evidence is weak, Detectives," he told them. "I can't believe the District Attorney's office wants to risk having these two dropped at a preliminary hearing.''

He was wrong. The D.A. had agreed that arresting Zimmer and Hessick might give them a better chance to turn the conspirators against each other. In the end the Fullerton investigators got their warrants and arrived back at the student dorm just as dessert, coconut-mango mousse, was being served in the dining room. Mrs. Monserrat tried to have them ejected for ''uncouth conduct during the dinner hour.'' ''The espresso hasn't even been served yet,'' she protested. ''Nor should young ladies of good family, no matter what they may have done, be treated like common criminals.''

All four young women fell into stunned silence as they were handcuffed, read their rights, and put into two unmarked cars for the trip to the County Detention Facility. Once the shock wore off, but before leaving for the jail, Zimmer and Hessick began to weep. Elena nodded to Leo; those were the two they'd work on. For the trip downtown, Zimmer and Hessick were separated from LaFaure and Chalmers.

Minette, from the back seat of the car, launched into a stream of indignant protest, demands for a lawyer, and scathing comments on the intelligence of police officers who could come to the ridiculous conclusion that she would endanger her future by doing anything so foolish as to murder a creep like Graham Fullerton.

Only Barbara Chalmers showed no shock or dismay at the course of events. There was a certain defiant resignation about that one. *Another interesting dramatic performance?* Elena wondered.

The situation at the County Detention Facility, as the jail was called by those who cared to be formal and correct, was unfortunate. The holding cells were full, with only one reserved for females. Although Elena would have preferred to keep the four apart until they could be interrogated, a female deputy sheriff shrugged off the request and hustled the H.H.U. contingent all into the same enclosure. While male prisoners whistled and cat-called at the pretty, well-dressed young women, they held a hasty conference. After that, the booking deputies suffered a stream of complaints about everything from the "tacky" nature of the questions asked the prisoners to the quality of the pictures taken by the jail photographer. However, the prisoners refused to talk to the arresting detectives. They all demanded lawyers and bail but refused to answer any questions or even listen to anything the detectives tried to say.

Cathy Zimmer pretty much summed up their attitude when she said to Elena, "You're mean. Why should I talk to you?"

46
..

Friday, April 18, 8:15 A.M.

Elena and Leo parked in the police garage on Campbell across from Central Regional Command, a red, three-story building that had once been a fire station. The ramps and traffic bumps in the garage were so formidable that both detectives could remember Ford Escorts belonging to the department that couldn't get past the second floor without dying, their fuel pumps turned off by the mechanical mis-apprehension that the cars had been in an accident.

From the garage they walked to the underground entrance of the jail, where they stowed their guns in lockers before being admitted. Once inside they were immediately told that Sheriff's Deputy Ana Laura Sombrano, who ran the women's floor, wanted to see them. Elena and Leo glanced at one another apprehensively.

"You don't think one of them tried to commit suicide, do you?" Elena asked. The four coeds had been through book-ing late enough that any lawyers they hired, and Elena was sure that legal talent would have flocked to their banner, wouldn't have been able to get them out on bond, if bond was even possible. The charge was conspiracy to commit murder and murder, the evidence good but not great. The detectives still hoped to firm up the case after talking to the young women separately. Elena had thought the diabetic the most likely to break, the one who had called Elena mean. But what if the girl had gone into a coma? Maybe through some screw-up, she hadn't got her insulin and—

Before these speculations got out of hand, Deputy Sombrano stalked in wearing her crisp tan uniform and looking thunderous. "Have you any idea," she demanded, "what you wished on me when you brought those four kids in?"

Elena and Leo tried to look innocent.

"Of course you do," fumed the deputy, a stocky woman in her late thirties with skinned-back hair and a forceful jaw. "If they're not weeping, they're complaining. The food isn't fit for human consumption; the beds are hard and lumpy; the place smells bad; they can't be expected to use toilets that aren't enclosed; the clothes don't fit and aren't stylish; their daddies are going to hear about this. They've kept the whole floor in an uproar all night. So you damn well better talk to them; that's all I can say. If you don't, I'm going to put them in a cell block with the crazies."

"Now Ana Laura," Elena murmured soothingly.

"That's Deputy Sombrano to you," said the jail officer coldly. "Are you sure that bunch is guilty of anything? They strike me as the ultimate wusses."

"We'd like to talk to them," said Leo. "One by one."

"Well, you'll have to take the Chalmers girl first because she's the only one who's willing. The rest are telling everyone who'll listen that they'll never talk to another law-enforcement person without a lawyer present. This is what they're saying between bouts of hysterical weeping. I tried to tell them that I and my deputies are law-enforcement people, but unfortunately, that didn't shut them up. Damn, I hate noisy crybabies." The deputy stamped out, calling over her shoulder, "We'll send down Chalmers."

"Think she's going to confess?" asked Leo hopefully.

"More likely she's going to sue the county for cruel and inhumane treatment. An H.H.U. student would consider not having freshly squeezed orange juice for breakfast akin to torture."

Leo sighed. "I haven't had freshly squeezed orange juice since the babies were born. Concepcion used to do stuff like that. Now the only orange juice I see is made by Gerbers."

"There's an upside to all this," said Elena.

"I don't see what. Have you ever tasted baby food?"

"I mean about the fuss our prisoners made last night.
They may cut the rate of female recidivism in half."

"Anything I can't stand, it's a Pollyanna," Leo grumbled.
Before he could enlarge on that subject, the prisoner was
brought into an interview booth.

Barbara Chalmers said, in response to a question Elena
felt obligated to ask, "I don't need a lawyer to say what I
have to say." She looked terrible, hair uncombed, face pale.
The jail togs did not become her.

Elena nodded. Leo turned on the tape recorder.

"You want to know who poisoned Fullerton? I did. But
he'd be alive today if he hadn't lied."

"Explain that," said Elena.

"I asked him if he had AIDS. He said no. So if he didn't
have AIDS, he wouldn't have taken the AIDS medication in
the bathroom, would he?"

"How did you know it was AIDS medication?" Leo
asked. "The bottles weren't marked. Could have been as-
pirin for all you knew."

Barbara shrugged. All the verve of her previous perform-
ances was gone; she now seemed without emotion of any
kind, her face expressionless. "I followed him for two
weeks. Found out where his doctor was. Morton Conway,
the AIDS doctor."

"When did you do this?" Elena asked.

"Right after I got the call from Barton Marquis, and in-
cidentally, the other three were telling the truth. He told them
only that Amy was pregnant because that was what I told
him to tell them."

"So they didn't know they could be—"

"They're not infected. We all got tested at my suggestion."

"That still doesn't explain how you knew the pills were
for HIV."

Barbara stared at Elena with hard eyes. "The others may
not be infected. I am. Conway's my doctor, too."

"You have AIDS?" Leo asked.

"I'm positive, and I'm taking medication to stave off the

disease.'' She looked grim. ''I asked the doctor what happened when I started to have symptoms, and he told me about this new program he connected up with because of a patient of his from Chicago.'' Chalmers smiled grimly. ''He even showed me the medication in the little room at the end of the hall, explained the dosages and the tests and everything, and how the stuff was keeping that bastard Fullerton symptom-free.''

''He named Fullerton?''

''No, of course not, but how many HIV patients from Chicago could the doctor have? If the medication had looked different when I got into the son of a bitch's bathroom, I wouldn't have fixed it up with cyanide.''

''What if his roommates—''

''I spread a rumor that those chastity freaks were poisoning AIDS medication, and I made sure Pete and Lawrence heard it, but not from me. Ironic, isn't it? The chastity bunch had it right. Abstinence is the only safe alternative. Fullerton used a condom, and he still infected me. And if I hadn't been having myself such a high old time at prep school, I'd have been able to get into a better university than H.H.U., and I'd never have met Fullerton. Hell, I didn't even like him that much. I was just curious because he had a reputation for being an exceptional lover.''

''Was he?'' Leo asked curiously. Elena frowned at him.

''He wasn't that great, and I told him so.'' Barbara Chalmers laughed bitterly. ''He said I was a cold bitch and not to call him if I turned up pregnant. That was after the condom broke. But what he didn't tell me was that I had a lot more to worry about than pregnancy. Same with poor Amy. If he'd warned either one of us, we could have started AZT right away, maybe kept ourselves from getting infected.''

Chalmers had stopped looking at them. As she talked, she stared at her hands.

''How does Zimmer come into it?'' Leo asked.

''I borrowed some syringes from her to see if I could inject my AZT with cyanide. It didn't work.''

''So she knew what you had in mind even if she didn't do the actual—''

"I told her we were going to have a midnight watermelon party on the floor—watermelon injected with vodka."

"It's not watermelon season," said Leo. It was obvious he still thought Chalmers had co-conspirators.

Chalmers laughed humorlessly. "Right. Poor Cath was real disappointed when I discovered I couldn't get melons shipped from southern Mexico. And then she got the dumb idea of throwing a baby shower for Amy. I had to steer her away from that."

"Because you didn't want us following up the Marquis connection?" Leo asked.

"Right."

"And the cyanide?" Elena prompted.

"Hessick got it for me. I told her I wanted to kill a rat, and that's exactly what I did with it. Of course, she thought I meant a four-legged rat."

"And where did she think this rat was?" Leo demanded.

"Gnawing on the scenery at the theater."

"What did she say after Fullerton died of cyanide poisoning?" Elena asked suspiciously.

"Nothing. Matter of fact, I don't think she's said two words to me since then."

"So it was just you and Minette LaFaure. Is that what you're telling us?" asked Elena.

"Minette had cause to hate him."

"Is she HIV positive, too?"

"I told you. Just me. And Amy."

"So Minette—"

"—thought I was putting laxative into whatever I could find in his bathroom. She thought we were going to give him the world's worse case of diarrhea. Maybe we did. You could probably tell me what the cyanide did to him besides kill him."

"So there was no conspiracy. Just you using your friends to get even with Fullerton?"

Chalmers nodded.

"Then what about this mysterious group, the Friends of Amy?"

Chalmers shrugged. "Amy had lots of friends. I don't

know about any group. Maybe it was the baby-shower thing.''

''Amy's dying,'' said Elena.

Chalmers blanched. ''Are you sure? Her brother didn't say—'' She stopped. ''What about the baby?''

''They'll try to deliver it HIV-free,'' Elena replied. ''But they won't know for a couple of months after it's born.''

''Maybe I'll write to her and tell her I got even for both of us,'' Chalmers muttered. ''Because I'll be dying too. One of these days.''

''Fullerton seemed to be doing pretty well.''

''Not anymore he isn't.''

''You realize you've just confessed to premeditated homicide?'' said Leo.

Chalmers stared back at him. Then tears began to pour down her face, as suddenly as a summer storm falling from one cloud in a blue sky. ''I was protecting myself,'' she sobbed.

Elena was momentarily confused by the abrupt change until she remembered that Barbara Chalmers was a drama major. Then it occurred to her that this young woman, with a good lawyer, whom she would undoubtedly be provided by doting and wealthy parents, might well be able to twist a jury around her little finger. After all, she was a victim too, and Elena was sure that the lawyer would point that out, repeatedly. Before the trial was over, Fullerton would be seen as a dangerous, callous predator; Chalmers, as a fear-wracked victim.

''Anything else you want to say?'' Leo asked.

''Not a word,'' commanded a gray-haired man, entering the booth behind Barbara Chalmers.

Oliver Formalee. Elena knew him from previous criminal cases in Los Santos. He was a brilliant litigator.

''Why are you talking to my client when I'm not present?'' he demanded.

''Because she asked to speak to us,'' said Elena.

''My client is not in any psychological state to make decisions of that sort, Detective. I hope you realize that that tape will be worthless in court when the defense psychiatrists get through testifying.'' He cast a fatherly eye on the weeping girl. ''Look at her,'' he commanded.

''All I want is for them to let the others go. My friends didn't do anything.'' Chalmers continued to sob, accepting a handkerchief from her lawyer, who gave Elena and Leo a rebuking glance.

''I've seen the performance before,'' said Elena dryly. She wondered if the D.A. could have put Fullerton in jail for killing Amy Marquis if Barbara Chalmers hadn't killed him first. Because Fullerton was a murderer too.

Epilogue

Elena had been invited to the wedding of Gus Mc-Glenlevie and Linda Morell, as had Leo, but Leo refused to go. "I'm not buying that jerk a wedding present," he said. Elena commissioned her mother to send down one of the Mexican spotted-owl ceramics made and sold by Elena's brother and sister-in-law. It was the two-foot version in which the owl held a hapless Hispanic villager in its claws, symbolic of the dispute between native wood-gatherers and the environmental owl-fanciers who wanted wood left on the forest floor to encourage the proliferation of rodents that fed the owls.

When the owl arrived, in all its tasteless splendor, she wrapped it in silver wedding paper and enclosed a card saying that she thought Gus and Linda might enjoy this original piece of Sangre de Cristo folk art. Linda evidently didn't, but Gus loved it, called Elena to thank her for her "fanciful" gift, and informed her that he had arranged to have a ledge built over his office door on which the owl was now ensconced. Elena amused herself by imagining the bird perched and apparently ready to drop down on student poets who came to consult with their professor.

On the day of Gus McGlenlevie's nuptials, as Elena drove through the H.H.U. gates after presenting her wedding invitation to the guard, she reflected that they had a lovely day for the wedding. The untimely cold spell having disappeared

269

over the northern horizon, the campus was a riot of spring flowers. Although she hated to see water wasted to keep the landscaping lush, Elena had to admit that the quadrangle looked beautiful.

On such a nice day, she should be feeling cheerful. After all, she'd discovered who killed Graham Fullerton, who hadn't killed Wayne Quarles, Jr., who had tried to kill her, and who'd shot at the bridegroom-to-be, Angus Mc-Glenlevie. The sight of Angus giving up his freedom to a pale and ethereal bride, who had tied him up in so many prenuptial knots that he'd never get loose, promised to be very entertaining.

However, Elena was fretting over a serious professional dilemma. The results of the sergeant's exam had come back, and she had scored so well that they had to offer her a post, which they did. Traffic. They wanted to make her a traffic sergeant. She'd been stewing for three days. She didn't want to transfer to traffic. Even though the corpses, murderers, and violence, some of it directed against her, were nerve-racking, she had to admit that she loved working in Crimes Against Persons. So what was she to do? Becoming a sergeant would be good for her ego and her pocketbook. Her father would be proud of her. Some of her colleagues would be envious, but she herself would be bored to death.

Before she could pursue the decision-making process any further, she saw that something was definitely wrong at the chapel. She parked her truck in a visitors' parking area and headed toward the small mob of arguing, gesticulating people, arriving in time to hear the bride say in slightly hysterical tones, "You can't have a sit-in on the day of my wedding. It's unfair."

"This is where the Virgin is, so this is where we're sittin' in," said Socorro Rascon, who was wearing red polyester stretch pants and a T-shirt embellished with the words MAIDS' RIGHTS above a silk-screen print of the Virgin of Guadalupe handing roses to the lucky Mexican peasant to whom she had appeared. Underneath the Virgin and peasant were the words, "Union de la Virgin de El Paso del Norte."

Neat T-shirt, Elena thought. She wished that she had one.

"Dear lady," said Gus, putting his arm around Socorro
Rascon's shoulder; he had just forced his way through the
crowd. "Much as we sympathize with your cause—"

"What are you doing here, Gussie?" demanded the bride.

"Making a timely appearance for our wedding," Gus replied.

"You're not supposed to see me before the ceremony."

"I won't look."

"And you're flirting with that maid. I consider that an
infringement of our prenuptial agreement."

"But we're not yet wed, sweet Linda, so the agreement
hasn't yet gone into effect."

"Get your hands off me, *gringo*!" ordered Socorro Rascon.

"Yes, do that," Linda agreed. "Otherwise, I'm not marrying you."

"Let's not make any hasty decisions here," said Vice-
President Harley Stanley. "The wedding and reception are
all planned."

"If you planned 'em for this chapel, forget it," said Socorro. "My people ain't budgin'."

"But we've met all your terms," said the vice-president.

"Yeah, mostly, an' we went back to work. But we still
ain't got free access to the Virgin."

"She isn't the Virgin. Professor Castor Apulonia has
come to the conclusion, on the basis of the most meticulous
scholarly investigation, that she is the goddess Demeter,"
said Harley Stanley. "Your bishop would be horrified to
think that you are—"

"He's lyin'. You're all lyin' 'cause you don't want *la raza*
in your chapel."

"Who's *la raza*?" asked Linda. "I don't want anyone at
my wedding but invited guests."

"Then have it somewheres else, 'cause we ain't leavin',
an' you—" she poked a finger into the chest of the vice-
president, "don't think you can send some Anglo heathens
in to wash off the Virgin's tears. We seen through that.
You'll all go to hell for screwin' with a miracle. It's—it's
blasphemy."

The vice-president turned red. "Young lady, those young men were sent in to wash off the tears because they put the tears there in the first place. An ill-conceived fraternity prank, I'm sorry to say."

"Liar!" snarled the union leader. "An' we know how to take care of Protestant blasphemers. We knocked those *pinche* bastards right off their ladders."

"Good lord!" cried the vice-president. "Were they injured? Detective Jarvis, you must go into the chapel immediately to ascertain the state of the young men in question."

"Siggies, by any chance?" Elena asked, grinning. She had run into the Siggies and their pranks before, the turning on of the sprinklers during the first graduation, for instance, the result of which was an explosion of sprinklers and shrubbery.

"I'm afraid so," said the vice-president.

"No one goes in," said Socorro Rascon.

"But my wedding," wailed the bride.

"Maybe we can reach a compromise here," said Elena. "I'll go in and check on the frat boys, and you can move the wedding to—" She thought a moment. "How about the lobby at the Administration building?"

"What about the flowers?" Linda demanded. "I can't get married without flowers."

Elena looked at the bride's bouquet and those of the bridesmaids, who had been standing around watching the labor union-bridal dispute, checking their makeup in the mirrors of gem-encrusted gold compacts, flirting with groomsmen, and giggling among themselves. The wedding bouquets were composed of waxy red flowers that looked vaguely lascivious.

"How many flower arrangements are there? Maybe I can move them out myself. If the frat boys who came to scrub off the Virgin's tears are mobile, they can help me. That suit you, Socorro?" Grinning, she winked at the union leader.

Socorro looked taken aback and dubious, but Elena added persuasively, "Then *la raza* can have the Virgin, or Demeter, or whoever she is, all to yourselves, and without any weird-looking flowers to screw up the devotional mood."

"Those are very expensive and exotic flowers," protested the bride. "I had them flown in from Hawaii."

"Are they the kind that eat flies?" asked Socorro Rascon.

"No!" exclaimed the bride.

"Too bad." Socorro shrugged and flipped her long hair over her shoulder with queenly disdain. "We don't care if you take them out, Elena. You're on our side, after all."

"She is not," said the vice-president. "She's on the university's side."

"We're all connected in one way or another with the university," said Elena diplomatically.

"You can take the *pinche* bastards who tried to interfere with the Virgin, too," said Socorro generously. "Makes no skin off our asses. An' that ain't Dem—whoever in there. Miracle tears don't fall outa the eyes of pagan goddesses." Socorro then marched back into the chapel, having had the last word.

Elena followed her and was appalled to see how many arrangements of the dangerous-looking red flowers there were. However, she freed the traumatized frat boys from their captors and set them to work. Within an hour the wedding had been transferred to the Administration building, while the maids remained in possession of the chapel.

Now seated on a folding chair, surrounded by buzzing students and faculty, her feet aching from standing too long in high heels on the pink marble floors while supervising the placement of the flowers, Elena returned to thoughts of her professional problems. *Do I become a traffic sergeant?* she asked herself, *or*—well, no. She wasn't going to do it. She definitely wouldn't earn enough additional money to make up for the boredom.

Just as she reached her decision, Sam Parsley slipped into the seat beside her. He was wearing a dark blue blazer with a nifty red tie and gray slacks that actually had a crease. She'd never seen Sam look so well turned out. The man was constantly surprising her: first with how much he ate, then with how smart and kind he was, later by proving to have more muscle than fat on that bear body of his, and finally by being a good kisser.

"I hope you've got a hankie," he whispered. "I always cry at weddings."

Elena giggled at the idea of Sam in tears at the sight of a bride.

"Don't laugh," he said reprovingly. "I'm a romantic guy at heart."

"Well, Sam, this isn't a very romantic wedding. The chapel has been taken over by devout domestics, the bride is pregnant, and the groom is trussed up so tight in a prenuptial contract that he won't recognize himself a year from now."

Sam smiled. "One can only hope for a happy ending."

Linda Morell, looking very pretty, floated down the aisle behind sixteen bridesmaids, all of whom held bouquets of those phallic flowers. Gus was wearing a tuxedo instead of his aviator jacket and silk scarf. Had another codicil been added to the contract?

Happy ending? Elena thought of Barbara Chalmers. She'd engineered a happy ending for the three other Friends of Amy by taking all the blame for Fullerton's death. Elena still wondered where the truth lay in that case. But the ending wasn't very happy for Barbara, who was still in jail for murder and still HIV positive. She had lots of visitors: lawyers, coeds who had dated Fullerton themselves and stood behind her, relatives, even Dr. Conway. Oliver Formalee, who headed her legal team, had managed to arrange for private medical treatment.

Maybe it would save her life—for a while. But she could lose that life to the death penalty. Or maybe Formalee would plead her temporarily insane and get her off. Whatever happened, a happy ending wasn't in the cards for Barbara.

Or Amy. That sweet girl. So sick.

Gus and Linda were exchanging vows, vows they had written themselves, vows that caused Dr. Sunnydale to look puzzled and sometimes offended. Had the bride really said something about oral sex? Had the groom actually promised to get the bride's poetry published in a prestigious periodical?

Elena closed her ears to the ceremony. At least it would

be followed by terrific food at a gala wedding reception to be held upstairs where President Sunnydale conducted his biweekly prayer and cocktail parties, instead of in the Sacred Vestibule at the chapel.

Elena decided that she'd call Barton Marquis tomorrow and tell him about the treatment that had kept Graham Fullerton healthy. Maybe it wasn't too late for Amy. The drug company had an open slot in their program; why shouldn't Amy fill it? Could she take those red capsules while she was pregnant? There was a certain justice in the idea. And hope—for her and her baby. Hope was the important thing.

Elena put her arm through Sam's as the bride and groom kissed and the president beamed at the audience. Much to her astonishment, when Elena looked at her therapist and friend, she actually saw tears in Sam's eyes.